MADE FOR TV

Also by Richard Breen

Adam's Child

MADE FOR TV

A Novel
RICHARD BREEN

Beaufort Books, Inc.
New York / Toronto

No character in this book is intended to represent any actual person; all incidents of the story are entirely fictional in nature.

Library of Congress Cataloging in Publication Data

Breen, Richard, 1936–
    Made for TV.
    I. Title.
PS3552.R3646M3   1982   813'.54   82-4325
ISBN 0-8253-0103-3   AACR2

Published in the United States by Beaufort Books, Inc., New York.
Published simultaneously in Canada by General Publishing Co. Limited
Printed in the U.S.A.   First Edition
10 9 8 7 6 5 4 3 2 1

For my mother, Genevieve Breen
And my wife, Camille Breen
Age before beauty.

MADE FOR TV

1

"Hello," the girl said. "My name is Tawny."

She looked to be seventeen or eighteen, certainly no more than nineteen or twenty. Her hair was a maze of stringy dark-blond shoelaces, her eyes hard green pits, her features sharp, angular. Perhaps Scandinavian. More likely German. "This man I know says he may kill me. And then again he may not. It depends on how I do, how convincing I am."

A nervous smile revealed teeth that were slightly bucked and dulled by too much tobacco and too little personal hygiene. She wore a Groucho Marx T-shirt and blue jeans cut off in raggedy edges at midthigh. The nipples of hard little lumps poked dots beneath Groucho's glasses. The T-shirt was dirty, the jeans scrunched up in mean little folds around the crotch, creating the impression that they had been the girl's entire wardrobe for days, maybe weeks. The nervous smile faded into a blank stare as the girl tried to concentrate.

"I'm coming out of hiding tonight," Tawny began. Her voice had a nasal twang but no discernible accent that might reveal her origins. "For two years, ever since I split from my parents' nest in the North, I've done some numbers you wouldn't believe. Nothing I'm too proud of, anyway. But this—this has got to be the weirdest gig of my life. Of anybody's life." She closed her eyes. Her lips, which were much too full for the angular planes of

1

her face, pursed as if they were about to whistle, then relaxed. She took a deep breath, held it for about ten seconds, and exhaled, the air rushing out in a jet of relief.

"The fact is, I had to run away to find myself. I had to get away from what everyone else thought I was, to find out for myself who I really am. There I was, sixteen years old, and I'd wake up every morning and for fifteen minutes or a half hour, I'd lay in bed trying to figure out who I was." She tugged at the strand of dirty-blond hair next to her left ear and with forklike fingers twirled it into a hard little rope to squeeze in her hand. "I've done it all. Glue. Uppers. I've done coke. H. I've made money from men—I've taken money from women. But I've never, ever done anything like this. It's a trip. It's . . ." The girl lost her concentration for a moment. Her expression grew worried, as if what she had been saying had failed to please.

"Listen, what I really want to get across is that there must be half a million parents in this country who don't know where their kids' heads are at. Don't have any idea. Zip—zilch—zero. And for everyone like me who split, there's a dozen going through the motions at home and at school and with their families. But listen. Those kids' heads are really zonked out. And I don't mean on grass or booze or hard drugs or any of that crap. I mean we just don't understand who we are or what we are, or even why we are."

Tawny spoke rapidly, running words together rather than lose spontaneity for the sake of clarity.

"Like I said, my name is Tawny. But it could just as well be Debbie or Melissa or Jesus H. Christ or Charlie Manson. Know what I mean? My parents loved me. Or they thought they loved me. But they didn't know me from diddly. They've probably been looking for me for a couple of years now. Gone through a lot of bread. Probably cried a lot and blamed themselves and fought with each other and for what. For what?" Once again taut fingers squeezed and rolled erratic strands of hair into a neat little rope. "But the thing that knocks me out is that the girl they cried over and fought over and spent their money trying to find never really existed. She wasn't me. They made her up and called her me. But she was never me. She had nothing to do with me, nothing at all, except that I had to make believe I was her. For years. Do you know what kind of a number that does on your head? I mean, you make believe you're someone else long enough and you forget who you are."

Tawny smiled and tucked the loose edge of her T-shirt back into the waist of her jeans. She closed her eyes, then opened them. Her mood changed, the hard green eyes had become softer, yet more brazen. Something exciting was going on behind those eyes.

"People tell me I'm good-looking. Men pay attention to me. Even some women. Know what I mean? But the thing is, I wasn't born good-looking. I wasn't a pretty kid, the kind everyone fusses over. I was like a bowling ball with pimples. But then I think I actually willed myself into being pretty. No jive. I mean it. Both my mother and father had that whole Hollywood number about a girl's looks. So did their friends. And you know why? Because my daddy was in the Air Force. Yes sirree, The United States Air Force. Now how do you like them apples?"

Tawny snapped to attention, saluted an invisible flag, then relaxed.

"Now let me tell you the way it was for a fat homely young chick on an Air Force base. It was the end of the world. You learned how things worked there pretty fast. The pretty young things with nice round boobs and pinchable little fannies got the handsome young pilots and officers with terrific careers ahead of them. And the plain-looking Janes got to sit home alone or go to bingo or go bananas. So I became pretty. Because I had to—I had no other choice. I just couldn't take that bingo crap." A faint, humming sound, perhaps from a straining air conditioner or a plane passing in the distance, distracted the girl a second. She cocked her head. "What's that?" Tawny didn't wait for an answer. "All you'd have to do is take one good look at my mother and father and you'd know I wasn't meant to be good-looking. You'd wonder where I came from." She smiled.

"My mother has one of those bitchy faces all squeezed in tight like she's always biting on the inside of her cheeks. You could tell it was never a pretty face. But the truth is that it wasn't always that ugly either. It got that way over the years from all the frustration and hate she felt being married to a mousy twerp like my father, and bouncing around military bases playing happy homemaker."

The girl sucked in her cheeks in an obvious imitation of her mother and narrowed her eyes into a spiteful squint.

"She's five years younger than Daddy but she could pass for ten years older with no sweat. And I'll tell you how she got so old so fast. Pay attention! This is Tawny's beauty secret for America. She got so old so fast because she was furious at herself and him and me and everyone in the whole goddamn world that she didn't have a pretty face." Dark semicircles had appeared near her armpits on either side of Groucho's head. "Pretty women got ahead. Their husbands got promoted. Their families were happy and secure. She never said it. I mean she never came right out and said it in so many words, but she always wanted me to be pretty so I wouldn't have to settle for someone like my father, for some deadbeat with no ambitions, no brains, no money, no talent, no spirit, no nothing—"

The tone of Tawny's voice grew mean. She could see her mother and father as if they were right in front of her "He didn't even have enough guts to answer my mother back when she told him she was sleeping around because that's the only way he'd ever get promoted. Twenty-four years in the stupid Air Force and still a major. Twenty-four years without once piloting a plane or seeing action or doing anything but issue underwear at places like Texas in the forties, and Labrador in the fifties, and Kansas in the sixties—before he finally sucked up enough nerve to retire."

"Excuse me, Tawny," the man's voice interrupted, "don't you think you might be starting to bore your audience?"

Tawny's eyes moved slightly to the left as if she could see the man who was speaking to her from a distance of perhaps fifteen to twenty feet from where she was standing. Tawny was frightened.

"What do you suggest?" she asked softly.

"Can you sing?" the man answered with a question of his own.

"Yes," Tawny said in a low voice, "a little. But there's no music. I'd need some music."

"My dear," the man answered, "sing, hum, whistle. Do anything. But please don't bore us with any more sordid details about your childhood."

Tawny spoke. "I'm sorry. It's just that I'm nervous."

"Nervous, why should you be? There's nothing to be nervous about, because none of this is real." The man's voice was flat, emotionless—the monotone of a late-night weather forecaster from the Midwest.

Tawny bit her lip, then spoke. "What do you mean none of this is real? Of course, it's real. What's not real about it?"

Again the man's voice, clear but barren. "My dear, I'm afraid you'd never understand what I'm talking about. But the simple face is that the only thing that can make any of this real is what I choose to do with it."

"I don't understand."

"Of course you don't understand. And why should you? After all, you're only seeing a glimpse of the whole picture. You're merely a bit player. You don't know the entire script. You've never met any of the others."

Tawny raised her right hand and shielded her eyes, as if by doing so she might better be able to see the man who spoke to her. "What others?" she asked.

"Oh, there are others," he answered. "But there is no need for you to know anything about them. Whether they came along before you or after you is of no real consequence, because the important thing is simply that it all fit together in one harmonious whole. You are an integral part of something far bigger than yourself. Something that will make your face an enigma to millions."

"My face. An enigma to millions. Do you mean I'm going to be famous?"

"In a manner of speaking."

"What's an enigma?'

"It's something that no one understands. A mystery. A puzzle."

Tawny raised her voice. "What kind of a turn-on is this anyway? You're not following the script. You're playing games with my head." Tawny no longer looked or sounded frightened. She seemed irritated.

"I'm only doing it to help you my dear. To make you feel more relaxed, more spontaneous. I want to give you every chance. Because so much depends on what you say. And how you say it."

Again, Tawny shielded her eyes with her hand. "So?" she said in honest curiosity. "So, where do we go from here? Do I go back to talking about my family? Or do I sing? Or dance? Or what?"

"How about die" the man said. "Can you die well?"

"I don't know," said Tawny. "I've never died before."

"You can do it, I'm sure you can do it really well," the man answered. "You look like a natural. And there's got to be a first time for everything."

"Yeah, sure" said Tawny sarcastically. "Should I die in a slow agonizing way. Or would you prefer it sudden, spectacular?"

"Sudden and spectacular, I should think," the man answered.

"Natural or violent?" asked Tawny.

"I don't see that there's a difference" answered the man. "Violence is natural."

"That's not what I meant!" snapped Tawny. "Natural like in 'heart attack.' Or violent like being ripped apart by a cage full of lions or having your head blown off by a shotgun."

"Having your head blown off by all means," answered the man. "It's sudden, it's spectacular. And if you don't mind my saying so, it's quite colorful."

"Thanks" said Tawny slapping herself playfully on the face. "I needed that."

The explosion that followed ripped half of Tawny's head off and gouged great chunks of flesh out of her face. In the second or two before she fell, the whiteness of bone and skull were visible beneath bits of eyes and flaps of skin and strings of hair. Blood gushed out from the area where her nose had been and ran down Groucho's face. Then there was only the sound of Tawny's body crashing to the floor. Everything went blank.

2

The newscaster was a contemporary version of Don Ameche. Slick black hair. Trim moustache. Warm, reassuring voice. A handsome, fortyish face constantly projecting a blend of fatherly wisdom and mellow good-neighborliness. The suit was dark blue, the shirt a lighter blue, divided by a crisp red-and-white-striped tie. He held a sheaf of papers in his hands, but did not even glance at them as he spoke directly into the camera.

"As we said prior to the showing of the tape you have just seen, we had hoped nothing so gruesome would ever be seen on television—certainly, not on this program."

It was obvious to any regular viewer of Channel Eight's late evening news that Roger Tatum was not himself tonight. The voice was resonant, mature, as always. But the eyes were a dead giveaway. They didn't stare straight ahead in an authoritative gaze that had communicated to South Florida's largest late-night television audience for fourteen years. They were nervous eyes, unable to fix a gaze for more than a few seconds at a time.

"I can personally assure you that the executives of this television station underwent some horrendous soul searching before finally deciding to show this to our audience. As you know, it is the first time we have ever felt it necessary to caution parents that children should not be present when we were showing a tape on our news program. And, by the way, our program, because of its

7

special nature will run a full quarter hour longer than usual tonight.'' Roger Tatum placed the sheaf of papers he had been holding in his hands flat on the desk. The tip of an elegantly long, slim index finger unconsciously smoothed the right side of his moustache. He folded his hands in front of him, and took his audience into his confidence, a trait that had made him the most trusted commentator in the state and, some people felt certain, a good bet to wind up on one of the evening network news shows before long.

"What you have seen tonight is television history. A horrible piece of television history mind you. But history nonetheless. The only event even remotely comparable in my experience was the Jack Ruby slaying of Lee Harvey Oswald on live television back in 1963. But that was a case of killing, accidentally, or rather incidentally transmitted simply because television cameras happened to be there at the scene of the crime.

"What you have seen tonight appears to be a murder obviously planned and staged and fully executed for television.'' Roger Tatum paused for a moment, unclasped his hands, and rubbed them together in nervous agitation that none of his viewers had ever seen him exhibit before. "I am now going to read you a letter from the management of this station, explaining why we have chosen to let our viewers witness the sordid and inhumane event depicted on this tape, even though we know it will leave us subject to strong criticism from certain of our peers in television. And, of course, from certain members of the press. Nonetheless, we at WCQM felt a moral imperative to present this tape, in its entirety, to our audience completely unedited in any way, exactly the way we received it. We hope this letter will make our station's position, if not agreeable, then at least understandable to those who will surely judge us. But first, this message.''

There were three messages actually. The first consisted of twelve professional football players—six to a side—dressed in bathing suits and engaged in a furious tug of war. At the very center of the massive rope used for the event was a piece of luggage. The rope was entwined around the luggage handle in such a manner that the two teams, were, in effect, straining to pull the piece of luggage apart. The luggage defeated both teams of professional athletes rather easily. The second commercial featured a cream-colored cat with dramatic splotches of black around the eyes. Amazingly, the cat could sing extremely well when served one brand of cat food, but was horribly off key when served another. The third commercial was of a public-service nature, depicting a variety of positions that could be filled quite adequately by people handicapped by blindness, deafness, loss of limb and assorted other afflictions.

The image of Roger Tatum returned to the television screen. He was now staring directly into the camera. Once again authoritative, obviously aware that the message he was going to deliver transcended the ordinary evening's offering of rapes, murders, scandals, disasters, and personal tragedies. He picked up the sheaf of papers he had only moments before placed on the desk in front of him.

"I am now going to read you the official statement of this station concerning the taped event you have just seen. The statement will tell you how we came to be in possession of this tape, what action this station took regarding the contents of the tape, and why, finally, and regrettably, we decided that it must, no matter how painful its impact, be presented to our audience." Tatum paused for a moment, staring straight ahead with great solemnity, and then, looking down at the papers he held in his hands, began to read to his audience in a tone much lower and softer than that of his usual news delivery.

"On the morning of June eighteenth, some twenty-three days ago, this staton received, through the mail, an unsolicited videotape cassete. It was marked Attention: News Director. There was no return address, no indication of who had sent us the package— except that the postmark indicated it had been mailed from Miami International Airport at four forty-one P.M. on June seventeenth. Since there was no message accompanying the package—no request for action of any kind—there was no great sense of urgency at the station to see what was on the tape. It was a standard cassette, one used by television stations and private production companies across America. For all we knew, someone could have simply been returning a blank cassette that was the station's property and had somehow gotten misplaced. In any event, no one at the station paid any attention whatsoever to the cassette for three days. Then, on June twenty-second, one of our news editors happened to notice the cassette when he accidentally knocked it to the floor during a news-editing session. Because there was nothing written on the outside of the cassette to identify its contents, and because there was no written message attached, the news editor routinely decided to play the cassette so he could identify it and label it properly for future use.''

Roger Tatum glanced up at his audience, cleared his throat quickly then once again focused on the sheaf of papers he held in his hands.

"Once the news editor viewed the tape, he quickly called in four other station personnel who happened to be in the immediate area at the time." Once again, Roger Tatum looked up at his audience. "I was one of those four people" he said. "It was an experience I will never forget. Just as I am certain that none of you out there watching will ever forget what you have seen tonight on this program.''

Roger Tatum returned to the letter. "Obviously there was a good bit of confusion and shock at first. Was someone playing a monumental prank on the station? The entire news department and executive management of this station was called, in secret, for a private screening of the tape. We sought to determine if what we had witnessed was truly the event depicted—that is, an actual on-camera murder of an unknown person—or was merely a ghoulish prank, carefully rehearsed and skillfully executed to simulate an actual murder in a manner so realistic as to deceive us all. We sat in the screening room with twelve monitors in front of us. We ran the tape in its entirety more than twenty times. We ran it in slow motion. We used stop action repeatedly, especially in every frame at the violent conclusion. We ran it backwards. We looked at it from every angle. And when we came out of that viewing room there was unanimous agreement among seventeen people—unanimous, mind you—that what we had witnessed was not a dramatic simulation of a murder, but rather an actual murder within the setting of a dramatic presentation.''

Again, Roger Tatum looked up from the letter and spoke directly to his audience. ''I was at that meeting. And I can assure you after having seen isolated portions of the tape in slow motion, blown up enormously and in stop-action sequence, that no trick photography, no special effects, no make-up man could have created what we witnessed. We have not shown you that tape in slow motion or stop-action simply out of a sense of propriety. But I think the remainder of this letter will verify that what we all saw—we here at Channel Eight—and you the viewing audience at home, was in fact a murder.''

Roger Tatum paused. ''Let me get back to the letter.'' He read more quickly now, because the excitement of the events he described had touched some hidden coil of emotion behind his otherwise totally calm professional facade, or perhaps simply because he had become conscious that the news was running longer than even the special fifteen-minute extension could accommodate.

''Once we had agreed that there was no deception involved— that we had indeed witnessed a videotaped murder—we immediately contacted the police. Prior to their arrival we made a dupe—or duplication—of the tape, anticipating correctly that the police would confiscate the original cartridge as evidence. The management of this station cooperated fully with them, granting them use of our telecasting facilities so that police experts might analyze the tape in as many ways as they deemed necessary. Against our better judgment we agreed not to announce or make public the contents of that tape, allowing the police sufficient time to circulate the victim's picture to other police departments and various missing person agencies throughout the country. Every person from this channel who was at our private screening vowed to keep their lips sealed, believing that by doing so we might best aid the police in locating the killer as quickly as possible. Unfortunately, the cartridge itself contained no other physical evidence beside the tape itself. There were no fingerprints. No foreign substances on the cassette. No way of tracing where or when or to whom it was sold.''

Roger Tatum paused in his reading for a moment, sighed audibly, as if with great weariness, then continued. ''One week went by. Two weeks. Three weeks. After checking with the FBI and virtually every police department in the country, as well as with the Bureau of Missing Persons, a total of fourteen reasonable leads as to the identity of the female victim on the tape were produced. These leads were systematically checked out, and each, in turn, proved to be a dead end. In some cases, the missing persons had returned home. In three of the cases, positive identity had already been made by next of kin; on two accident vicims and one murder victim. Finally, segments of the tape and enlarged still photographs from the tape were shown to the parents of four runaway teenagers who had never been found, and whose appearance bore some resemblance to Tawny—the girl on our tape. All of these parents gave statements to the effect that while there may have been superficial similarities between their daughters and the girl on the tape, they were absolutely certain beyond any doubt that the victim was not their daughter.'' Roger Tatum's eyes moved slightly to the left, a mannerism longtime viewers could identify as an attempt on his part to see how much time he had left without glancing down at his watch. Even under extreme pressure, he remained the total professional.

''We have, as our letter indicated, done everything possible to cooperate with the police. And we would have continued to maintain silence as long as was reasonably prudent, but something happened recently that made our silence seem almost criminal.''

Roger Tatum stopped talking. He rubbed the forefinger of his right hand slowly across his moustache. When he spoke again, his voice lost all semblance of authority. In fact, the next day, people would comment that it didn't even sound like Roger Tatum speaking.

"A few days ago," he said, "this station received another unmarked videotape cassette in the mail. We immediately played this second cassette on one of our monitors. Our worst fears were confirmed. Another murder. Obviously male. As in the first tape—the one you saw a bit earlier—the victim appears to be play-acting, almost auditioning. And then suddenly, shockingly, he, too, received a massive shotgun wound in the head. Obviously fatal. In fact, on this second tape, the camera lingers slowly over the body on the floor focusing on the fatal damage as if to underscore a point. Once again, we duplicated the tape and called the police. They in turn asked us to once again remain silent. A meeting of the executive management and news staff of this station was called. We decided that we could be silent no longer. And for a number of reasons. Here to explain those reasons to you in detail is Mr. Edmund Laurenson, executive director and chairman of the board of WCQM."

There was a quick cut to a slender gray-haired man with sharp features and an extremely pronounced nose that distracted viewers from the soft, nervous expression in deep blue eyes that stared out from behind narrow wire-rim glasses.

"Good evening. My task tonight is most unpleasant and I shall attempt to make it as brief, yet as thorough, as possible. This station has no desire to cater to the whims of a perverse murderer, who, even as I speak, is probably watching this program. There can be little doubt that he, or she, or they, or whoever sent us these tragic tapes, wanted them seen on the air. It saddens and sickens all of us at Channel Eight that we are forced to conform to those wishes at this time. But we are doing so only to protect our audience and to speed the apprehension of the killer as soon as possible."

Edmund Laurenson adjusted the narrow wire-rim glasses perched on the ridge of his impressive nose.

"For one thing, the girl on the tape you saw tonight has not been identified by the police, the FBI or virtually every missing person's agency in the United States and Canada. I know it is a gruesome thing to see. But perhaps someone watching this news program tonight will be able to identify that girl. By tomorrow, the networks will surely be running the tape on their news shows so that the rest of the country will see it. The press will run pictures of the poor unfortunate girl on their front pages. Virtually everyone in America will be exposed to that young lady's face. Certainly someone will recognize it. And when someone does recognize it, we will have taken our first step toward locating the twisted mind that took her life.''

Shiny dots of perspiration were visible along Edmund Laurenson's forehead, as the powerful TV lights and the tenseness of the situation combined to make his discomfort apparent.

''But there are other reasons as well'' he continued, ''for making the contents of the tape you have seen tonight public. Is it possible that someone in our audience might recognize the voice of the unseen man asking questions on the tape? His voice or manner of speaking was probably disguised . . .but still . . .perhaps someone might recognize a key phrase or the pronunciation of a particular word.'' Mr. Laurenson removed a white handkerchief from his lapel pocket and dabbed at his forehead in a mindless, totally mechanical manner, as if unaware that he was addressing a live television audience.

''If you remember the man's voice on the tape, you may remember that he made reference to the girl only being a bit player, that she couldn't understand the whole picture, that there were others involved. Since viewing the second tape, the one in which an unidentified man is killed, we have come to the conclusion that more of these tapes—perhaps many more—will be forthcoming. We have discussed it with the police and with a number of criminal psychiatrists and they agree: there is no way, at this time, of determining how often the killer may have killed. We have run laboratory tests on the age of the tapes we have received, and while the tapes are both approximately four years old, there is no way of determining when the footage on them was taken. It could have been four years ago. Or four months ago. Or four weeks ago. What we do know is that one young lady and one man, both unidentified, have been murdered. It is entirely possible that the person who sent us the tape has videotaped a number of similar murders over a period of time. It is also possible that these are the only two tapes of their kind. And finally, it is also possible that the person responsible for these tapes is now actively trying to convince people—young people primarily, we would think—that he can help them get into television or films if they will audition or make a screen test, if you will, for him. For that reason, we urge all of you watching tonight to make sure that your children are aware of the dangerous type of person who may try to lure them into his company with the promise of being on television. We all know how very excited children—and even many adults—can get about the idea of being on television. But warn them to be extremely careful. It could cost them their lives.''

Mr. Laurenson paused for a moment. He folded his hands softly in front of his face and then rested his chin on them. When he spoke again, it was in the manner of a father talking calmly to his children about the problems they were going to have to face together as a family, but that if they all behaved properly, everything would be fine in the end.

"Obviously, we are dealing with a very sick person in this matter. It is regrettable that we have been forced to show you the contents of the first tape, but unless the police or the F.B.I. or someone produces a valid lead as to the identity of the killer within the next forty-eight hours, we will consider it our moral duty and public responsibility to run the second videotape cassette, which carries the scenes of a man's murder. As of now the man has not been identified through any conventional search methods, and we think you will understand why once you have seen the tape. Computerized searches have scanned every file of every young man reported missing in the past four years. So far it seems as if both this girl and this man came out of nowhere to shock our sensibilities with their tragic deaths. But they did come from somewhere, that we can be sure of. And when we find out where they come from, we will be on our way to finding their killer. Thank you.''

There was a sudden click and the solemn image of Edmund

Laurenson disappeared from the screen. The slender man seated in the elegant bowl of an Eames chair placed the remote-control TV channel selector that he held loosely in his hand on the stuffed black leather ottoman at the side of the chair. The room was now in total darkness. There was complete silence except for soft sounds of the man settling back in the chair. He was deep in thought, trying to remember exactly how long it had been since he had taped the Channel Eight eleven o'clock news with Roger Tatum. Was it a week ago? Or a month. Or a year? What matter? He had captured Roger Tatum and Edmund Laurenson on videotape as they related the awful events of the televised killings to their audience. So now they too were his forever. He owned them. Not as he owned the others, of course. He owned the others absolutely. All of them. But still, it was nice to know that he had Roger Tatum and Edmund Laurenson in his videotape file. All the pieces were beginning to come together. There was no doubt in his mind that it would all work out as he had planned. Sitting in the silent darkness, the man moved stiffly. His hand reached over the edge of the chair and fumbled along the edge of the ottoman until he found the remote-control TV channel selector he had placed there only a few seconds earlier. He pressed the "on" switch, and a sudden expanse of light erupted on the large screen in front of him. Within a millisecond, the features of Edmund Laurenson appeared before him. A sudden click-click and Edmund Laurenson disappeared, to be replaced by the familiar face of Ed Sullivan. Another click-click, and Ed Sullivan vanished, to be replaced by the image of Ernie Kovacs with a giant cigar standing out straight from beneath his bushy moustache. The man in the chair pressed the remote-control buttons impatiently, aware that he had arranged better programming for his evening's entertainment. When he recognized the face that appeared on the screen, he settled back into his chair. This was one of his all-time favorite shows, the kind he could watch over and over all through the night, night after night. And it was just starting. He hadn't missed a moment of it.

"Hello" the girl said "my name is Tawny."

3

Gavin Risen was born in the Bronx, New York, in April of 1940.

A quarter of a century later, in April of 1965, a communications satellite named Early Bird was sent into orbit around the earth, making possible commercial transatlantic transmission of television messages. Human isolation, as well as human privacy, were on the verge of becoming extinct. Soon, every point on the globe—every village, every valley, every city, every street, every house, every room, every eye, every mind—could be connected with every other point on earth by means of live television. The family of man, all watching one event, one shared moment of experience. Natives of Africa would now be Gavin Risen's neighbors. Astronauts making history would now be his Saturday night companions. The world, the moon, the universe, were, quite literally, coming into Gavin Risen's living room. And oh, how he welcomed them. Because it was only then, at the age of twenty-five, that Gavin Risen began to form a clear concept of who he was, and for what purpose his life was being lived. And for the very first time he felt a sense of urgency, a need to participate in his own life rather than merely observe the lives of others, as he had been doing for as long as he could remember. Since 1949, anyway.

Three events of lasting importance in Gavin Risen's life took place in 1949.

First, early in the summer of that year, Gavin's father deserted Gavin and the boy's mother. One Sunday afternoon, Gavin's father simply walked out the door and was never seen nor heard of again. Second, in the early fall of the year, young Gavin raced his bicycle into the rear of a parked garbage truck on Bruckner Boulevard in the East Bronx, with the result that the boy's right thigh was badly broken, necessitating painful weeks in traction in the hospital, and months of boring recuperation at home in a cast that ran from the tips of the toes on Gavin's right foot up to his neck, and down to the knee of his left leg. Obviously, the boy had to remain virtually immobile for months. And so he did, nearly dying of boredom and loneliness until the third big event of the year. One month after Gavin was sent home from the hospital— in an ambulance—and carried to his mother's apartment by two husky black ambulance attendants who placed him in a specially rented hospital bed, Gavin's mother purchased a television set. It was a nine-inch Philco with a rectangular screen set in a black plastic box and it was easily the most beautiful thing Gavin had ever seen. And, as time would ultimately prove, it was not only a bigger event to Gavin than breaking his thigh or being deserted by his father, it was to be the happiest event of his youth.

Of course, Gavin Risen's first nine years on earth had not been filled with rip-roaring, knee-slapping, hugs-and-kisses happiness. By the time Gavin reached the age of five, he had begun to perceive that his father really didn't like him all that much. It had to do with the feel of the man's hands when he touched Gavin's body. Hard and stiff, as if the young flesh the hands occasionally brushed against was foreign and unpleasant. Too, there was the way the man clenched his mouth whenever he was listening to the radio and the little boy happened to walk into the room. It was obvious to Gavin that the radio was far more important to his father than he could ever hope to be. There were a few bright moments, of course; the man wasn't totally without feeling for his son. There was an occasional day at the zoo. An afternoon at

Yankee Stadium. And a week at a summer cottage in Milford, Connecticut, where the man tried to teach the boy to swim at Bayview Beach. Gavin was eight years old then. And he could actually feel that the man's hands were less stiff, less tense. The man laughed a lot that week, more than Gavin could ever remember. So did Gavin and his mother. They all ate hot dogs and Gavin's mom and dad drank beer every night at a screened-in roadside restaurant named Jack's where the mosquitoes only paused momentarily to circle the yellow-balloon light bulbs at the door before proceeding in like good paying customers. Gavin always remembered that the mustard smelled funny and the night air seemed so much softer on his skin than it ever had in the Bronx. And his dad gave him nickels and Gavin kept playing the same song over and over again. It was called "Fuzzy-Wuzzy Was a Bear, Fuzzy-Wuzzy Wasn't Fuzzy Was He?"

They rode the New York Central from Milford back to the Bronx, and while the trip took under three hours, to Gavin it was a journey through another continent. Connecticut was wood, the Bronx was concrete. Connecticut was tan, the Bronx was sunburned. It was on the trip back that Gavin realized that his father worked for the company that ran the trains. He realized this because when the conductor came through the car to punch holes in the passenger's tickets, Gavin's father merely opened his wallet and showed the conductor a card. The conductor and Gavin's father then exchanged a few brief words about mutual friends who worked for the railroad and how one of the few breaks anyone ever got working for the company was that at least they and their family could get free travel out of the city once in a while. And with the heat in the city that summer, a week in Milford was a week in heaven.

They never went back to Milford again. They never went anywhere for an entire week again. "And why should we be wasting money going to faraway beaches when we have a beach right at our back door," Gavin's father would say. And he was perfectly right, of course.

Doctor's Beach was to beaches what ghettos are to suburbs.

True, it was located on the water, on Pelham Bay, in the Throgs Neck section of the Bronx. True, it had a kind of coarse gray sand and a wooden float that bobbed in the waves some forty yards from shore. True, there was a rickety little pier where young Gavin had once seen a man strolling in a bathing suit struck by lightning and rendered instantly dead on a sweltering Fourth of July afternoon. But it was not a beach in the classic sense of the word. It did not really remind one of nature and freedom and fresh air. It was really nothing more than a stretch of dirty sand about seventy-five yards wide and fifty yards deep that happened to run to the edge of Pelham Bay where seaweed and condoms flowed freely around children splashing away late summer afternoons.

And when Gavin's father said this beach was at their back door, he was totally accurate. Because Gavin and his family lived in a small four-room apartment that was situated directly over Doctor's Bar and Restaurant, which, in turn, was situated directly on Doctor's Beach. In the twenties, Doctor's Bar and Restaurant had been a fairly distinguished drinking and dining establishment, accessible only by car. By the late thirties, a neighborhood class of petty thieves and loan sharks known as "the water rats" had made the place their semiofficial social headquarters, discouraging the appearance of more respected clientele. And by the mid-forties, when Gavin and his parents moved into the small apartment directly over the bar and restaurant, it had deteriorated to such a state that it would have failed to qualify as the setting for a Eugene O'Neill waterfront play. The facilities were sufficiently decrepit, but the characters who populated them lacked any sense of drama or destiny. The move into the small apartment atop the bar and restaurant had an effect upon young Gavin. He did not quite understand why, but he knew he had been disgraced and dishonored in the eyes of his classmates at school. Even though the relocation represented the distance of only a mile, it may as well have been a move to another country. Children who used to visit Gavin at his family's previous apartment were forbidden to visit him at his new home. It was never stated openly, but Gavin understood nonetheless. He was invited to other homes, to birthday parties, and to watch a wonderful new machine called television that was just like going to the movies except the pictures were smaller and you didn't even have to leave your living room to see them. But the children whose homes Gavin visited never seemed able to come visit him. Gavin understood the reason without having to have it explained to him. It had to do with the people who sat at Doctor's Bar drinking and playing poker as early as ten o'clock in the morning. And it had to do with the people who worked there. "Will, the Indian," was a fast-talking, dark-skinned, forty-two-year-old man with a half-moon scar on his left cheek the size of a silver dollar. It was rumored that Will had spent time in prison for doing something dirty to a twelve-year-old girl, but as far as Gavin knew, it was just talk. Will was the porter at Doctor's Bar and Restaurant, cleaning the barroom and restrooms every night in return for a small allowance and a one-bedroom apartment immediately adjacent to the Risen family's apartment atop Doctor's Bar. In fact, Will shared the bathroom with the Risen family, courteously trying to limit his use of it to the early-morning hours before the family awoke, and to the late-night hours when they were asleep. Actually, Gavin didn't dislike Will in spite of his reputation, just as he didn't dislike Mattie, the combination waitress, dishwasher, and short-order cook. Mattie was deformed in two ways: one, her left leg was a good four inches shorter than her right left—the result of an injury in infancy—causing her to walk in a rolling gait that made her the butt of raucous barroom jokes. Two, her face was one of those unfortunate combinations of features that are a source of embarrassment to everyone who comes in contact with them for the first time. There was something of a female ape in Mattie's face, and with her badly dyed bright-orange hair and worn-out fifty-five-year-old body she was not the sort of person most parents of young children would want those children to come in contact with after school, or for that matter, after anything. What with the presence of people like Will the Indian and Mattie keeping his school-age friends at a distance, Gavin began to become a young recluse.

There were only two ways for Gavin to reach the long, narrow stairway that led from the downstairs bar and restaurant to his family's apartment. One was through the restaurant kitchen, the back-door entrance to which was often locked, denying him access. And the other was through the bar, where Gavin would often be stopped by customers who recognized the boy and offered to buy him a Coke and tell him how lucky he was to be living over a bar where there was so much fun and action. The swirling colors of the jukebox blinking out a background for the Andrews Sisters and Vaughn Monroe and Harry James. The whoop and holler of shuffleboard combatants as one last weight slid the length of a highly waxed wooden surface to eke out a victory by a fraction of an inch. And now, of course, there was that new thing right up there in the corner on a special platform above the bar, the focal point of every sober eye's attention for Friday night's fights and Saturday afternoon football. The fourteen-inch television set with a huge magnifying glass set in front of it to make the picture larger, so large in fact that one could stand at the far end of the shuffleboard and still see what was happening if the picture was clear. It was a miracle, there was no doubt about it. And Gavin, the regular customers thought, was a lucky boy to be able to enjoy it simply by walking downstairs whenever he wished.

Of course, Gavin didn't believe himself so lucky. He couldn't understand why his parents had moved to this place that shamed him so. Why couldn't he live in a normal apartment or house the way his classmates did? Why should he have to walk through a loud, smoke-filled bar crammed with dirty-looking people to get to his bedroom, only to find that once there, the music from the jukebox could clearly be heard filtering up from below. Gavin never dared tell his parents how miserable he felt at their new "home" because by that time there were awful arguments between his mother and father and those arguments began to reveal to Gavin, piece by piece, the reasons the family had moved into the apartment above Doctor's Bar and Restaurant.

"Goddamn you, I'll tell you why I drink so much," Gavin could hear his mother screaming at his father. Drink often enflamed her feelings when she thought her son was asleep. "I drink because I can't stand living in this shithole of a place you got us stuck in unless I'm drunk. Understand? Understand, you smart-ass son-of-a-bitch hot-shit poker player? Understand where your fucked-up big-deal card games get us. And where they're going to keep us for years. So you can pay back Big Teddy. You want me to pay back Big Teddy by putting out for him and his friends on top of the bar every Friday night? Is that what you'd like? Well, then keep your goddamn mouth shut and don't ask me why I drink so much. What else is there to do around here?"

Gavin would lie in bed, alternately straining to hear every word and then periodically covering his ears because he didn't want to hear his mother's voice or his father's voice ever again. Because as they shrieked at each other over the muffled din that arose every night from the bar downstairs, many of the unspoken parts of puzzles that had floated loosely on the edge of Gavin Risen's consciousness began to fall into place. He learned, for example, that he wasn't his mother's only child.

"God strike me dead, how stupid I was to ever listen to you, to ever think I was in love with you." Gavin realized that her speech was slurred, that she was drunk again. "I left a good man for you. And my little baby girl, my little baby. My God, I was insane. I am insane. How could I have left them for you? For this! I can't ever see her again. I don't even know where she is or what she looks like now." Gavin's mother began to cry.

"No one never asked you to leave. I never asked you to come with me or promised you anything." It was Gavin's father, his voice more controlled, but even at the distance that separated Gavin from his father, he could hear the man's quiet despair. "What about the boy in there? Doesn't he count for anything? Don't you care when he sees his own mother acting like a drunken slut?"

"Don't you shit me about that boy," screamed Gavin's

mother. "You never wanted him, you tried to make me get rid of him, you don't even like to be around him, and now you make out like you care for him."

"Shut up," the man snapped. "He's probably listening to every word you're saying." There was a long pause, as if the man realized that what he was saying might very well be true, the boy might be listening.

Gavin turned slowly on his side in his bed, eyes tightly shut, waiting in the tense silence for his door to open slowly and his parents, or at least his father, to step quietly into the room to see if he was asleep. For perhaps two minutes he heard no sound save for the muffled mix of jukebox music and jumbled conversation coming up from the bar below. Then he could hear his mother's voice again, not distinctly, but talking rapidly in a much more subdued tone than that she had used a few minutes earlier. He could not make out what she was saying, but he could tell she seemed less angry. Then there were a few seconds of silence, and he could make out his father's voice again, low and calm like the soft purr of an engine, but the individual words escaped him. He rolled over onto his back and raised his head to stare out his bedroom window at the thick blackness of night and the even thicker blackness of Pelham Bay. Below the sky, the silhouettes of a few small boats bobbed atop a sea of ink. He heard a dog, perhaps on the beach, howl in pain, and he wondered if the dog's howl could be heard by his parents in the kitchen, or if they were too busy fighting with each other or pouring drinks to notice. The next sounds he heard were the high pitched little laughs of young children squealing in a mixture of delight and pain as they splashed into the coolness of the morning bay. He opened his eyes and squinted at the bright-yellow presence of the sun in his room. He looked at the clock. It was ten-fifteen A.M. Sunday. Gavin Risen arose, got dressed, and went for a walk all the way to Pelham Bay Park. When he returned, his mother was sitting at the kitchen table reading the *Sunday News* and sipping a glass of scotch with three thin ice cubes in it. "Your father is gone," she said. "And he's not coming back."

The accident came two months after Gavin's father had left home. The thing about the accident that Gavin's mother couldn't really understand was how a boy Gavin's age could manage to get hit by a parked garbage truck? It became a kind of inside joke among all the regulars at Doctor's Bar. Veronica's kid is really some kind of "numbnuts." "Imagine racing your bike at full speed—maybe twenty-five miles an hour—into a parked garbage truck that must weigh in at about four tons? And then when someone asks you how it happened, you tell them you never saw it. How the hell can you miss seeing a parked four-ton garbage truck that's right in front of you? You know what the kid answered? He said, 'I nearly missed it.' Now is that a little nutbar, or what?"

It was a joke, of course, to everyone except Gavin and his mother. The boy's right femur had been broken diagonally, as if a knife had sliced the bone almost from top to bottom. He lay in lonely pain for seven and one half hours in an overcrowded ward at Fordham Hospital before his mother could be located and her permission granted to administer anesthesia. Veronica had been spending the day with a male companion at his apartment near Yonkers. It was her first "date" since Gavin's father had left, "and now this had to happen." By the time the hospital authorities finally located her, Gavin was so confused and exhausted from pain that he actually believed the doctors were going to amputate his leg. Wouldn't that be something, he thought. Then maybe all the kids in his class could feel sorry for him and come to visit him and his mother at their home. He could actually see himself on crutches, with one empty pajama leg dangling loose, while his classmates gathered around him, their faces reflecting equal parts of sympathy and envy and horror.

When he awoke the next morning, his ankle was painted orange and there was a funny looking wire running through his heel with weights dangling from either end. His mother was seated next to his bed. "Oh, my baby," she said. "My poor, poor baby. I'm so sorry I wasn't there when you needed me."

Gavin smiled. "They didn't take off my leg?"

"Of course not, silly. They don't take people's legs off just because they're broken. But yours is a very serious break. The doctor says that this thing your leg is in now is called traction. And that if it doesn't pull your bone back together and hold it in place, you may have to have an operation."

"I saw one man laying in bed yesterday when they brought me in. He only had one leg. I asked him what happened and he said they took his leg off and I thought they might do the same thing to me."

"Don't you worry, baby. No one's ever going to take your leg off. Not as long as mommy's around. Now tell me, how could you run into a parked garbage truck? Weren't you watching where you were going? How many times . . ."

The traction didn't work. After three weeks of setting and resetting the bone—once without anesthesia of any kind so they could see how the boy reacted—the doctors decided to operate. A pin was inserted in Gavin's right thigh, fusing the two daggerlike shafts of bone into a single unit. A cast was immediately placed not only over Gavin's entire right leg, but also over his left leg down to the knee and completely over his hips and stomach to the top of his chest. The idea was to make him virtually immobile so that his right leg could not possibly move in the slightest, preventing the pin from slipping and giving the bone time to knit. Medically, it was a sound decision on the part of the doctors. Psychologically, it was the worst thing that could have happened to young Gavin. He perhaps could have coped better had his leg been amputated after all. At least then he would have been somewhat of a heroic figure, hobbling about on crutches, inspiring others with his courage in the face of adversity. And at least he would have had a degree of mobility. He would have been able to go up and down the stairs. Out to a movie. Downstairs to watch the television.

Instead, he would have to lie flat on his back, unable even to leave his bed to perform his daily bodily functions. Fortunately, since his father's desertion, Gavin's mother had been given a job as a full-time waitress and part-time hostess at Doctor's Restaurant. She was given the job by the owner of Doctor's Restaurant, a man Gavin never knew by any other name than Big Teddy. And inasmuch as Gavin's father had been considerably in debt to Big Teddy, Gavin thought it was especially nice for Big Teddy to give his mother a job, while letting her know that he considered her in no way responsible for her husband's debt. The pay was fair, the tips poor, but the job was perfect for the time being, since it allowed Veronica to stay close to her son, who then required so much attention, and still be able to make a living. Had she found it necessary to travel to and from work, their troubles would have mounted, since the boy obviously needed someone nearby, someone who could reach him in a moment or two if he suddenly needed the bedpan, or if, God forbid, he should accidentally roll out of bed. And of course, there was always the possibility of a fire or other emergency. It was indeed a good thing that Veronica could earn a living only a few feet from where her son recuperated. A good thing, except for one thing. Veronica now managed to stay reasonably drunk from noon till closing time at four in the morning.

The more frequently Veronica got drunk, the lonelier Gavin became, lying solemnly in his hospital bed, encased in the massive white cast, staring up at a living-room ceiling that seemed like a cloud of pure white ice suspended in space a few inches above his eyes. It reached a point where Gavin actually felt lonelier when his mother, drunk, was in the room with him, than when he was left completely alone.

When Veronica was present she tried to make casual conversation and appear completely sober, but invariably the attempts were so strained that they began to fill Gavin with a sense of loathing.

He felt only relief whenever she left the room.

Big Teddy popped in for a minute or two every third or fourth day. Will, the Indian, stopped by from time to time, as did Mattie, the waitress. But Gavin didn't seem to care particularly. He much preferred his own company. He had, in fact, begun to shut the others out of his life as if they didn't exist. The emptiness of every day, the monotony of staring straight up at an empty ceiling from seven o'clock in the morning to well after midnight, gradually began to create a trancelike existence that neither bored or excited Gavin. He was there. He couldn't move. He had no choice in the matter, so he accepted it quietly. The only thing he couldn't accept were the infrequent appearances of his mother during the day. To feed him lunch. Empty his bedpan. Change his sheets. Bring him dinner. And always drunk. Not rip-roaring drunk, but drunk enough to mix up words. And drop a bedpan on the floor by the bed. And scream at Gavin that she wasn't meant to be a goddamn nurse. And one night to wind up crying at her son's bedside, sobbing out her sordid life story: all the details about the little baby and husband she had left behind for Gavin's father, and how her life had turned into a mess, and now all this on top of it was more than she could take. She looked up at Gavin. He was lying in his bed, eyes wide open, staring up at the ceiling. It was as if he hadn't heard a single word she'd said. It was as if she didn't exist.

In the next few days after the episode of the crying and confession, Veronica realized that Gavin was shutting her out of his world. He would speak to her, but only when absolutely necessary. He was distant to Will the Indian and Mattie. And Big Teddy. Could he have known or guessed about herself and Big Teddy? Well, a woman has to live, she thought, and after all, if it weren't for Big Teddy, both she and Gavin would be in a lot worse shape than they were. Maybe the kid's just got the blues, she thought, what with his father leaving and his leg and none of the kids in his class at school ever stopping by to see him. A full six-ounce glass of scotch gave Veronica a well-intentioned idea about how to cheer up her soon. As son as she had one or two more drinks, she would see Big Teddy and tell him she would do that special thing he was always asking her to do for him, if he would do her a favor to help her son. She didn't like the idea of doing the special thing, but shit, if you were drunk enough it wasn't all that bad. And besides, maybe her son would start to like her again. Was that too much for a mother to ask?

With the two hundred fifty dollars she borrowed from Big
Teddy, Veronica bought a nine-inch Philco television set. Black.
Rectangular. Really nothing special, even in those early days of
television, but to Gavin it was the most magnificent gift he could
imagine. Now he would have something to keep him company,
instead of someone. Now he could lie in bed and watch movies
and dancers and ballplayers and acrobats and not have to answer
dumb questions about how his leg felt, and how long did he think
he'd be in the cast and how in hell did he manage to run into a
parked garbage truck? He appreciated the gift so much, he almost
found it in his heart to forgive his mother for who and what she
was. He even managed to smile at her a few times during the next
few days, and say "thank you" when she fed him his meal or
washed his face. Of course, she was still drunk most of the time,
but no matter. As long as she didn't doze off in the living room
and snore so loudly that Gavin couldn't hear the television set.

The television set was on from the first show in the morning
until the last show at night. If he awoke too early, Gavin would
turn on the set and simply lie in bed watching a test pattern and
wait for a program to begin. The set was placed on a night table
opposite his head, so that Gavin could simply extend his right arm
to turn or tune the set, and turn his head to the right to watch it.
And because there was an outdoor antenna on the building for the
television set in Doctor's Bar, the reception on Gavin's television
set was exceptional. As day after day went by, people like Big
Teddy and Will and Mattie—and even Gavin's mother, Veronica
—began to fade into the background of Gavin's consciousness.

More important, finer, more obedient people began to domi-
nate Gavin's life. Turn a switch and they would suddenly appear
to ease his loneliness. Turn the switch again and they courteously
disappeared. But how could Gavin ever tire of people like Mike
Barnett, Man Against Crime? And Mary Hartline, the beautiful
bandleader on Super Circus, and Buffalo Bob, Howdy Doody's
friend?

And there were so many more, all living beautiful, exciting
lives inside the little black box. Captain Video; Kukla, Fran and

Ollie, big, fat Herman Hickman and nice old Conrad Nagel on "Celebrity Time." And those old people were smarter and funnier by far than anyone Gavin had ever seen at Doctor's Bar and Restaurant. Nice, funny old folks like George Shelton and Lulu McConnell and Harry McNaughton and Tom Howard. How they made Gavin laugh on a show called "It Pays to be Ignorant."

And it never seemed to stop, hour after hour, day after day: new faces to see, new places to go, new friends to meet. There was Maggi McNellis and Eloise McElhone on a program all about women. There were smart men named Clifton Fadiman and Sam Levinson. And cowboys like Hopalong Cassidy and Gene Autrey. There were scary programs like "Suspense" and "Lights Out." There were long stories for grown-ups like "Kraft Television Theatre," but Gavin loved them, too. And there was even a show about the Bronx where Gavin lived. It was called "The Goldbergs," but Gavin didn't know any Jewish people. Some of the people at Doctor's Bar reminded him a lot of the man who played Chester Riley on "Life of Riley." But he certainly didn't know any families like the family on "I Remember Mama." They were so nice and loved each other so much and they even made Gavin laugh out loud when he was all alone. But Gavin was never really all alone. From the day his mother brought the television set into the little living room where Gavin lay recuperating in a hospital bed, until the day he died, the young boy knew he would never be alone again. His father was gone. His mother was barely a memory. But he had found his real family.

4

He wore a long, black cape that reached to the ground. In the center of the cape was a bold white eye that covered his chest and seemed to gaze out in hypnotic silence. In his left hand he held a TV antenna, the size and type commonly referred to as rabbit ears. In his right hand he held a small globe of earth no larger than a softball. His face was covered with a stark black-and-white mask, leaving one side of his head entirely in black, except for a small circle of white around the eyes; and the other side of the head entirely in white, with the eye encircled in black. He looked very much like a costumed professional wrestler about to enter the ring.

"Hello, my friends," he said. "I would like to talk to you tonight about a problem that faces each of us here on earth." There was no sign of his lips moving beneath the mask, and his voice had the hollow, distant ring of someone talking through a speaker phone. "The problem is whether or not we exist as ourselves, if we are valid beings in our own right, or if we are creatures of someone else's imagination, conforming to the directions of an invisible creator who controls us without our knowledge." He extended his left arm straight out in front of him and moved it stiffly back and forth from right to left in a symbolic gesture that had meaning only for him.

"For example, take myself. I mean, am I truly standing here

before you, or am I a character, so to speak, acting out a role? Am I, as the saying goes, the real McCoy? Or am I merely a toy for your mind? And once you have seen me will you ever be able to forget me? Won't I become a part of your life for all of your life?''

The eerie and geometric black-and-white face remained almost motionless, the only evidence that the deep emotionless voice came from behind the mask being the barely discernible bobbing of the head when certain words were emphasized or spoken louder than others.

''And then there's the other part of the question. Do you really exist for any other purpose than to hear my words? Have you simply been created to hear what I have to say? Wouldn't that be something? Think about it for a moment. If, all of your life, every breath you've ever taken, every book you've ever read, every pain, every pleasure, every conscious act, every second of sleep, everything was simply so that you could bear witness to an event you don't understand: An event like me.'' The voice remained detached, droning on monotonously, the eyes behind the mask gazing at some invisible object in the distance.

''Things are happening that you don't understand. I don't understand them fully either. But be patient. Have faith. Because in time we will understand everything; that has been promised to me. And in time we will understand the roles that each of us must play. But for now, I must inform you that by all your standards— your present standards—I do not exist. Sincerely. As I stand here before you at the very instant you see me standing here and listen to me talking to you, I tell you in all honesty and candor that I do not exist.''

Again the ritualistic waving of the antenna. And then, inexplicably, a loud sigh that carried with it the sound of exhaustion. The antenna and the globe simultaneously dropped to the floor, making a brief clanging sound as they fell by his bare feet, the globe rolling slowly in a nonsensical circle until it came to a stop.

''But what is existence anyway? What is real and what is fake and why should we bother worrying about it anyway. I mean, does it really matter whether you and I exist at this moment? Life is too short to worry about things like that, isn't it? Life is too short. Or it's too long. If it exists at all. I mean it did exist once. But can we be sure it exists right now? Maybe immortality is simply a recorded announcement that can't be turned off.'' The man's thick fingers came to the collar of the cape and toyed delicately with the strings that tied it together at the neck.

"And now, I am going to reveal my true identity. Watch closely; this may be your only chance to see who I am.''

The fingers moved quickly and the cape peeled away, falling in a heap at the man's feet. His body was lean, muscled. The same stark white eye that had been displayed prominently on the cape was painted on his naked chest. The only clothing he wore was a pair of black bathing trunks. And the mask. He did not remove it.

"As you can see,'' the man said, "I am nobody. And that means I am everybody.''

Another voice. Male, also a monotone, coming from a distance. "Why do you say you're nobody? Everybody is somebody.''

The masked figure cocked his head slightly to one side. "Because I'm an illusion. I'm not real.''

The second voice spoke again. "But why are you talking in riddles? Beneath the illusion of your mask, there is a real face, isn't there? Beneath the illusion there is a reality.''

The masked figure shook his head. "You will come to realize, my friend, that illusion has become reality. And reality has become illusion. They are no longer opposites. They are the same.''

Again, the other voice, coming from a distance. "I don't understand.''

The masked figure again shook his head. "It's so evident. Reality always disappears. Illusions live forever.''

"I don't understand. You're twisting things around.''

The black-and-white mask remained motionless, except for the slightest movement around the lips. "Have you ever seen photographs of Civil War soldiers?''

"Yes, of course. Everyone has.''

"But have you ever seen any Civil War soldiers yourself? Have you ever touched one or spoken to one or heard one speak?"

"No. Of course not. They're all dead. They all died long ago."

The masked figure moved his head slowly from left to right. "That is exactly my point. You've never seen even one Civil War soldier. But you've seen their pictures. The soldiers die and disappear. But the pictures can live on forever in your mind and in the minds of millions of others. The lives of Civil War soldiers were nothing. Their pictures are everything. Immortality is a recording."

There was silence for about ten seconds and then the second voice spoke again. "Does that mean it's time?"

"Yes."

The bullet hole appeared directly in the middle of the mask in the forehead at precisely the instant the explosion was heard. The man's eyes turned white behind the mask and his hands started to move instinctively toward his head but they never quite made it before he collapsed to the floor, blood squirting from the neat, spherical hole in quick, pulsating jets. He tried to get back to his feet but his coordination was gone and his instincts could not manage the task on their own. After about twenty seconds, all body motion stopped, except for the quivering of his left leg. And then that stopped too. The blood continued to squirt in bright red streams, staining the black-and-white mask and spilling across the floor.

The camera panned up from the fallen body to show a white wall that had been partially obscured by the man in the mask while he had still been standing. Something was printed on the wall. The camera moved in closer until everyone in the viewing audience of 96 million could read it clearly for themselves. Three words in black type on a white background. It read, "To be continued."

For a moment there was absolute silence, then came a sudden outburst of canned studio applause and laughter. Then abruptly, all sound stopped. The screen went blank.

"Good evening, America, this is Roger Tatum, news anchor-man for Channel Eight in Miami, bringing you a special update on the videotape killings that have shocked our country during recent weeks, and have focused the eyes of the world on what some members of the press have now labeled 'the mass-media murders.' " Roger Tatum's voice was clear, resonant. No matter how distasteful the subject, he was the complete professional, communicating a sense of quiet, mature control.

"The tape you have just witnessed is by now quite familiar to most of us—and certainly to anyone who's been anywhere near a television screen this past week." Roger Tatum stifled a small cough with his hand and cleared his throat quickly. "It is, of course, the second tape mailed directly to our station, WCQM, Channel Eight in Miami, by someone unknown."

The television screen was suddenly cut vertically in half, with Roger Tatum occupying the left side of the screen and a large close-up frozen-frame shot of the man in the black-and-white mask an instant before the bullet struck his forehead on the right-hand side of the screen. Roger Tatum continued talking.

"By now, this masked figure has been seen not only by ninety percent of the people living in America, he has been seen by the vast majority of people who own or have access to a television set anywhere in the world. There have been literally hundreds of calls to the authorities by viewers who claim the victim's voice or physical build strongly resembles those of a missing relative. But as of this moment, the police indicate there has been no identification or even strong lead as to the identity of the victim."

The right-hand side of the screen was wiped clean and the masked face was replaced by a frozen-frame shot of the girl called Tawny. Again Roger Tatum spoke from the left-hand side of the screen.

"This, of course, was the first victim, a girl named Tawny, if that is her real name. No last name was given. Estimated age at the time of the taping between eighteen and twenty-one. Still no positive identification."

The figure of Tawny was washed away and the vertical line in the center of the screen disappeared with her. Roger Tatum's face now filled the screen, but only for a second or two. "I'll be back in a moment."

Then Roger Tatum's face also disappeared into blackness. White type appeared: MORE ABOUT THE TV MURDERS COMING UP.

There was a total of four commercials, three running thirty seconds, and one ten seconds. Between two of the thirty-second commercials there was a network promotion for a new comedy series based on the behind-the-scenes feud of two top newscasters, one male and one female.

When Roger Tatum appeared again on the screen, he no longer shared it with anyone else. "Before we continue by showing you close-ups and by recapping the cases of the other two victims— and before we bring in our criminal psychology expert to give us a profile on the kind of person we might be dealing with, I'd like to pause here to make a point that's going to affect all of us long after this case is history." Roger Tatum folded his hands in front of him and leaned forward as if to come even closer to his audience throughout the country. "As you are no doubt aware, the subject matter of tonight's program has become a cause of controversy not only in this country but in virtually every civilized nation."

Once again, Roger Tatum was delegated to the left side of the screen, while the right side carried close-up stills of some of the mastheads of the world's leading newspapers.

Roger Tatum's voice. "The London *Observer* noted that violence on television in America has now become an audience participation affair." Cut to slide of *Tass* masthead. Roger Tatum's voice: "The Soviet newspaper *Tass* stated, 'To exploit the American people's fear . . . under the guise of freedom of the press . . . to create huge audiences and therefore huge profits for the networks from this sordid episode is the ultimate mark of moral decadence." Cut to slide of *Le Figaro* masthead. Roger Tatum's voice: "*Le Figaro* said, 'Mass-media murderer dwarfs Son of Sam as world watches in horror.' " Cut to slide of *New York Times* masthead. Roger Tatum's voice: "And our own *New*

York Times editorial noted, 'Roger Tatum should be barred as a newscaster. He is literally cooperating with the most insane killer in our nation's history to build ratings for his station and propel himself into a network anchorman's job. Turn off your television sets, America.' ''

The last masthead disappeared and the image of Roger Tatum spread across the screen again. He unfolded his hands, and sat back in his chair. His manner was pensive, his voice unusually soft. ''I do hope America does not turn off its television sets. I believe that when the first break comes in this case, it will most probably come from a member of our audience, someone who recognizes a face or a voice or an article of clothing.'' Roger Tatum cleared his throat and leaned forward in his chair. ''So far neither the police nor any government agency has been able to uncover a single significant lead in this case. Nor has any newspaper made any contribution, save to criticize us for presenting these unedited tapes to our viewing audience.

''I would like to address myself for a moment to the editorial comments of the *New York Times*. They claim that my local station in Miami, and this network, have systematically used these tapes to build an audience, to increase our ratings. They point out that when we first aired the tapes together in sequence, we had the largest viewing audience of any news program in television history.'' Roger Tatum paused for a moment, then reached slightly to his left and picked up a folded newspaper that had been resting on the desk in front of him. He started to unfold the paper. ''Did you see this? I wonder how many of you out there saw this?'' He unfolded the newspaper and held it up in front of him so the viewing audience could see the large, bold black headline.

TV MURDERER STRIKES AGAIN.

''This is the headline the *New York Times* ran on its front page exactly nine days ago. Perhaps it was a mere coincidence, but the *New York Times* sold more issues that day than any other in its history. More issues than the day President Kennedy was assassinated. More issues than the day man walked on the moon. More issues than ever.'' Roger Tatum folded the paper and placed it again on the desk in front of him. He smiled faintly into the camera for a second, then his face once again took on a serious expression.

"The point I want to make is simply this. I did not seek to become involved in the reporting of this case to make a national name for myself. I will, like the rest of you, be extremely relieved when the person responsible for creating these tapes has been apprehended. But these tapes—all of them—were sent directly to the news editor of Channel Eight in Miami. And that is me. Why I was singled out or selected, I do not know. Why our station was selected, I do not know. But I do know this: Everyone at Channel Eight in Miami, and everyone I have talked to at the network, does not view the events of the past month as an opportunity to increase ratings. We see it instead as an awesome responsibility to bring whatever we know to the attention of the public. Because, you see, this is perhaps the first time in the history of television that a news station has found itself not just in the position of reporting the news, but actually of being a major part of the news itself. It is unprecedented. There are no case histories in the past upon which to base our current actions. We are trying to do what we think is the right thing, regardless of ratings, or political pressure, or criticism from the press and other members of the electronic media.''

Roger Tatum paused again and unconsciously smoothed his moustache with the tips of two fingers. He was aware, he could not help but be aware, that he was probably being watched at the precise instant by more people than any single individual in the history of the United States. ''But, now let's get back to our basic responsibility; bringing you all the important information we can concerning this case.''

The camera pulled back from a closeup of Roger Tatum to show that a wiry balding man of about fifty-two, dressed in a dated blue suit, was seated next to him.

"Tonight, we have with us one of America's foremost forensic psychologists, Dr. David Dukoff of Princeton.'' Roger Tatum turned slightly and nodded at his guest. Doctor Dukoff's slender fingers fiddled with his tie, smoothed his shirt, straightened the ashtray in front of him. "Doctor Dukoff, what kind of person, in your opinion, are we dealing with? Do we have any kind of theoretical profile? Can we make any educated guesses about age? Appearance? Can we venture a guess about marital status or religious background or anything like that?"

The camera moved in tight on Dr. Dukoff, fingers fluttering across an angular chin. Nervous blinking of eyelids behind large steel-rimmed glasses.

"We know very, very little at this time, Mr. Tatum. To say that we know much of anything—anything we can be sure of—would be misleading and even dishonest—at this time."

Roger Tatums's off-camera voice: "Certainly you must have some opinion, some theory as to why these murders have taken place, why they have been taped and then forwarded to a television station."

Dr. Dukoff drummed his fingers on the desk compulsively as he closed his eyes for a second or two to collect his thoughts. Then he opened them, looking directly into the camera. "I think it is particularly interesting how the press and other media—yourself included, by the way Mr. Tatum—have continually referred to, and I quote, 'the person responsible,' 'the killer,' 'the maniac,' etc. Note that 'the killer' is always described in the singular, never the plural. I find that quite interesting."

Roger Tatum's off-camera voice: "Why is that, Doctor? I realize that it could be more than one person. But isn't it more or less natural to assume that one person murders another? Isn't that the way it is in most cases?"

Doctor Dukoff smiled wryly, dark-brown eyes flashing bright behind his glasses. "Ah, Mr. Tatum. This obviously isn't most cases. Certainly the most significant aspect about this case is that the murders have been videotaped and then sent to a television station, obviously with the idea in mind that they would be shown to the viewing public."

Again, Roger Tatum's off-camera voice: "And this suggests

something to you, doctor. Some discernible reason or rationale, some perverted train of logic.''

"Well, Mr. Tatum, it has been our collective experience within the past decade or so to see political groups exploit and even seize control of television outlets to propagandize or gain sympathy for their particular causes. Certainly none of us will forget the ordeal of the American hostages in Iran, and how their captors staged what I can only call 'TV Specials' showing angry mobs of Iranians and despondent American hostages to millions of viewers around the world. In some instances, I'm afraid they used our media as if it were their own.''

"You believe these murders may be politically inspired?''

Dr. Dukoff's thin fingers straightened his glasses. "I can't say that with any degree of certainty. But I think it is a distinct possibility, perhaps even a probability.''

Roger Tatum's expression was intense and he asked the next question with a subtle suggestion of surprise, as if a new thought had just occurred to him. "Would that make the victims on the tape political hostages? Or rather political martyrs?''

"Not necessarily. They appeared to be unaware that their lives were in danger right up until the moment of their deaths. It's true that the girl named Tawny stated that someone might kill her, but she appeared to be play-acting. At least she certainly did to me.''

Roger Tatum's voice was low, his expression still one of deep concentration. "Then why . . .?''

"To attract our attention,'' Dr. Dukoff answered the incomplete question. "The person or group of people responsible for these tapes simply wanted to attract America's attention, so they chose the fastest, most effective means possible. Television. I suspect that these taped episodes of violence are merely prefaces to their main statement or demand, which will probably be forthcoming shortly, as soon as they are convinced that most of the world is tuned in.''

"Have the police or any government bodies expressed belief in your theory, doctor?''

"Yes, they have. Along with a number of other theories that

are also being explored. But there is a strong case for political terrorism, since television has so frequently been a target in the past." Dr. Dukoff paused momentarily, but Roger Tatum's silence made it evident that he wished the doctor to pursue the subject further. "Example," said Dr. Dukoff, referring to a small sheaf of notes on the desk in front of him. "Nineteen seventy-five. West Germany. The Baader-Meinhof terrorists in West Germany took a politician hostage to use in trade for the release of five of their comrades who had been imprisoned. As each prisoner boarded a plane to freedom, West German television was forced to carry their obviously dictated propaganda messages."

Roger Tatum nodded silently, indicating that he recalled the incident.

Dr. Dukoff referred to his notes again. "Patti Hearst was another case in point. Remember how the Symbionese Liberation Army used the media to make their message public through radio and televised reporting of tape-recorded messages?" Dr. Dukoff paused, looked away from the camera, and directed his next remarks to Roger Tatum. "There are numerous other cases. When the Arab terrorists took over the Vienna headquarters of OPEC, their game plan included continuing the siege until the television cameras could arrive. And perhaps the best-known example was the one in March of nineteen seventy-five in Washington, D.C. Remember how the leader was on the phone so much answering questions, and how he checked with his wife to see what the broadcasts were saying and showing? He even got public apologies from the government officials live on TV for everyone to see."

"I think your point is well made, doctor. But these killings seem to have no immediately apparent relationship to any political aims." Roger Tatum unconsciously smoothed his moustache and waited for Dr. Dukoff to answer.

"Remember, Mr. Tatum, at this time—until there is concrete evidence—everything I say is pure speculation and must be regarded as such. Still, I see here the possibility of political terrorists using television in a way in which we had never previously conceived. In the past, they staged violent events and had the television cameras come to them, or they interrupted televised events with violence calculated to attract attention. But what we may have here—and please note, I say *may* have—is a case where they are literally creating their own television programming—almost like syndicated packaging—and then having a network like yours act as an innocent dupe in projecting that message.''

"But so far, there have been no political messages, doctor.''

"No, not yet. But they certainly have our attention now, don't they? Whatever they may have to say, you can bet the world will listen to and watch very carefully.''

"Excuse me, doctor, we need to break here for a moment.'' Roger Tatum turned away from Dr. Dukoff and once again was speaking personally to every member of the viewing audience. "Our guest is Dr. David Dukoff, one of America's foremost forensic psychologists. We'll be right back.'' The first commercial was for a soon-to-be-released major motion picture starring Robert Redford as an IRA guerilla. The second commercial was for Preparation H and featured a middle-aged woman talking to a druggist. The commercial ended with a close-up of the product that faded into blackness. White type appeared on the screen. THIS SUNDAY, SEPTEMBER 23RD. THE MINNESOTA VIKINGS VS. THE MIAMI DOLPHINS. The type reduced in size rapidly until it took up only the lower portion of the screen. The middle section of the screen became animated with stills in rapid sequence of mammoth professional football players crashing into each other. The track was a mixture of martial music and the sounds of players grunting and groaning as their bodies collided.

The fast-paced physical action of the promotional spot for professional football faded, and the camera was once again on Roger Tatum. "Doctor, you were speaking about the way political terrorist groups have either manipulated or seized the media— generally television—to get their messages across to the masses. And you indicated that because they have operated in such a manner in the past, it is possible that some such group is responsible for the videotaped murders we have telecast for our audience. The implication then being that knowingly or unknowingly, we at this network may be aiding a group of terrorists.''

Dr. Dukoff nodded. ''It's a possibility, certainly. But there are many possibilities.''

''You are aware, doctor, that there have been numerous incidents where individuals with no political motivation have used television to focus attention on themselves and their crimes?''

''Of course,'' Dr. Dukoff answered, ''I was going to refer to individuals like that as representing another distinct possibility. I mentioned the political-terrorists possibility first because of the actual videotaping of the crimes. It seems to me that a sophisticated activity of that kind would probably be more easily conducted by a group than an individual. There'd have to be access to videotape equipment. Knowledge of how to use it. Proper lighting. Technical awareness. Plus, of course, actually taping the murders themselves. I don't rule out the possibility of one person's being responsible for it all. But it seems more logical that it's some type of group.'' Dr. Dukoff paused for a moment and referred to his notes. ''By the way, did you notice the reference in both of the tapes to the idea that what we were seeing were only 'parts of the total picture,' that we couldn't understand everything yet, but that in time we would. I think that fits in rather well with the theory that these tapes are merely to focus our attention on a main message yet to be delivered. And if that is the case, the message will most probably be political. If there's one thing these extremist groups realize, it's the power of television.''

''I'm sure, Doctor Dukoff, that many of us can recognize the rationale behind your theory of political terrorists at work here. But again, what about the possibility of a single individual, acting alone?'' Roger Tatum folded his hands on the desk in front of him and waited for Dr. Dukoff to answer.

Dr. Dukoff smiled. ''I wonder how many of your viewers recognize the name Stonehaffer? Edward Stonehaffer? Probably not too many. And yet for a number of hours he had the entire nation's attention. Remember?''

Dr. Dukoff and Roger Tatum disappeared from the screen and were replaced by a tape showing a stocky man in a T-shirt holding a sawed-off shotgun. The muzzle end of the shotgun was wired to the neck of a man in a business suit. The two men were moving slowly through a crowd of police officers and television crewmen. Across the bottom of the screen were the words, TAPED IN 1977. Dr. Dukoff's voice could be heard as the two figures, separated only by the length of a shotgun, marched through the crowd.

"Remember," Dr. Dukoff said, "the man holding the gun is Stonehaffer. The hostage in the business suit is a mortgage company officer. It was Indianapolis—middle America—in the winter of 1977. And do you know what Edward Stonehaffer was yelling as he moved through those crowds? He was yelling 'Get those cameras on! Get those goddamn cameras on! I'm a goddamn national hero!' "

The footage of Stonehaffer and his hostage disappeared, and once again the screen was filled by the figures of Roger Tatum and Dr. Dukoff. "I think the Stonehaffer case is a perfect example of an individual's committing a crime solely for the benefit of television. This crime did not happen to be reported *by* television. It was committed because *of* television, because Stonehaffer wanted everyone to see him. Had television not existed, I doubt the crime would have been committed." Dr. Dukoff looked up from his notes and turned to face Roger Tatum just before the two of them again faded from the screen, to be replaced by then-President Jimmy Carter.

"Yes, we all remember this," said Roger Tatum, as the video picture showed President Carter speaking at a press conference. White type across the bottom of the screen read: PRESIDENTIAL PRESS CONFERENCE, MARCH 1977.

Jimmy Carter's voice could be heard in the background, but Dr. Dukoff's voice spoke over his until the President's voice simply faded away. His lips moved, but the only words heard were those of Dr. Dukoff. "Here was a case where a criminal not only got the attention of national television, he also watched the

President of the United States promise in a televised press conference to speak to him. I wonder how many of us can recall how this man, who was holding hostages, actually got a television set so he could see the President speak directly to him on a national telecast. Do you remember, Mr. Tatum?"

There was silence for about three seconds, and then Roger Tatum answered. "He traded a hostage for a television set, didn't he?"

"That's right," Dr. Dukoff added as the image of Jimmy Carter faded from the screen. Once again, the camera was on Roger Tatum and Dr. Dukoff. "Certainly," Dr. Dukoff continued, "there have been cases where isolated individuals have sought to manipulate and seize the media to gain attention for themselves. Perhaps this is what's happening here. But I rather doubt it. I think it's a little far-fetched to imagine one individual out there among all your millions of viewers who has systematically arranged to select victims, apparently rehearse them, and then videotape the executions. The others made the TV cameras come to them and their victims. This one would have to be using his own TV camera to bring the events to us. It's a little hard to imagine one person bringing this kind of thing off."

Before Dr. Dukoff or Roger Tatum could say another word there was a sudden click and they quickly disappeared from the screen. The slender man sat alone in the darkness, settling deep into the Eames chair. He placed the remote-control channel selector back on the stuffed black ottoman. He closed his eyes, and on the secret screen behind his eyelids he watched another kind of news report, one he knew would soon make television history.

And wouldn't Roger Tatum be surprised.

But for now, it was time to turn to another channel.

5

These were the wonderful years for Gavin. His mother and Big Teddy and his classmates all faded neatly into a small compartment of his mind that he grudgingly acknowledged but paid as little attention to as he possibly could. Gavin knew they were there, but they weren't real. Only the people who performed for him on television were real. He laughed at Sid Stone, the pitchman on Milton Berle's "Texaco Star Theatre," who rolled up his sleeves every Tuesday night and said directly to Gavin: "I tell you what I'm gonna do." And Gavin loved ventriloquist Jimmy Nelson and his dummy Danny O'Day on the same show. He also liked a man named Jackie Gleason who was Chester O'Reilly on the "Life of Riley" show. And he was disappointed when he turned on the show one night and Jackie Gleason wasn't there. There was a new Chester Riley, a man named William Bendix. But it all turned out fine because Gavin grew to like the new Riley very much, and then Jackie Gleason began appearing on a lot of other shows. He could make Gavin laugh inside almost as hard as anyone, except, perhaps a man named Sid Caeser who had such silly friends. There were other funny people, too. Bob Hope and Red Skelton and Jackie E. Leonard and Red Buttons and Jimmy Durante and Ken Murray and Jack Benny and Eddie Cantor and Joe E. Brown, who had, Gavin thought, the widest mouth in the world. And there was a really crazy lady with a big mouth named

Martha Raye. But his favorites—the ones who could make him laugh so hard inside that his blank face would almost form an expression of amusement—were two men named Dean Martin and Jerry Lewis. He really loved Jerry Lewis. But Gavin never actually did laugh out loud. Maybe it was because there was never anyone in the room with him. Or maybe it was because he could tell if something was funny in his mind, and he was perfectly content to enjoy it there—in his mind—without making any kind of noise of approval or changing his expression. If someone had watched Gavin Risen's face as he watched those television shows, there would have been no way of telling what kind of shows Gavin actually was watching. Whether it was a comedy, drama, news, sports, musical, documentary, or quiz show, Gavin's expression remained placid, emotionless. The excitement was completely inside him, but it was constant, intense and totally private.

Those early television shows and stars paraded before Gavin's eyes, a seemingly endless source of information and entertainment. And the people he'd meet! People he knew he'd never have a chance to meet at Doctor's Bar or at school. People like Art Baker of "You Asked for It." And Arthur Godfrey and Rex Reed and James Melton and Morton Downey and Captain Video and Kathi Norris and the mind reader Dunninger and Sherman Billingsly. There were Laraine Day and Faye Emerson and Dave Garroway and Jack Lescoule and Jerry Lester and Dagmar and Milton DeLugg and Roberta Quinlan and Kate Smith. There were Lee J. Cobb and Reed Hadley and Jack Webb and David Brian and Sgt. Friday and Mr. Peepers and Lucy and Mr. DA, and so many more there was no way in the world to count them or keep them straight.

It was during the spring of 1952 that Gavin Risen began to seek sexual excitement and gratification from the glowing tube that was now located on a night table in his bedroom. His first climax came as a popular television hostess named Faye Emerson talked quietly with the composer of a new Broadway show. Miss Emerson's blouse slipped low in front and pulled away from her ample bosom as she frequently changed her position from facing the camera to turning to her guest. Each time she pivoted slightly in her seat, the soft white mounds of her full breasts came close to spilling out of her blouse. For reasons he didn't understand, Gavin Risen began to feel short of breath. His heart pounded heavily in his chest and his head became light. A sweaty hand moved beneath the bedsheets that covered his slender body. He tensed with sudden pleasure. Miss Emerson made a slight turn to her left to speak more directly to her viewers. Gavin's stomach trembled and his hand began a slow, shy, rhythmic stroking motion beneath the bedsheet. Miss Emerson bent slightly forward. Gavin's hand moved faster, harder. He could hardly breathe at all. The line between her breasts was deep and Gavin knew somehow it would be warm and soft. His hand moved even faster. Something terrible or wonderful was going to happen any second. And then the door to Gavin's bedroom flew open and his mother stood swaying in the doorway. "What the hell are you doing up at this hour watching that stupid thing for. Don't you know you've got school tomorrow?" Her speech was drunken, slurred. Miss Emerson moved forward in her chair and Gavin knew it was too late to stop what was happening inside him. His face remained a mask of calm but his body trembled until the bed rattled softly and he sighed deeply and pulled the sheets tightly around him when it happened.

"Are you all right, Gavin?" his mother asked. She almost fell as she backed out of the room and started to close the door. "You don't have a cold or chills or anything do you?" Gavin didn't answer. His mother closed the door and he could hear her heavy, uneven footsteps in the hallway outside his bedroom. He didn't care. He was alone with Faye Emerson again. And happy and sad at the same time in a way he'd never known before. Faye Emerson wished Gavin good-night. He said good-night to her and closed his eyes and went to sleep without getting up to turn off the television set. He had never done that before.

There were others—scores of others—who aroused the young man's passion that spring. Some of them had names. Like Roxanne, the tall, exquisitely lovely blonde who appeared on the quiz show, "Beat the Clock," with a very nice man named Bud Collyer. And there were others without names who danced in chorus lines or assisted emcees, sleek taut thighs gleaming white beneath black mesh stockings. Circus shows were especially good because the acrobats and trapeze artists and tightrope walkers wore the briefest of costumes, with firm, hard buttocks protruding from tights that literally clung to the performers' bodies with such intensity that Gavin was certain he could see clear outlines of those parts of a woman's body he had seen only on his mother when she had passed out on the toilet or in the tub. But these girls were so different from his mother. They were young and pretty and their flesh giggled under satin. Their breasts swelled out over the tops of gowns. Their sweet milky white bellies moved sensuously through foreign dances and their hips vibrated with incredible mobility.

There was a singer–piano player named Nancy Laurie who appeared three nights a week after the late news. She was not a particularly pretty girl. Her lips were a bit too thick, her nose too prominent and somewhat more fleshy than the pert Doris Day type of button nose that was then so popular. She was Gavin's favorite. Not only because she had extremely large breasts, which she displayed with great generosity through a wardrobe obviously created to merchandise her figure, but because the cameraman on the show was obviously as enamored of Nancy Laurie's breasts as Nancy was herself, not to mention Gavin and a few million other late-night viewers. The camera would often start out high at the beginning of a song, shooting down at Nancy as she sat playing the piano, looking up soulfully into the eyes of her audience. As the song progressed, the camera would move slowly down, down, down, taking Gavin's eyes literally inside Nancy's blouse or dress. Always, Gavin's face stayed calm, without any trace of feeling or emotion. But his hand moved frantically, night after night, bringing him momentary relief from the tension that constantly attacked his body and which caused him to walk in a stiff-legged, straight-back way that suggested arthritis.

His leg had healed, but not properly. It had been two years

since the doctors had taken off the cast and surgically removed the plate from his leg. The bone had knit successfully, but his right leg had not kept pace with the growth rate of the rest of his body while it was encased in the huge cast, with the result that his leg was one and a half inches shorter than his left leg. This handicap did not interfere with Gavin's life in any way, except that it caused him to walk with a slight but clearly discernible limp. The doctors said that perhaps the limp would disappear in time. Gavin knew better. He knew it would be with him for the rest of his life. And he liked that, because he often fantasized about how the women he saw on television would be sympathetic and somehow attracted to him because of his leg.

As the fifties rolled along, Gavin moved deeper into the world of television and further away from his mother and classmates and the habitués of Doctor's Bar. He became fascinated for a while with the frenzied activity that surrounded professional wrestling—the ranting old ladies screaming hysterically for their favorite to rip off an opponent's arms and legs. He enjoyed the obvious battle between good and evil with living legends like Antonio Rocca and Gorgeous George and the Swedish Angel leaping around the ring, ricocheting off the ropes, banging each other's Adam's apples, sticking thumbs in eyes, biting ears, kneeing testicles, twisting necks while appealing to the referee and the audience for fairness. Baseball, football, and basketball captured Gavin's fancy for a short time, although he would never consider playing any of these games with his classmates at school. He realized that if you were playing the game you couldn't watch it. And he had realized for a long time now that it was far more interesting to be a spectator than a participant in events. Perhaps one day, he would often think to himself, it will be possible to observe and participate in an event at the same time; to be both audience and performer simultaneously. Now that would really be something wouldn't it? To climb a mountain and see yourself climbing it; to catch a touchdown pass and see yourself catching it at the precise instant the football reached your hands. To sing and dance and be able to see yourself singing and dancing at the same moment millions of others watched you perform. Even to die and to see yourself dying right up to the split second that separates "right now" from forever. But until that time came—and Gavin somehow knew even then that the time would come, he would always choose to watch rather than do, to observe rather than act. His mother and schoolteachers were always expecting him to *do* something: to make his bed, to eat his breakfast, to solve math problems, to clean his room, to write more neatly, to speak more clearly. Only the small television set on the night table in his bedroom gave to Gavin without asking anything in return. Day after day, night after night, it provided him with so many nice companions, so many exciting moments, so much sexual satisfaction and happiness and laughter, although the laughter always remained locked quietly in Gavin's mind. It was no wonder then, that Gavin considered the nine-inch Philco his one and only close personal friend, as well as his true family.

Even though Gavin was now moving into his teens, the subject matter of the programs he watched was of no great importance. He watched shows for preschoolers with as much attention as he focused on Westerns or comedy shows or late-night movies. He loved them all. Captain Kangaroo and Howdy Doody and Kukla, Fran, and Ollie. He loved a new show about a lovely dog named Lassie, and another about a Western sheriff named Wyatt Earp. There was the Mickey Mouse Club and Commando Cody and "The Millionaire," which was all about a mysterious billionaire named John Beresford Tipton who gave money away—a million dollars a week—to people he never knew. Of course, no one ever saw John Beresford Tipton's face; just his back, and hands and a big brown cigar. The man who actually gave the money away was Mr. Tipton's ever faithful executive secretary, Michael Anthony. Gavin knew what he would do if Michael Anthony ever knocked on his door and handed him a check for a million dollars. He would move as far away as he could from his mother and Big Teddy and Will, the Indian, and Doctor's Bar. And he would never see them again. He lay awake nights hoping that somehow Mr. Tipton and Mr. Anthony would realize just how much he wanted to be free of his mother. If they did, they would surely give him the money.

Then, one night as he was lying in bed quietly watching a new show called "Alfred Hitchcock Presents," Gavin's mother knocked on his door, entered his room and practically handed him a million dollars. Or at least she gave him a million-dollar idea.

"Son," she began, sitting down softly on the edge of Gavin's bed, unaware of how furiously she irritated him by interrupting his concentration on the program. "I know I haven't been the best mother in the world, and I know I can never undo so many of the things I've done to turn you away from me."

She sounded sober, thought Gavin. Sad, but sober. The light emanating from the television set on the night table cast an eerie glow over her face, outlining features that once had been considered quite pretty but which now seemed bloated and battered beyond saving by alcohol. Still, she sounded sober.

"We don't have much money, never have had. Your father left us with nothing more than his debts and I've worn myself out trying to repay them. But I have managed to put a little aside each month. Not much, but enough so that if anything happens to me you'll be taken care of."

Gavin's gaze remained riveted to the television screen. A seriously overweight bald man with a priggish moustache was talking to the audience with a slow, exaggerated British accent. His voice had been competing with Gavin's mother's voice for the boy's attention.

"Gavin, are you listening to me? Please pay attention to me for once. I swear that television set means more to you than your own mother."

Gavin's face remained a mask of indifference but his mind smiled at how his mother had unknowingly spoken such an evident truth.

"The money I've put aside has gone into an insurance policy on my life. God only knows how I got anyone to insure me. I think he must have been watching over you. Anyway, if I die, there'll be money to take care of you for a few years until you're old enough to earn a living for yourself. It's not a fortune. It's around fifteen thousand. But I wanted to tell you about it so that in case anything happens to me, you'll know that you have some money coming to you. Do you understand?''

Gavin turned his head from the television set and looked at the pathetic stoop-shouldered woman sitting on the edge of his bed. "I understand, mother," he said. "But don't say that you haven't been a good mother. You've been a wonderful mother.''

There was a moment's silence, and then Veronica spoke softly, her voice barely audible above the fat man speaking on the television set. "Do you mean that, Gavin? Do you really mean it?'' Every word that Gavin had spoken a few seconds earlier was from a play he had seen on a program called "Playhouse 90" only a few days before. And he knew that the lines he was going to speak were lines the main character had spoken on the television program he was watching just a few moments before his mother had entered his room.

"I meant every word of it," said Gavin. "I've never meant anything more in my life.''

Veronica felt tears spilling across her cheeks in the semidarkness of the room. She stood and bent to kiss her child. Gavin remained motionless, his face revealing no more feelings than a television test pattern. Veronica bent forward and kissed him on the lips for the first time in years. Gavin suppressed a feeling that he might vomit violently, forcing his mind's eye to reconstruct the image on the television screen, which his mother's body now blocked. Veronica pulled back suddenly after making contact with her son's lips. They were ice-cold. And yet she had felt the unmistakable quick jolt of an electrical shock. She looked down through the darkness at Gavin to see if had felt anything. His face was impassive.

"Didn't you feel anything, then, Gavin. A kind of shock.''

"No," answered Gavin. "I didn't feel anything, mother. I don't feel anything at all.'' The voice on the television set stopped talking. There was silence in the room. Gavin had already made up his mind about what to do with his mother.

He didn't do it right away, of course. He waited patiently for the right time, watching his favorite detective and mystery stories, hoping to pick up some idea of how to do away with his mother while making absolutely certain he would never be caught. All kinds of ingenious ideas showed up on "Alfred Hitchcock Presents," the very show Gavin had been watching when his mother first gave him the idea to end her life. And there were others—"War Against Crime," "Doorway to Danger," "Fabian of Scotland Yard," "Boston Blackie," "Mr. and Mrs. North," "The Line-up," "Paris Precinct," "The Telltale Clue," "Crime Photographer," and many more. But somehow, the exactly correct method of doing it to Veronica eluded him. Weeks passed, then months. Months became years, until finally, by 1957, when Gavin was seventeen years old and ready to graduate from high school, he made the decision that, right or wrong, he had to do it at once. And once he had made the decision, the method became immediately apparent to him. He would kill her with the television set. Sure, it would be painful to lose his closest companion, but once he had collected the insurance money on Veronica, he would be able to afford dozens of television sets, all much bigger and clearer than the tired nine-inch Philco that labored each day to keep Gavin entertained.

The opportunity came a week before Christmas. Veronica had spent the afternoon drinking with Big Teddy and "the boys" at Doctor's Bar. By the time Gavin returned from school, she had already reached the point where she was making no sense whatsoever when she spoke.

"Hey Gavin," said Big Teddy, his own voice hoarse from too much alcohol, "Veronica's gone numb in her noggin again, know what I mean?" The "boys" at the bar laughed. Saliva slipped from the corner of Big Teddy's mouth as his own laughter caused the sloppy butt of a cigar to fall from his mouth to the floor. Veronica was seated next to Big Teddy at the bar. "Donna," she said to no one. "Donna wanna Donna's mamma." She turned her head slowly to the left. Her eyes tried to focus on Gavin, but the boy had no way of knowing whether she recognized him or whether she could even see him. He spoke softly. "Please, Mom, let's go upstairs."

"Donna wanna Donna's mama" she said. And then she lowered her head slowly to the bar, where she rested it on the backs of her hands. It took two of the boys and Gavin about five minutes to get her up the stairs and onto her bed. She was still mumbling when Gavin thanked the boys for their help and told them that everything would be all right, that Veronica would sleep it off in a few hours. As soon as the boys had gone, Gavin began to make arrangements for Veronica's sleep to last a lot longer than a few hours.

First Gavin went into the bathroom and started the water running in the tub slowly. He adjusted the faucets so the water was a soft, lukewarm stream that would take about twenty minutes to fill for a proper bath. Then he left the bathroom, stepped out in the hall, and stood silent for a moment, straining to hear if Will, the Indian, was about in his room. He could hear nothing, so he stepped up to the door to Will, the Indian's, room and knocked gently. No answer. He knocked harder. Still no answer. "Will, are you there?" Silence. Gavin smiled in his mind and walked slowly back to Veronica's room. She was snoring softly, her skirt yanked up to her hips, revealing stockings rolled to the knee and bloated thighs streaked with splotches of veins and bruise marks that Gavin imagined were caused by bumping into tables when she was drunk, or by Big Teddy's mean and greedy hands. For a moment he felt like he wanted to vomit. Then he began to undress his mother, starting with the stained white blouse that buttoned to her neck. When he lifted her back off the bed to make it easier to slip off her blouse, Veronica opened her eyes and looked at Gavin. "What are you doing, what are you doing to me, Gavin?"

She was a dead weight in Gavin's slender arms, but he held her steady and said, "Easy Mother, easy. I'm just helping you get ready for bed." Veronica started to say something, but instead smiled and closed her eyes and drifted back into a drunken sleep.

When Gavin had undressed her down to her bra and panties, he moved her body into a sitting position on the side of the bed. She started to come round again, and Gavin spoke to her softly, patiently, as if he were the parent and she were the child. "O.K., now Momma, try to stand up and walk with me. I'll hold you good. But please try to get up. You've got to get up."

Without understanding why she had to get up or where she was going, Veronica leaned against her son and managed to get to her feet, however unsteadily. It was a long, lurching walk to the bathroom, with Gavin barely able to keep Veronica from collapsing. Once inside the bathroom, however, things went more smoothly. He eased his mother onto the toilet and in less than a minute had removed her bra and panties so that she was completely naked. Gavin tried hard not to look at her large, sagging breasts or pubic area for fear it would make him sick. He tried, instead, to concentrate on her eyes, which were open again, and staring at him in a strange, uncomprehending gaze.

"C'mon, Mama," he said softly, "it's time to get up again." It took all his strength to get her on her feet again, but he managed to get her into the bathtub, which was now three-quarters full, with less difficulty than he'd imagined. She'd actually been able to lift her foot over the tub and put her hand against the wall to help hold herself up until Gavin could guide her gently, gently down into the water. Gavin looked at her face closely to see if the water might shock her into a more sober state. It didn't. She rested her head on the back of the tub and smiled stupidly, her dull grey eyes glazed over almost as if she were totally blind. Gavin started to leave the bathroom, but halted abruptly when he heard her say, "You're a good boy, Gavin. I should be a better mother to you."

He looked down at her lying motionless in the tub. She was talking, but she really didn't know where she was. The water was high enough. Gavin bent and turned off the faucets. The sound of the water stopped. Veronica was mumbling something, but Gavin couldn't quite make out what it was. "You've been a wonderful mother," he said, "you've given your son everything he could ask for."

When Gavin returned to the bathroom carrying the nine-inch Philco in his arms, Veronica was asleep in the tub. He bent slowly and lowered the television set to the floor. Then he quickly slid the hamper over next to the tub, and lifted the Philco again and placed it atop the hamper. Then he took the wire and plug attached to the television set and walked with them to the bathroom sink; he bent and placed the plug in the outlet beneath the sink. Then he turned on the television set and sat down on the toilet to watch the evening news while his mother slept peacefully in the tub a few feet away.

When the evening news was finished, Gavin got up from the toilet and walked over to the hamper. Next to the hamper, perhaps a foot or so away, was a bathroom scale. With his foot Gavin pushed the scale to the base of the hamper, then, very carefully holding the hamper and TV set with his hands, he tipped the hamper ever so slowly. Again using his foot he pushed the edge of the scale beneath the legs of the hamper, so that two legs of the hamper were on the ground, and the other two legs, nearest the tub, rested on the edge of the scale. This accomplished, he took a towel from a rack on the wall and wiped down the television set and the hamper, pushing the Philco softly so that it extended over the edge of the hamper nearest the tub.

Gavin returned to the toilet and sat down. There was one more program he wanted to watch. And besides, the show was only on for fifteen minutes. Veronica could wait. Now if only Will, the Indian, didn't come up the stairs during the show everything would be all right. Gavin sat on the toilet watching the show, his face blank but his mind happy. Will, the Indian, never came up the stairs. When the show was finished, Gavin got up from the toilet. He walked over to the hamper. He drew his left foot back and kicked the scale, but not too hard, just enough to nudge it out from under the legs of the hamper, which in turn, hit the floor rather hard, causing the nine-inch Philco to totter precariously for a second or two on top of the hamper, before dropping into the tub. Veronica's body stiffened suddenly, and then her head slid beneath the water, and that was the last Gavin ever saw of her because Will, the Indian, was the one who discovered the body, and Big Teddy and everyone else thought it best that the casket be closed and the boy be spared the painful experience of viewing his mother's body.

Of course, Gavin cried in his mind the night his mother died, because, after all, that was the night he lost his nine-inch Philco and was the first night in years he couldn't watch television. He vowed it would never happen again.

6

Three months after Veronica died, Gavin Risen completed high school. He did not graduate but was issued a certificate of attendance instead. And since he had already turned eighteen—having lost a year in school when he had severely injured his leg years earlier—Gavin was left pretty much on his own. He had made no close friends during high school and was considered by his classmates to be a "loner," a "weirdo." So no one paid any attention when he failed to make an appearance at any of the numerous parties that took place during the last few weeks of school. He was not actively disliked by his classmates, nor did he actively dislike them. It was as if his classmates and he were only vaguely aware of the other's existence and quietly respected the distances that separated them. No one seemed to know or care very much whether Gavin ever dated. He paid no attention to girls at school, and whether or not he had a girlfriend outside of school was anybody's guess, if anybody cared to guess. But no one did.

The money from Veronica's insurance policy still hadn't been straightened out by the time Gavin finished school, but Big Teddy let Gavin stay on in the apartment, until he could find a job.

The first few weeks after school were absolute paradise for Gavin. He seldom moved from the apartment, because everything he wanted and cared about was right there, from early-morning weather reports to afternoon soap operas to evening variety shows to news reports to late movies that often stayed on till after four in the morning. People like Perry Mason and Peter Gunn and Richard Diamond and Elliot Ness visited Gavin in the apartment. And so did a handsome young man named Kookie, who reminded Gavin of a student in his geometry class. But Gavin realized it was so much easier to get to know the people like Matt Dillon and Major Seth Adams and Flint McCullough who came to spend time with him in the apartment than it had been to get to know any of the kids in school or even the people around Doctor's Bar. The people with whom he spent so much time in his apartment were so much nicer, so much friendlier, so much more real. About the only person from his school or Doctor's Bar that he could feel anything at all for was Big Teddy, and that was because Big Teddy—in a burst of compassion—had bought the boy a television set to keep him company after Veronica died. "After all," said Big Teddy at the time, "the kid's got no one now. He's strange enough as it is without being left alone in the world. At least the television will keep him company, will keep him entertained. Maybe it'll help take his mind off his mother."

It was a regular customer at Doctor's Bar—a personal friend of Big Teddy's—who helped Gavin get a job six weeks after school was out. Big Teddy was greatly relieved when the boy finally went to work because he knew it wasn't doing the youngster any good just sitting around the apartment day and night, week after week, brooding about his mother.

Gavin, of course, was quite disturbed that what had clearly been the happiest period of his life was coming to a close. But he knew that it was expected that he should hold a job, and it was also expected that once he had settled into a job, he would be moving from the apartment. Actually, the job wasn't anywhere near as bad as Gavin had imagined it would be. It was on an assembly line, making concrete conduits for underground installation. The job required no particular skills. It consisted, in fact, of a series of very basic and monotonous motions that were repeated approximately twenty-four times an hour, every hour, five and a half nights a week. But the job suited Gavin perfectly because it was a night shift. He started at midnight and worked through until eight in the morning. Of course, Gavin did not like being away from his television for any extended period, but at least this way, he rationalized, he was away when little or nothing was on. Sometimes Gavin and his co-workers would manage to make an extra number of conduits over and above their specified quota and would then store them away until they had enough to gain almost all of Saturday night off simply by adding the secret surplus conduits to the number they made that particular night. Gavin worked especially hard to make the extra conduits, because on Saturday nights there was always an excellent selection of late movies on television.

A month after taking the job, which was located in Queens just over the Bronx-Whitestone Bridge, Gavin moved into a one-room garage apartment located in back of a typical two-family house in a quiet section of Queens just twenty minutes' walk to work. From the day he moved, Gavin never again saw Big Teddy, or Will, the Indian, or any of the regulars from Doctor's Bar, or any of his classmates. He disappeared into his own world, which is exactly what he'd wanted to do ever since those days years before, when he lay in a long white cast and met so many exciting and interesting new friends while Veronica drank downstairs with Big Teddy and the boys.

The next few years rolled by swiftly and satisfactorily for Gavin. He received his inheritance from Veronica soon after starting his new job, and apart from spending six hundred and eighty-five dollars for the clearest, large-screen television set he could find, he placed the entire amount in a savings account until he could decide what he wanted to do with it. He knew, in some way, that the money would be very important to him, but for the time being he couldn't figure out how. But he didn't worry. It would come to him. Meanwhile, he kept toiling faithfully at his job night after night, grateful that the nature of the work required him to think very little, and talk very little to his co-workers.

Gavin measured the passage of time not by conventional dates such as Christmas or his birthday, or by the change of seasons, but rather by the arrival of new shows on television. Nineteen fifty-nine would be forever fixed in his mind as the year "Bonanza" first rode across his TV set, with Ben Cartwright and his boys making Sunday evenings Gavin's favorite time of the week. That was the year that Rod Sterling introduced "Twilight Zone," another show that communicated with Gavin far more clearly than any of his co-workers ever could. Nineteen-sixty saw the arrival of "The Andy Griffith Show," "The Third Man," and one show in particular that caught Gavin's fancy: "Surfside 6." Often as he sat in his sparsely furnished one-room apartment watching the show, he would glance out his window, and the ice-coated telephone poles would become bright-green palm trees. He could even feel the very floor beneath his feet rise gently, then fall, as if he too were living on a houseboat in Florida.

In 1961, Gavin became fascinated by two brilliant young doctors; one calm, modest; the other mercurial, outspoken, angry. In addition to "Dr. Kildare" and "Ben Casey," Gavin found himself fascinated by what he was certain was the most authoritative courtroom show ever presented, "The Defenders."

More and more, his night work blurred into a kind of monotonous dream. Over a number of years, all of the employees who had been on the job when Gavin was hired drifted away. Some were fired within weeks or months. Others quit to seek better opportunities. Some were laid off during slow periods and never returned. The work was of such a repetitive nature that the employees soon found themselves bored or frustrated, and few lasted more than a year to eighteen months on the job. A relative handful did manage to hang on for a few years or longer, and one even stayed for almost five years. For the most part, the men who managed to stay on the job for extended periods did so only because of family responsibilities, or because their age or abilities made it virtually impossible for them to find work elsewhere. Gavin stayed on the job seven years, a company record. But the frequent turnover of employees, combined with Gavin's total indifference to those around him, enabled him to pass the time without forming even a single friendship, or for that matter, any kind of meaningful personal relationship. He was content to spend eight hours a night doing his job so that he could spend all his free time watching the people he loved so dearly in his apartment. When he went on vacation every year during the first two weeks in August, Gavin went nowhere. He remained in his small, sparsely furnished apartment staring at the television set for marathon stretches, leaving the room only to fix some food in the kitchen or relieve himself in the bathroom. But that didn't really matter because he had installed small television sets in those rooms, as he had in the tiny bedroom. In fact, there was no area of the apartment that didn't have a television set, save for the closets.

Vacation, of course, was Gavin's favorite time of year, even though most of the shows were reruns or summer replacements. The reruns in particular fascinated Gavin. As videotape came into greater use, it became increasingly difficult for Gavin to separate what was happening "live" on television and what had been recorded or taped at an earlier time. People who were already dead and in their graves paraded before his eyes with the same vivid sense of reality and immediacy as those whose live images were being sent instantaneously into his room from thousands of miles away. The living and the dead became totally interchangeable; past and present became inseparable; fact and fiction, education and entertainment, information and fantasy and reality all merged into one continuous force of energy that was now available to Gavin twenty-four hours a day, seven days a week. Small wonder, then, that Gavin finally became interested not only in what was being shown on television, but how it was being shown. For the first time he started to become fascinated with the technical aspects of the medium. How were images transmitted from a football stadium in California into his living room in a split second? How could something that was telecast live be shown again to the audience within a matter of seconds? How did it all work? What made it happen? And as he wondered about the mechanics of the daily miracle that unfolded before his eyes, he wondered if somehow there might be a place for him within that miracle.

Gavin had always hated to read. It was such a slow and ponderous way to get information or be entertained, especially since television had always made it so easy for him. All he had to do was turn a dial and sit back and someone would tell him or show him all kinds of interesting things. But now he needed to know something about television that television wasn't telling him about. And so, reluctantly, he turned to books for the information he needed.

Television, Gavin learned, had taken over from radio as the most popular form of entertainment in the home in 1949, the same year Veronica had brought a set into their home. By now, 1965, it was estimated that there were 65,000,000 television sets in the United States—at least one in each of 50,000,000 homes. But Gavin didn't care about that—he wanted to know how it worked. And then he found a book that told him how, in simple words and pictures. The book said that a television picture was taken by a camera that changed the light waves into electrical energy that could be sent through the air. This electric energy traveled through the air until it reached the picture tube in each home, where it was transformed back into light waves, which then showed upon the television set's screen as the picture. Beneath a basic diagram, which Gavin had very little trouble following, was a slightly more detailed explanation of the process.

"The image of the subject is received by the ionoscope. The quantity of light which moves through the modulator from the generator is dependent upon whatever quantities of light is reflected from the various elements of the image. The transmitting antennas send out waves which are promptly received by the receiving antennas. These waves are then significantly amplified and converted back into light in the kinescope, which in turn produces the picture on the screen."

The words were at once mystifying and magical to Gavin who now was beginning to realize that he might be able to do more than sit back and watch television. He realized that now, somehow, he might become a part of it. His imagination soared and he sought out more books and articles about all the technical advances that were being made. About this time, color TV had become a practical but costly reality, and Gavin became perhaps the first person in his income bracket in America to purchase one. From his books he learned, too, that transmitting color television images was a more complex and costly process than regular black and white transmission. And he learned that television meant "far-seeing." But perhaps the most important thing Gavin learned that year was that he could actually attend technical schools that would teach him everything he needed to know about television. How fortunate that he had never squandered the money Veronica had left him. It was all there when he needed it, and somehow he had always known he would find the way to use it properly. Now he wasn't just going to watch television. He was going to study television to get inside it and learn about how the cameras worked and all about lenses and mounting equipment and videotape and film and editing and optical effects and script preparation and an endless stream of fascinating subjects he read about in the brochure sent to him by the Evans Television Production School. Who knows, thought Gavin, one day I might actually make television programs myself. Or appear on them. Wouldn't that really be something? To make my own television shows that would be seen by millions upon millions of people. A charge of excitement rolled through Gavin's body and brain. It was as if he had gone into a half sleep immediately after Veronica's death years ago and was only now coming back to full consciousness. He could literally feel a million nerve endings tingling throughout his body like the light waves that were converted into electrical energy so they could be sent through the air to become pictures on television screens. Gavin put down the brochure and glanced for a moment at the television set. "Route 66" was on, but, oddly, Gavin barely noticed. Instead he got up, put on his heavy woollen black-and-white checkered jacket and left the apartment quickly.

He walked to work in the bitter cold of a New York winter night, never noticing the icy slush that slipped inside his well-worn shoes.

When Gavin arrived at work, the foreman immediately looked at his watch and wondered what Gavin was doing there so early: he wasn't due in for another forty-five minutes, and no one ever showed up early for this kind of work. Gavin walked directly up to the foreman, paying no attention to the assembly-line workers and the whirring of machinery and the low monotonous roar of the huge cement mixer overhead. When he spoke it was the first communication he had had with the foreman in the last eighteen months, but the words were lost amid the noise of steel forms clanging shut and iron-wheeled carts rolling over cement. It didn't matter. Over the years the foreman had become an expert at reading lips, and he had no trouble reading the message from Gavin's lips. "I quit," they said. The foreman shrugged his shoulders in a gesture of massive indifference. Gavin turned and walked quickly out of the plant. Tomorrow, he thought, he would enroll at the Evans Television Production School. But tonight he would simply settle back in his favorite chair and watch television all night long. For the first time in his life, Gavin realized he was going to be somebody. Somebody important.

Physically, the school itself was something of a mess. It was located in a shabby old warehouse on the West Side of Manhattan, near the Port Authority building. But to Gavin it was the most beautiful structure he had ever seen, especially inside, where students and instructors were busy wheeling cameras into place, adjusting lights, building sets, applying makeup, and shouting out a whole new language that was music to Gavin's ears. Words and phrases like "dolly" and "sweep focus" and "zoom" and "split screen" and "playback" and "vertical sweep reversal" echoed across empty sound stages and lingered in Gavin's ears long after he had left the school to take his ride home on the subway each night. But the ride was never lonely for Gavin, because he passed the time by silently framing the different passengers' faces in his mind's eye. He would zoom in tight for an extreme close-up of the puffy-faced woman in red; so close in fact that the cameras that were his eyes would see the small bead of perspiration forming on her upper lip near the light-brown mole. Those two little black kids sitting next to each other he would shoot from a distance, dollying in slowly to capture their look of being slightly afraid and alone except for each other in a big people's world. The pretty Puerto Rican teenage girl in the shiny jacket open in front to reveal a white sweater covering melon-sized breasts he would shoot in color, the gleaming green satin of the jacket, her ochre skin and the white of the sweater creating an interesting contrast. Soon after Gavin started school, perhaps by the third or fourth week, he was taking each day's lesson and translating it into practical terms on the subway ride. He even found himself using his fellow passengers not merely as models, but also as characters for TV shows he would write in his head. But even more exciting, Gavin's eyes were acquiring a power that gave them the same range and freedom of television cameras. No longer did he merely imagine zooming in for a tight shot on a passenger's face, his eyes actually did it for him. Not only that, but his eyes could now also create a variety of effects such as soft out-of-focus shots, or a split screen, or even a quad—splitting the screen in his mind into four areas, each of the areas framing the face of a different passenger, and in each case the passengers would not be sitting side by side, but rather at a good distance from each other. Gavin's eyes could bring them together. It was, he realized, a unique and great gift—and it was entirely possible that he was the only person in the world who possessed such a gift. It was not a gift to be treated lightly, he knew. It was a gift to be used wisely.

The days, of course, were filled with the excitement of exploring a new universe and learning a new language. "Alpha wrap" and "audio track" and "cue track" and "dubbing down" and "instant replay" and literally thousands of other phrases like them became an extremely important part of Gavin's environment. But more than the mere words, it was the constant interaction of images and the precise patterns of camera technology that kept Gavin's brain working at fever pitch. After brief sessions on theory, students would begin to handle cameras themselves, working with film, and videotape, and even videodiscs for instant replay, which was just coming into popular use. Gavin learned the importance of lighting. He learned the various functions of back lighting, how it helped to distinguish between the shadow of the object and the dark outline behind it by accenting the contours of the object. He learned too, that lighting angles of forty-five degrees are best for most normal lighting situations. And that the name for the light that supplied the primary source of illumination—showing the basic form or shape of the object—was the "key" light. He learned about light ratio and vertical key light position and fill light and the lighting triangle, which was simply the triangular arrangement of key, back and fill lights.

Now, when Gavin sat at home night after night watching "Beverly Hillbillies" and "I've Got a Secret" and "Peyton Place" and "The Rogues" and "The Man from U.N.C.L.E.," he could make more critical observations about the lighting, which he realized the vast majority of the viewing audience could never appreciate. It gave him a feeling of great power and urgency to understand that he was becoming part of the same world as Walter Cronkite and Tina Louise and Jim Nabors and Robert Lansing and Richard Basehart and even Flipper. "Hello," he could hear himself saying, "hello, Mr. Cronkite, this is Gavin Risen speaking. Frankly, I think it's only fair to let you know that the back lighting on your last news special left a lot to be desired." Or, "Miss Ball, this is Gavin Risen and I just want to say that the people who handle the lighting on your show are absolute wizards. I don't think I could do a better job myself. However, if you ever need . . . "

Of course, Gavin never actually made these calls because he was finding it increasingly difficult to speak to anyone. It was fine, if they were safely inside a television set—and fine, if they were working in a video drama inside his mind. He could talk to them at considerable length and with considerable expertise. But he had reached the point now where he had virtually tuned out the outside world, except for his instructors at the Evans School of Television Production. His fellow students at the school tended to avoid Gavin as much as he avoided them. They all admired his work at the school, because he was easily one of the most technically efficient student cameramen in the class. And they all respected his competency in set decorating and costume design and sound recording and dubbing. But they all acted as if they would prefer not to have to spend any time alone with him. He was too cold, too distant. Gavin was delighted that they stayed away.

After almost two years of intensive full-time study at the Evans School of Television Production, Gavin Risen graduated in April 1965, the same date that the first Early Bird communications satellite was hurtled into orbit. Gavin considered it a good sign, but it certainly didn't prove to be one, at least in the immediate future.

In spite of his excellent qualifications, Gavin could not seem to land a job connected with any phase of television production. He applied to the networks and local stations as a cameraman. No experience, so no dice. He applied as a lighting assistant, but found that the list of applicants ahead of him could almost form a single-file line across the George Washington Bridge. He applied as a sound technician, and that's when he began to get the message that maybe there was more to his rejections than a lack of experience or an oversupply of qualified personnel.

When his application for the sound technician position was turned down, the station's production manager gave it to him straight. "It's easy to see that you know what you're doing, Mr. Risen, and if there's one thing we respect at this station, it's professionalism. But there's also something else I respect when I'm hiring someone. And that's my stomach. If my stomach tenses up when I'm talking to someone about a job, I just know it's not gonna work out. Too many times in the past I went against my stomach and it just caused everyone a lot of pain in the long run." The station's production manager patted the solid sphere of fat just above his belt. "Please don't take this personally," he continued. "It's no rap against you. It's just the chemistry of the thing. But don't feel bad, because you'll catch on somewhere. You know what you're doing. It's as simple as this. My head says hire you and my stomach says don't. And over the years, my stomach has turned out to be a lot smarter than my head. Sorry. But like I said, don't worry, you'll catch on somewhere."

But Gavin didn't catch on somewhere. He was upset but not destroyed, because his failure to find a job left him with an enormous amount of free time to watch television. And he knew that in the final analysis he could happily spend the rest of his life doing just that and precious little more. But unfortunately, money from Veronica's insurance was finally running out and he realized that it was only a matter of a few weeks or at most a month before he would have to find some kind of job to support himself. Sooner or later he would find something in television. But in the meantime, he'd just have to be patient and keep trying, and maybe he'd get a break. And then, just as his money was about to run out completely, Gavin's break came along.

Gavin had sent a résumé to a local station in Miami, Florida. The résumé had been reviewed by the station's assistant manager, who in turn wrote Gavin informing him that there was a definite opening at the station for a cameraman, and that if Gavin's qualifications were faithfully reported in the résumé, the job was almost certainly his. There was only one small step to be satisfactorily completed. It was the station's policy not to hire anyone prior to holding at least a rather informal interview. The letter made it quite clear that the interview was merely a formality but that, nonetheless, it was also the station's policy not to pay travel expenses for prospective employees, since so many people obviously wanted to visit Miami and Miami Beach, and as the station had learned, an all-expenses-paid job interview was as good a way as any for insincere snow-birds to finance a free vacation in Florida.

Gavin received the letter in late November, 1965. For seven months he had tried unsuccessfully to find any kind of employment in the field of television and had come up empty-handed. Only four hundred ninety-two dollars remained of the money Veronica had left him. The first frozen fury of winter had already iced its way around and even into the lonely barren little apartment where Gavin sat huddled in front of the color television set, his thin white body wrapped tightly in a dark-blue woollen blanket. The letter from the Miami television station lay on his lap as Gavin watched the honey-skinned girl in the clinging white bikini run directly at him, the flesh around her navel jiggling softly, her entire body vibrant and glowing with health as she raced almost into Gavin's living room before she faded away and the screen filled with the words: MORE ABOUT JACKIE AND MIAMI BEACH IN A MINUTE.''

Gavin's hand reached from beneath the blanket, and he held the letter at such an angle that he could read it in the glow coming from the television screen, where a cowboy was riding a gallant brown-and-white horse through a field dotted with cattle, while the music in the background played the familiar strains of *The Magnificent Seven*.

As Gavin read the letter for the seventh time that day, he became conscious that his fingers were trembling from the cold and that the letter itself was actually making a wintry sound as it rattled in his hand. The girl in the white bikini returned to the screen, along with other young girls similarly dressed and as voluptuously shaped. They were accompanied by tanned muscular young men in bathing trunks, and all were doing one of those modern hip-shaking, breast-waving, pelvis-snapping, buttock-grinding dances that Gavin always loved to watch. Quickly his hand moved back inside the blanket and began the slow, steady familiar stroking motion as the bronze bodies bounced and wiggled and bent and revealed generous glimpses of soft white flesh that hadn't been exposed to the sun and that quivered with excitement as the music grew more frantic and the dancers' bodies grew bolder and more uninhibited and Gavin's hand moved faster and faster and then he was there, right on the beach in Miami, the cold winter in his room fading as the warm sensations in his body grew warmer, wilder. He could feel those breasts, touch those buttocks. The sun suddenly exploded all round him and deep within him. And even before he managed to slow his breathing and relax his grip and realize that the room was still painfully cold, he was on his way to Miami with his last four hundred ninety-two dollars.

When he got there, the assistant station manager told him the job had already been taken.

7

The change from the frigid black and white of New York in winter to the clean, clear technicolor warmth of Miami was almost as much of a shock to Gavin as the fact that he found himself over twelve hundred miles from the only world he had ever known, without money, without work, without a place to stay—and worst of all, without a television set of his own.

He applied immediately for jobs at the other two television stations in Miami, knowing even before he was turned down that it would probably be hopeless. Why was it impossible for him to find work—any work—in television? Was it the way he looked? The way he spoke? Gavin Risen made a secret and solemn vow to study the people on television more closely so that he could act properly and not make others feel uncomfortable when he made contact with them in the outside world. And, of course, the outside world was an extremely painful place for Gavin. If he came across a particularly uncomfortable situation—like the one on the plane coming down from New York, when the fat lady next to him kept trying to make conversation—he could not change the channel to a more pleasant program. Nor could he turn off her volume. Or even simply turn her off. He had to sit there and endure pain that was beyond tolerance, with no avenue of escape except for three trips to the lavatory. And now, Gavin was more frightened than at any time since he was a young boy and feared he was going to lose his leg. Because now he would have to go back out into the outside world, to make contacts, talk to people, listen to them, perhaps from time to time even touch them, at least until he could earn enough money to find a place to live here in Miami, or to return to New York. The thought was so upsetting that he seriously considered suicide.

Then, in a moment of quiet desperation, Gavin Risen walked into a rundown tavern named Reinhart's in South Miami, near Coral Gables, to spend perhaps his last few hours on earth quietly watching the large television set that loomed over the rectangular bar. Gavin made every attempt to avoid eye contact with any of the handful of customers who had barely noticed his arrival. Even when the bartender stopped in front of him, Gavin kept his eyes focused on Johnny Carson and Ed McMahon whose conversation, to Gavin's irritation, was constantly interrupted by a coughing air conditioner that groaned and sputtered just a few feet away from the large RCA. Gavin said, ''Give me a beer, please,'' still without looking at the bartender, and pushed his last five-dollar bill in the burly man's direction. When the five dollars was gone, Gavin realized, and when the last of the late night movies was over, and the final prayer said, and the national anthem played behind the waving flag, and the television set turned off, Gavin Risen would turn off his own life. ''It should be that simple,'' he thought, ''just like turning a dial and the picture you see before your eyes fades quietly away forever.''

And then there was a sudden eruption of noise a few feet from the large RCA. Gavin's eyes were involuntarily drawn to the loud air conditioner screaming out at the warm night air. And then he saw it, just to the left of the air-conditioning unit, a piece of white cardboard tacked to the wall. There was red ink on it, and the red ink said NIGHT PORTER WANTED. Gavin reached for the glass of beer in front of him and his mind made a journey back through the hundreds of thousands of hours of electronic information that had poured into his brain since Veronica had first brought home the magic black box. And he thought of Will, the Indian, the dark-skinned man with the half-moon scar on his face, who had been the night porter at Doctor's Bar all those lonely years ago in the outside world. For a moment Gavin's mind became his own television screen and he could see Will collecting half-filled glasses crowded with cigarette butts, and mopping floors and cleaning the vomit and unclogging the stopped-up toilets in the rest rooms, and then without realizing he had spoken he heard his own voice speaking.

"How much does it pay?" his voice asked the bartender. "How much does the night porter's job pay?"

It was an incredible piece of good fortune for Gavin, because while the job as night porter at Reinhart's Tavern only paid $1 an hour for a total of thirty-five hours a week, it also included free rent for a small one-bedroom apartment in the rear of the tavern, plus access to an unlimited supply of hamburgers, hot dogs and frozen pizza. But perhaps even more important to Gavin was the nature of the work. He had the days and nights entirely to himself, and then at one-thirty A.M., after the last customer had left the tavern, he would let himself in, turn on the television set and begin to pick up the beer bottles, sweep the floor, and empty the ashtrays. Very few people in America, he realized, were fortunate enough to find work that so suited their nature. Because now he need not miss a single hour of scheduled television during the week. While he swept and washed and scooped and lifted, he could always keep one eye on his constantly entertaining companion who performed for him every morning from one-thirty until five-thirty A.M. True, there was some disappointment when Gavin compared the handful of channels in Miami to the great number of channels broadcasting in New York. There was just no comparison. Only now he had a job that was so much better than the one he had left in New York. He made $175 a week less. But now he need never wonder and worry about what he might be missing on television.

The similarity between his youth at Doctor's Bar and his job at Reinhart's Tavern was not lost on Gavin, but he attached no special significance to it. He spent most of his time, when not watching television, adjusting to the sunshine and warmth and outdoor atmosphere of Miami, although for the most part he failed to notice the blooming bougainvillea and the brilliant red poinsetta trees and the towering coconut palms and the golden yellows and vibrant greens and royal blues all around him, because there was no way they could compare to the rich color tones in the large RCA that whiled away the weeks and months for him at Reinhart's Tavern, until he had saved enough to replace the small second-hand black-and-white set he had bought soon after starting the job, with a thirty-six-inch Magnavox color console for his small apartment.

Gavin might as well have been living in Keene, New Hampshire, or Lafayette, Indiana, or even back in New York, for all the advantage he took of Miami's climate and beaches and outdoor life. He never stayed outdoors long enough to develop a tan and actually developed a strong dislike for sunshine, its hot rays burning his skin and stinging his eyes. Just as he had spent seven invisible years in New York after high school working and watching television, so, too, he disappeared into a world without people in Miami. He stayed in his apartment all day and night watching television, waiting until the last customer had left Reinhart's Tavern. Then, after five or ten minutes, he would hear Mac the bartender rap gently on his door informing him it was time to start cleaning up. Days and even weeks could pass without Gavin Risen seeing another human being in person. The saloon would be empty when he entered it and empty when he left, except for his television companions. And his apartment was nighttime dark, even during the day, except for the soft glow of the Magnavox. It was a wonderful way to live. It was everything he could hope for. Everything except one thing. But he was working on that. It would take time. But he had plenty of time and patience and he knew that one day he would be the biggest thing that ever happened in television. Or ever would happen in television.

There were the months and years of "I Dream of Jeannie" and "The Avengers" and Martin Luther King talking about civil rights and "Dark Shadows" and "Star Trek," "The Smothers Brothers Comedy Hour" and "Bewitched" and "Mission Impossible." These were the days and nights of "Search for Tomorrow" and "Judd" and "Laugh-in" and "Batman" and the deaths of Martin Luther King and Robert F. Kennedy and "The Goldiggers" and the riots at the Democratic Convention in Chicago and the journey of Apollo 8 around the moon, all conveyed to Gavin by the magnificent Magnavox proudly dominating the center of his bleak one-room apartment.

As the sixties rolled into the seventies, and Nixon replaced Johnson, and Vietnam kept exploding each evening in Gavin's room, the slender and by now slightly graying man began to grow impatient again at his own inability to become part of television. By now, the city of Miami and its surrounding areas had added a number of new TV stations as well as independent production companies, which might be potential employers for Gavin Risen. He bought a new suit. He rehearsed in front of the mirror on his bathroom door, even turning the knob as if it were a television dial, but whenever he came face-to-face in an interview he froze in fear. And consequently, there were no jobs for Gavin as a cameraman, or lighting assistant, or makeup man, or sound technician, or anything else. Each time he returned to his apartment after a job interview, he would simply turn a dial, and the pain of defeat in the outside world would disappear, while Zsa Zsa Gabor and Mike Douglas made him feel as if he were a part of their family.

Now he knew there was only one way. He would have to acquire his own television cameras, build his own sets, create his own scripts, find his own cast, direct his own programs in his own studio, with himself as the cameraman, crew, and audience.

But how could he possibly do all that? In the years since he had come to Miami, he had saved virtually every dollar he had made, existing night after night on hamburgers and hot dogs and pizza and beer and soft drinks. And still he had managed to amass only $2,763, probably one-tenth of what he would need to buy the necessary cameras and equipment. He was ready to abandon any hope of ever having his own studio, when he turned on the television in Reinhart's Tavern one night after the place had closed and watched a man named Neil Armstrong walk on the moon. Gavin watched the astronaut and his companion bound around the moon's surface, then he quietly slipped out the front door of Reinhart's Tavern and stared up at the lonely white sphere shining down on him from thousands upon thousands of miles away. There were cameras up there. Television cameras up there on the moon, sending pictures back to Gavin Risen. It was a sign. If someone could send television pictures of the moon back to him, certainly there must be a way for Gavin Risen to get a television camera so he could send his messages to the world. He knew now that nothing could stop him. He would become better known to the world than Neil Armstrong. He looked up at the moon and smiled. His life was ready to begin.

8

The voice had an unquestionable ring of authority, and the delivery was every bit as smooth and professional as Roger Tatum's. She sat behind the standard TV news desk, her eyes seeming to focus on each member of the viewing audience, a sheaf of papers held in well-manicured hands.

"Today," she began, "police authorities claim they have made their first major break in the bizarre case of the so-called television murders that have shocked the nation and the world in recent weeks." The man sitting in the Eames chair in the darkened living room stiffened suddenly and leaned forward intently. "Through a process which is too complex to explain in detail at this time, but which calls for magnification of the audio portion of the video tape literally hundreds of times, investigators were able to pick up background sounds that were positively identified as airplane engines."

The man in the Eames chair remained motionless.

"Through further sophisticated sound analysis the investigators were able to determine that the tapes were made within reasonable proximity—say within ten to fifteen miles of a major international airport. At first appearance this might not seem to be much of a break, but there are other factors which the authorities have taken into consideration.

"One, the sound of a number of jets in the background were isolated and broken down, and finally each one was identified by a consensus of aeronautical authorities. There were two seven-twenty-sevens and three seven-forty-sevens. So obviously, the airport had to be a major facility. But then came the big one. The big break. Positive identification was made on the engine noise of a Concorde.''

The man sitting impassively in the Eames chair rose to his feet slowly and began to walk around the darkened room in slow circles, never taking his eyes from the screen and the familiar face of the woman speaking to him and millions of others.

''In this country, the Concorde has flown in and out of only a handful of airports, on either a regular or test basis. Miami is one of these cities. By now everyone in America knows that all the videotapes in question were sent to a Miami station, even though they were mailed from various places in the country.''

The man pacing the darkened room stopped for a moment, then moved quickly to the TV set, where he knelt and gently turned up the volume. His face was so close to the TV screen that he realized he could lean forward and kiss the face of the woman talking to him. He resisted.

''Now,'' the woman continued, ''authorities have not ruled out any of these airport sites as areas within a ten- or fifteen-mile radius of which the tapes may have been made. But obviously the prime area of concentration right now is Miami.'' The woman coughed slightly to clear her throat, then continued. ''You may be wondering right now why we have revealed this information on a regular newscast, since it is certain to alert the person responsible for the creation of these tapes and encourage him to move to a safer place. Well, the reason is simply this: He created this tape, too.''

The sound of the blast was by now quite familiar to America's ears, and it echoed across the darkened room and across the nation as the woman's face and head erupted in an explosion of flesh and blood. It was evident that she was dead before her head bounced off the desk.

And then large white type appeared across the screen: STAY TUNED FOR THE WEATHER, it read.

9

The sky was a high, clean Miami blue and the breeze off the bay brushed across Gavin Risen's pale white face as he lowered the slender line of hose down into the empty swimming pool. Dry leaves and flowers and dead baby tadpoles washed toward the drain. Overhead, the sun was a large yellow spotlight beaming hotly down on Gavin Risen's shaved skull, a tribute to one of his great television heroes of the midseventies, Kojak.

Gavin had already finished his chores in the main house, waxing and polishing the floors, dusting the great book cases, applying rat and termite poisons in all the appropriate places. As he had moved about his cleaning chores, Gavin found the unique ability of his eyes to zoom in for close-ups like a television camera to be a valuable aid in spotting dirt or insects from a good distance away.

But now it was time to acid-wash the swimming pool: fill it with water and apply the appropriate chemicals. While the pool was slowly filling, Gavin would be mowing and trimming and hedging and pruning the bougainvillea and poinsettia and hibiscus and banana and banyan and citrus trees that grew in colorful abundance all over the six acres of the old Valiburn estate, which had remained uninhabited except for Gavin Risen for nearly three years now, or ever since Henrietta Valiburn died at the age of eighty-three. The battle for ownership of the estate had been raging in a series of seemingly endless court confrontations among surviving relatives. Gavin had applied for the position as caretaker for the property and, much to his amazement, had been selected. He suspected that he may have been the only person to apply for the job. But no matter. It paid him significantly more than his night porter's work at Reinhart's Tavern, provided him with even more privacy, and most important, gave him the space and secluded location he required to put into effect the plan that had been forming in his mind for years.

It was during his first few months at the Valiburn estate, isolated from all human contact except bi-monthly trips into Miami for food and supplies that Gavin began to hear the voices even when the television sets were off.

The first voice, he remembered, came to him at five-thirty in the morning as he lay awake waiting for the day's telecasting to begin. The voice didn't have to identify itself. Gavin recognized it immediately. Mr. Spock, from "Star Trek." "Good morning, Gavin," the voice began, "I appreciate your patience, waiting for me all these years. But I couldn't come to you until now. For one thing, Captain Kirk would have gotten suspicious. And, for another, passing through the time and space warp from television to the outside world presents some very special problems, even for a Vulcan."

Gavin listened in silent fascination, his face revealing no signs of surprise or delight, but his mind was smiling with an intensity he knew Mr. Spock would appreciate. He sat up slowly and looked around the semidarkness of the bedroom as slivers of dawn started to slip into the room between cracks in the drawn drapes. Mr. Spock was nowhere to be seen. But Gavin could feel his presence everywhere around him.

"You and I are very much alike in many ways, Gavin," the voice continued. "Both of us recognize the foolishness of show-ing emotions, and even the danger inherent in having them. Both of us are strangers here on earth. We find it difficult to understand the people, to share their values."

"And we both recognize the illusory nature of so-called real life and the potential of immortality through technology and the recording of images and sounds,'' Gavin added, his voice every bit as dry and expressionless as his visitor's.

"I must go for now Gavin. But I will be back. I just came this time to let you know that I do approve of your plan. The logic of it is impressive. And it could make you immortal. Good-bye, Gavin.''

Gavin strained his eyes and for just a split second he could see Mr. Spock move swiftly to the black drapes and then he was gone.

But there were others over the next few months. Arlene Francis dropped by to tell Gavin how wonderful she thought it was that today's young people, like Gavin, were so imaginative and innovative and not content to sit back and take things lying down, the way their parents had.

Walter Cronkite awoke Gavin one morning to tell him that he, Gavin, had the power within him to create one of the biggest news stories in television history. "Perhaps the biggest, because it combines so many of the things all of us are looking for today. And I promise you this, Gavin. I'll be there to cover it.''

But Gavin's most significant visitor during that period didn't say a word. It was David Berkowitz, the infamous Son of Sam. He simply appeared over Gavin's shoulder in the mirror one morning when Gavin was shaving. He smiled at Gavin, a mischievous grin that communicated clearly to Gavin the thought, "You and I know what's going on. The others are living in a dream world. Reality is seeing yourself in other people's eyes.'' Gavin knew all this had been said, though not a word had been spoken.

As the months turned into years, Gavin's role as caretaker of Valiburn estate grew even more comfortable. He had few chores. He had seven television sets. And he had such wonderful visitors.

After he had finished with the pool and the gardening, Gavin put away the tools, ran the hose quickly over his hands to wash away the dirt and flecks of plants that clung to them, then returned to the large old Spanish building on the rear of the property that had originally been constructed to house seven or more servants, but which for the past few years had been occupied solely by Gavin Risen and occasional guests from the outside world.

One of those occasional guests was lying facedown in a pool of blood when Gavin entered the main dining room, which he had transformed into one of the finest professionally equipped TV studios in the Southeast. There were two cameras: a Philips LDK-5 mounted color camera and a 1VC 700P broadcast-quality portable. An area to the left of the cameras housed the audio control board, where Gavin frequently spent nights selecting various sound inputs, then amplifying and mixing them before distributing them to line-out, reel-to-reel tape machines. It was, in essence, a small TV station, complete with tape-cassette machines, turntables, speakers, and intercom controls.

Around the set, which consisted of a series of modules and nondescript chairs arranged to simulate a newscasting layout, were a number of standing lights, and above was a lighting grid. The main performer in the drama which had been videotaped the previous evening lay absolutely still, his body splashed here and there with blood, the strange black and white mask still covering his entire head and face ripped open at midforehead where a bullet had burst into his brain.

Gavin walked over to the audio control board and flipped a switch. For a second or two there was a whirring of tape, then a sudden explosion of static and finally Gavin could hear his own voice informing the selected performer of the uniqueness of the project in which he was about to participate. "What I am attempting to do is to cross, once and for all, the fine line between fantasy and reality, between fact and fiction, between theater and what we have mistakenly referred to for years as real life."

A second voice spoke. "This is really quite an impressive setup you have here. The camera. The lights. Everything. Who'd ever expect anything like it in a place like this. When you said you would put me on television, I thought you were a bit whacked out. You know, maybe high on something. Out for some weird kicks or whatever."

There was a second or two of silence, and then Gavin's voice could be heard filling the otherwise silent room. "What I am doing, in effect, is filming a variety of people in individual sessions. Each, like you, is unaware of any of the other parts the others are playing. You are to concern yourself only with your own role, your own lines."

Again the second voice. "But what's so different about that? I mean, isn't that the way movies are made? I mean I read somewhere that when one of those big movies is made with dozens of different stars all over the place, a lot of those times those stars don't even meet each other. One is shot one day in London. Another is filmed two weeks later in New York. A third might do his part on location in the desert six months later. And yet when the whole film is finally put together, it looks like they were all in the same place at the same time. And they may never even have seen each other."

Gavin abruptly flipped a switch on the audio control panel and then spoke, his own voice sounding exactly as it had on the sound track, a tribute to both the quality of the equipment and his own technical recording abilities. "What you don't understand yet, my friend, is that I am putting together an original work of art, a new art form if you wish. My work will feature real people so to speak, performing as actors. It will have definite entertainment value, and it will also be a major news story, attracting attention perhaps around the world.

Gavin smiled and pressed the button and again the second voice was heard, an electronic ghost challenging the statement Gavin had just made. "But how can you be so sure that your work or whatever—as you call it—will ever be seen? You told me yourself that you don't know anyone at the networks, or even in local television. Just because you film your own show doesn't mean it's ever going to be seen."

Gavin let the tape continue to run, but this time he moved his own lips in synchronization with his own voice on the tape. "I know my audience," said the recorded voice of Gavin. "And I am perhaps the first person to recognize that immortality is available to all of us. Not through prayer. Not through meditation. Not through reincarnation or religion or anything like that. But through film. And videotape.'' There was a pause. Again Gavin pressed the button. Again he began to speak in his own voice, looking toward the blood splattered figure in black and white lying a few feet away on the floor.

"If you can orchestrate your life into a dramatic presentation that is captured and preserved on film, you can live forever among all the generations of man for all time to come. Your physical body may wither and die, but your image will be there for everyone to see forever and ever. I want to cross that line demarcating the outside world and enter into the infinity of images.'' Gavin stopped speaking, pushed the button. The taped voice of the man lying dead in the middle of the room once again spoke out.

"Look you must be either a genius or a fruitcake or something I've never run across before. I agreed to come here for two reasons. First, I think I could do every bit as well on the tube as some of those male models I see in those commercials, if I ever got the chance. And second, because I can use the hundred fifty you promised me.''

Gavin pushed the button, abruptly silencing the dead man once again. He moved away from the audio control center, stepping quietly around the set and walking to an area well out of camera range, where he opened a narrow door. Behind the door was a maintenance closet filled with cleaning supplies and assorted brooms and mops. He moved back toward the dead man, pausing as he did so to turn on a TV set that was sitting in front of a large black Eames chair. He turned on the television set and watched for a few seconds as the figure appeared on the screen. He wore a long black cape that reached to the ground. In the center of the cape was a bold white eye that covered his chest and seemed to gaze out in hypnotic silence. In his left hand he held a TV antenna, the size and type commonly referred to as rabbit ears. In his right hand he held a small globe of the earth no larger than a softball. His face was covered with a stark black and white mask, leaving one side of his head entirely in black, except for a small circle of white around the eyes and the other side of the head entirely in white with the eye encircled in black. He looked very much like a costumed professional wrestler about to enter the ring. "Hello, my friends," he said. "I would like to talk to you tonight about a problem that faces each of us here on earth."

While the masked figure on the television screen continued to speak, Gavin Risen walked to where the masked figure lay sprawled in his own blood. He bent and spread the cape laying near the man, then half pulled and pushed the man onto the cape. Slowly, with considerable effort, he dragged the dead weight across the floor until he positioned it between the television set and the large black Eames chair. Then using what amounted to a bear hug grip from behind, he lifted the masked figure and sat him down in the Eames chair. It was as if the masked man in the Eames chair was the audience for the masked figure on the television screen who droned on. "Sincerely. As I stand here before you, at the very instant you see me standing here and listen to me talking to you, I tell you in all honesty and candor that I do not exist."

Gavin smiled at the figure in the chair. "You are," he said, "more alive than ever."

As Gavin busied himself cleaning the set and the entire old Spanish house that had been his home for three years, he made mental notes about the number of people he had in his permanent library. There were five already in the can, so to speak, but he knew he couldn't release even one of them until the full set had been assembled. Then, of course, his achievement would be recognized world-wide. As he moved through the rooms, dusting here, sweeping there, he reminisced about the years he had lived here. Years in which the money he saved at Reinhart's Tavern was added to dramatically by his salary of $550 per month as caretaker of the Valiburn estate. As he accumulated sufficient cash to transform his dream into reality, Gavin began to acquire the equipment he needed, some second-hand from Miami production houses, some brand new from television production supply companies, and gradually it all came together. The makeup, the props, the costumes, the lights, the videotape-editing equipment, the cameras, everything.

There he was, alone on a grand estate that was visited once every three months or so by a representative of the trust company responsible for the upkeep of the property. The visits were totally predictable, since the trustee made it a policy to call Gavin at least a week in advance of his arrival—so that by the time he did arrive the cameras and other equipment were always safely wrapped in heavy canvas and tucked away somewhere out of sight amid the thousands of subtropical trees and plants that surrounded the Valiburn estate. Then after the trustee left Gavin would immediately set up his studio again, often donning costumes himself and applying makeup for hours before recording himself in a variety of roles, ranging from that of distinguished news-caster to enthusiastic sportscaster to emcee on a quiz show.

"Good evening, America. This is Gavin Risen with perhaps the most startling news program of the century. Right before your very eyes I shall display a series of vignettes that will make the Middle East situation look like a cross between the "Hollywood Squares," "Let's Make a Deal," and "Kojak." But first, a word from your good friend and mine. Here he is. . . ."

10

The music was a raucous and raunchy version of "Rhinestone Cowboy," with a mostly off-key and semidrunk chorus of male voices rising high above the rock group playing on the elevated stage in the middle of the large rectangular bar.

The three bartenders moved rapidly, pouring beer and mixed drinks in a blur of professionalism, as the crowd at the bar began to move now in rhythm with the music, arms draped over shoulders over and over again until a human link was formed around the entire bar, and the mass of men became one swaying and singing unit, until the final high note was reached and ravaged. The chain of musical companions broke up to scattered applause and cheers. One of the bartenders, dressed in a Miami Dolphin football shirt, gold lamé stretch pants and elevated shoes, glanced up at the clock in the corner of the room to check how much longer until closing. Only an hour and forty-five minutes.

The slightly built, slightly graying man wearing large steel-frame glasses sat at a quiet booth, sipping a gin and tonic. It was the first time he had ever been in a place like this, although he had heard about them on television newscasts when there was an infrequent raid. He tapped his fingers nervously on the table and hoped nothing like that would occur tonight. Especially not tonight, which was after all, his first night out in years. And, if he were fortunate, tonight he would begin to act on the great plan that had been forming in his head for years. He sipped at his gin and tonic and looked at the empty seat across from him and at the banana daiquiri that sat waiting for his expected guest, who should be arriving any minute now.

And then his guest arrived. In the flickering shadowy light of Club Adonis it was difficult to be precise about age, but the man rising from behind the gin and tonic estimated his guest to be about nineteen, perhaps twenty. "Please sit down," he gestured. "I can't tell you how much I enjoyed your performance."

The figure was slender, feminine. The features sharp, angular. The voice slightly hoarse, but still somewhat erotic. "Your message said that you could get me on television. How? Are you an agent?" Long, thin fingers tightened around the stem of the glass holding the banana daiquiri. The glass lifted and a pink tongue slid slowly over bright moist red lips before dipping into the froth of the daiquiri.

The man pushed his gin and tonic away in a gesture that revealed his inner tension. "I am about to become an independent producer," he said. "I have my own studio, my own equipment, cameras, videotape, a minicam, everything. For years, I have studied TV production. I know everything it takes to make a television show."

The banana daiquiri was poised just below the bright red lips. "Are you proposing we make a pilot film of some sort for a shot at a series?"

"No," the slightly built man said, the reflection in his glasses from a cigarette lighter a few feet away making it seem as if his eyes were on fire. "What I'm proposing is basically nothing less than a new art form, a way of using television that has never been attempted before, perhaps never been imagined before. Have you ever seen yourself on television? Can you imagine the thrill of knowing that millions of people everywhere may be focusing their eyes on your face, listening to your words, reacting to you and to you alone? To capture their attention, to hold the center of the stage, of the world, even for an instant. Isn't that worth everything? Especially for someone with a desire to perform. To be seen. To be admired. To become a part of everyone else's life. To have your image imprinted in their minds forever. And I can help you do it. I can help you become immortalized so that even when you and I are dead and gone, your image will be seen by other generations, by people perhaps as yet unborn. This is what I mean when I say I have it in my power to make you timeless. This is the adventure, the revolution in creativity I am about to begin. I can use your help, your talent. But if not you, there will be others.''

''I don't follow you; I'm afraid,'' the hoarse voice answered in a frightened tone.

''It's not necessary that you understand everything; it is only essential that you participate and follow my directions. If you do, I can promise you this: there is a very good chance that your face will become known all over the world.''

The banana daiquiri returned to the table. ''What is it exactly that I have to do? And why me? Why am I getting such a big break?''

''As I said, all you have to do is follow my instructions. I have all the equipment we need. And I have a script, the kind of a script that has never been used before on television, I can promise you that. But all of my performers must be unknown, at least until I have completed my work. After that, they will all be famous everywhere.''

''You didn't answer my second question. Why me?''

''Because you fit almost exactly the qualifications of a particular character or role I need filmed.''

The stem of the banana daiquiri glass twirled again in the slender fingers. ''How did you know I'd be here tonight? Did you know that this is my first night here? The first night that I've ever performed in public?''

''No,'' the slightly built man answered, a soft smile almost forming on his lips in the darkness. ''But I can assure you that if this is the first time you have ever performed in public, it is an incredible piece of good fortune. How long have you been in town?''

"Only two days. I don't know anyone here. That's why I came here. I've always had this urge to perform. But my parents, my friends, everyone, would have been ashamed of me." Again, the banana daiquiri brushed the red lips. Soft rock started playing in the background. "I've been on the run for a long time, but this is the first time I've had the nerve to really let my hair down. To come out as what I really am."

"How long have you been gay?" asked the thin man.

"Forever," came the answer. "Or longer."

"And how long have you wanted to be a female impersonator?"

"Since I first tried on my mother's dresses when I was six or seven. But to do it professionally? Oh, maybe two or three years. Ever since I left home to find out who the fuck I really was. Like I said, tonight was my first appearance this way in public."

"That's really fortunate for both of us. Now. Are you ready to come with me and create greatness? And even if we don't, you'll at least be able to see yourself on videotape, see exactly what you look and sound like to your audience."

"That sounds O.K. to me. But lookit, you better not be shitting me. Don't let this dress fool you. I can handle myself all right."

"I am not shitting you. I'm going to make you famous. Perhaps even immortal."

"But I don't even know your name."

The slightly built, slightly graying man extended his hand across the table. "I'm Gavin Risen," he said.

"And I'm Joe," said the man in the silk dress. "Joe Tawny. That's how I got the name for my act. Tawny. Sounds like a real bitch on wheels, doesn't it?"

"All right, Tawny," said Gavin, moving his chair closer and letting his hand fall softly onto the silk-covered lap, his insides tightening at the act of making physical contact with another human being. "We'll go to my studio. I have a script and set and costume all ready for you."

Gavin began to move his hand boldly in Tawny's lap. "And when we're finished," he said in a husky voice, his head bobbing up and down rhythmically, "I'm going to blow your brains out." He smiled at Tawny in the semidarkness.

Tawny's pink tongue made a slow circular motion around her full wet lips. "Is that a promise?" Tawny asked.

"That," answered Gavin, "is a promise."

11

There were three photos pinned to the wall. On the far left was the female newscaster, in the middle was the girl named Tawny, next to her was a close-up shot of the man in the black and white mask.

The police chief, substantially overweight and perspiring heavily under the hot white lights, tried vainly to force the waist of the shirt that had pulled out from beneath his belt back into his pants. He took a quick nervous sip from the water glass by his side. It was evident that he was apprehensive, that he preferred to be somewhere else, anywhere else, rather than trying to explain his position to an unsympathetic and even hostile audience.

"We are not at a dead end," he began. "We have made some progress—not as much as we would all like, of course, but we're working twenty-five hours a day and our big break could come at any moment." He picked up the pointer at his side by the desk and turned toward the photos on the wall. The tip of the pointer stabbed the female newscaster in the chin. "This is the one, the only one, we've been able to make a positive identification on. Name: Camille Sheridan. Age: thirty-seven. Residence: Toronto, Canada. Vocation: Schoolteacher. Last seen: The night of January seventh, 1980, at the Wreck Bar of the Castaways Motel on Miami Beach. She was seen in the presence of a baldheaded man in glasses. Approximate age, thirty-five to forty. He is believed to have walked with a slight limp, and witnesses claim he may have left the Castaways with Ms. Sheridan. When she did not return to the motel after two days, her traveling companions—a group of six female schoolteachers—reported her missing. She had not been seen since that time until she appeared three weeks ago as the victim in one of the videotape murders. Again, like the others, she seemed to believe she was participating in some type of dramatic presentation and was totally unaware of what was going to happen to her.''

There was a scrambling of voices trying to get in the first question, but one voice rose above the others, and the police chief nodded in his direction. ''Has there been any further detailed description of the man who was seen with Ms. Sheridan that night at the Castaways? Have the police artists been able to sketch any kind of facsimile based on witnesses' reports?''

The police chief held a large artist's sketch pad up in front of his own face. The head was bald, the glasses large, with circular frames, the lips were thin, tight. The face itself was slender, with no distinguishing characteristics. The nose was a million noses. The chin straight, but neither firm nor pronounced.

''This is the head-on shot,'' the chief commented before flipping to a page that showed a sketch of the subject from the side. ''And this is the profile.'' The chief brought the sketch pad down so his own face became visible and the profile shot of the subject blocked the view of the chief's substantial stomach. ''Of course, the thing to remember,'' the chief continued, ''is that both these sketches were made a few years ago, shortly after Ms. Sheridan disappeared.'' The chief glanced down at the sketch and continued talking. ''By now, the suspect may have grown a full head of hair if he was not naturally bald, but shaved instead. And the glasses themselves may or may not have been used merely to help shield his identity. In any event, we have had our artists work up some new sketches of what our suspect might look like two years later, with and without glasses. And in different hairstyles.''

During the next sixty to ninety seconds, the chief flipped through a number of sketches, pausing on each one for perhaps ten to fifteen seconds. The hairstyles ranged from Afro to crew cut to partially bald. There were sketches with glasses—from Elton-John-type superspecs to narrow horn-rimmed glasses one might picture properly on a fifty-year old conservative accountant.

When he had finished showing the sketches, the police chief placed the artist's pad back on the desk and again picked up the pointer. "We can reasonably assume that the videotape of Ms. Sheridan was made shortly, perhaps immediately, after her disappearance. But what about our other two victims?" The chief placed the pointer between Tawny's tiny pointed breasts, right above Groucho's eyebrows. "As you know, we have had no luck for a month or so tracing the identity of this young woman. But now, finally, we may be on the right track. Because finally, we may be looking for the right man, instead of the right woman. That's right. Tawny may be a man." The chief paused for a moment to let his words sink in, and then pushed his pointer up higher, to Tawny's neck.

"Only today, at ten twenty-five this morning, to be precise, an anonymous phone caller stated that he remembered seeing a female impersonator named Tawny in a gay bar called the Adonis Club in South Miami approximately three years ago. The caller said that the person in the videotape scene strongly resembled the female impersonator he had seen—in both looks and voice." The chief twirled the pointer in his hand for a split second, and then brought it to rest at his side. "The Club Adonis no longer exists. It closed eleven months ago upon the death of its owner. We are now trying to track down former employees and possibly club customers who may recall seeing Tawny perform there. Our anonymous phone caller said that as far as he could remember, Tawny wasn't a regular. She may only have been there for a week or weekend. He said he remembered that she wasn't there long because he thought she was an excellent performer and couldn't understand why the club let her go so quickly. The caller refused to identify himself, he said, for fear that his patronage of the Adonis Club would establish him as a practicing homosexual and perhaps cost him his job."

Again, there was a collision of voices as unintelligible questions poured out at the perspiring police chief. "Hold it, hold it," he said, raising his hands in a gesture that was as much a request for patience as it was a demand for order. A small smile formed on thick pink lips. "I'm not leaving yet. I'll try to answer any reasonable questions as candidly as I can. But I think you'll understand—I hope you'll understand—that if the answer to a question could hurt our investigation, I'll respectfully decline to answer." He patted a folded white handkerchief against the left side of his neck, letting it slip for a second beneath the collar of his shirt. His eyes acknowledged those present, and then his free hand pointed toward the center of the room. "The tall gentleman in the very rear. Speak up so we can all hear you."

The voice was low but clearly audible. "Ed Porter, *Jacksonville Post*. To what extent are the FBI or any other government agencies involved at this time? Are they involved in seeking to verify Tawny's identity as a man?"

There was silence for a moment or two except for the quick sharp interruptions of a hacking cough in the background. The heavyset chief nodded as if to acknowledge the question, and then began to speak in a slightly softer voice than he had used previously. "I don't think it is any secret that the FBI and other federal government agencies have been involved in this thing for a good time now. And with good reason. One, there is strong evidence of kidnaping, with the possibility that victims may have been taken across state lines. Two, and this is perhaps a technicality, but an important one; the videotapes were sent through the U.S. mails, thus making it a federal matter on another level. And three, while the person responsible for creating these videotapes did not actually televise them nationally, it was obviously his intent to use the networks to display his crimes, and the FCC feels there is definite cause for a full-scale investigation on those grounds alone." The chief paused, then smiled nervously, and continued speaking. "About the second part of your question. Yes, the FBI and other federal government agencies are now trying to help us ascertain whether the girl known as Tawny is in fact a man. And if he is—or was—to help us further determine where he may have come from, how he might have become involved in this entire affair, and if his life had been connected previously, in any way, with the life of Camille Sheridan.''

Again there was a brief period of silence followed by the murmured intermingling of questions as the police chief's eyes scanned the room in front of him, before nodding to the left. ''Go ahead—the gentleman in the turtleneck sweater.''

''Charles Denoyne. *Paris Match*.'' The accent was decidedly Gallic. ''There is a great curiosity in my country as to why you allow these tapes to be shown publicly. Certainly you can carry on your investigation without creating mass hysteria over a few isolated murders. And are we sure they are even murders? Is it not possible that we are all being tricked by some good acting and special effects? How long will you allow these tapes to be shown, until you turn every television set in the world into an eyewitness to murder?''

The police chief's conciliatory manner seemed to harden perceptibly as the Frenchman spoke. ''Are those questions, sir? Or opinions? In any event, I'm glad you brought up those points. For one thing, we have not only discouraged the television stations from showing these tapes, we have sought an injunction in court to stop them. To no avail. It seems as if the First Amendment is at issue here, and the judge, in his ruling, stated something to the effect that the police cannot determine what can or cannot be broadcast, no matter how they perceive it will effect the public interest. But I thought everyone knew that by now. Perhaps you were en route to this country when the court made its ruling.'' The chief paused and again tried to tuck his shirt in tightly beneath his belt. His voice had grown more confident during the last answer. He felt in control again.

''To answer your second question. Of course it is always possible that we are being tricked, until such time as we have flesh-and-blood evidence, or a corpse or a confession. But the chances that we are in fact being tricked are exceedingly slight. These tapes have been analyzed and dissected in every manner possible by videotape experts and objective medical and police authorities. There is unanimous agreement in each case that murder was committed. The fragments of skull, the gaping wounds, the immediate and subsequent reaction of the victims were all consistent with being shot fatally in the head at close range.''

''What about the man in the mask? Are there any new leads as to his identity?'' The unidentified voice caught the chief slightly off guard. He covered his mouth with the back of a fist to stifle a cough and then proceeded to answer, turning slightly as he did so to glance up at the still photo of the masked figure behind him.

''The masked figure has been an absolute dead end. We have been able to determine nothing for certain, but we are reasonably sure that he is a Caucasian male, probably no more than twenty-five, perhaps even younger than twenty. Our guess is that he is—or should I say, was—about five feet, nine inches tall and weighed approximately a hundred sixty pounds. From his speech patterns we have been able to determine that he probably came from the East. Pennsylvania would be a good guess. Possibly New Jersey. Other than these observations, which are by no means definite, we know nothing more about this masked figure than do the millions of people around the world who saw him on their own television sets.''

''I have something here that may be of interest to you, chief.'' The plain, soft-spoken voice came from the same area where the Frenchman had spoken a few moments earlier. ''It is a mask that is identical to the one worn by the victim on the videotape.''

There was a sudden eruption of excited voices and the chief shielded his eyes from the hot lights so he could look out to see if the speaker did indeed have a mask that looked like the one worn in the photo directly in back of him.

''Come up here,'' the chief said, ''and let all of us get a good look at it.''

There was a period, perhaps twenty seconds or so, when there was relative silence except for the low mumbled sound of dozens of voices conferring with each other about this significant new piece of evidence that had been presented in such a surprising manner.

The chief stepped back a bit on the platform stage so that the person presenting the evidence could clearly be seen. When he did appear, he was dressed exactly like the masked man in the videotape, complete with the long black cape with the bold white eye covering his chest. He carried a similar TV antenna and a small globe. But he wasn't carrying the black and white mask. He was wearing it.

The chief's shock was immediately evident from the expression on his face and the incredulous tone of his voice. "What the hell. . . What's going on here. . . Where did you. . . How did you. . . Who are you?

The masked figure spoke. "With all due respect to the police and the federal authorities, I have been busy conducting my own investigation. It seemed clear to me that I had seen a costume and mask similar to the one worn by the second victim, but I couldn't remember where or when. I thought that if I could locate where I had seen the costume, it might bring me closer to some kind of answer. The mask especially stuck out in my mind. It haunted me night and day. Every time I saw the scene acted out again and again on television I tried to remember where I had seen that mask. And then, suddenly, I remembered."

The police chief edged closer to the masked speaker. "You mean that there were two masks exactly alike?"

"No," answered the speaker. "If you'll look closely. Right up here in the forehead area, you'll see where it had to be patched up after the bullet blasted a hole in it."

The chief's eyes widened in an expression that combined a strange mixture of horror and hope. "You mean that's the same mask that was used in the actual murder scene? How did you get your hands on it?"

The masked man spoke deliberately. "I took it off the poor boy before I buried him." The TV antenna and the small globe in the masked figure's hands fell to the floor with an ugly clanging sound. The great black cape opened and a long gleaming steel sword suddenly appeared from beneath it, shining like a laser streak as it swung in a quick wide arc and then moved precisely into the chief's overweight neck at the exact point the soft layers of fat bulged out over his collar. The sword moved with a speed and power that the human eye could barely follow, cutting through the chief's thick neck so cleanly that his head actually seemed to balance for a long second on his sweat-stained collar before it teetered slowly to the left and then fell to the floor, leaving the chief a headless spectator for still another second or two. The body jerked spasmodically and crashed to the floor. The masked figure stood dramatically alone, his sword gleaming like silver as he held the blade in front of his face in a silent salute to his audience. The voice was that of a ghost, unholy and unnatural, echoing through space with electronic speed.

"Good day, my friends. Or is it goodnight?" The sword moved away from the front of the masked figure's face and disappeared beneath the cape.

"This is the first time I've had the opportunity to speak to you directly, although by now I'm sure that most of you are already familiar with some of my work." The mouth of the mask moved as the words were spoken, but the actual sounds seemed to be coming from a machine rather than a mask, so oddly devoid of emotion or any other recognizable human quality were they. "I assume there will be, or has already been, a sense of moral outrage about the killing of a few people whose lives literally had no significance whatever until I made them "household faces," so to speak. I imagine that by the time you see this, newspaper and television commentators will have labeled me a madman, there will have been a great outcry for action and a great bit of wailing and breast-beating by politicians. Rubbish. Absolute rubbish." The eyes behind the mask were hypnotic in the fixed intensity of their stare. They were hard eyes, like hazel marbles. "What I have done is simply create great drama for the world to enjoy. And don't deny it, you do enjoy it. You enjoy the suspense. You enjoy the violence. You enjoy the mystery. And I have created it for you. And so I ask: how do you measure the importance of the

lives of a few essentially useless people compared to the entertainment and involvement of millions.''

The voice still had the hollow ring of a robot, but it was
speaking faster now, caught up in the bizarre logic it explained.
''Of course the police are looking for me now. Of course the
government authorities are looking for me now. Of course everyone is looking for me now. But I'm the only person on earth who
knows who I am. All of you can see me. But none of you knows
who I am. And none of you can stop my actions, because I have
already acted. You have no way of knowing how many more
tapes there are, how many more programs I have written and
directed and recorded. In fact, you have no way of knowing if I
even exist any more. You don't know how long ago I taped this
show. Two months ago? Or two years ago?'' The masked figure
stopped talking for about ten seconds, staring silently straight
ahead as if to let its last statement register fully with whoever
might be listening. Then abruptly, he turned and walked off
camera.

When he returned a few seconds later, he was carrying a black
case about the size of a portable typewriter. There were a number
of dials and buttons visible on the case, and the masked figure
held it up in front of his chest so that viewers might see it more
clearly. ''This is how I keep you entertained,'' he said, and then
he pushed one of the black buttons and tilted his head slightly to
the left as if to listen more closely to the message that came from
the small black box. ''Charles Denoyne. *Paris Match*. There is a
great curiosity in my country as to why you allow these tapes to be
shown publicly.'' The masked figure again pushed the button on
the small black case and the voice with the French accent suddenly stopped talking. But only for a moment. Because the
masked figure again began to speak, only this time the ghostlike
voice of a moment earlier was replaced by the familiar voice of
Charles Denoyne. ''Certainly you can carry on your investigation
without creating mass hysteria over a few isolated murders.''
Again a button was pushed and there was the sound of voices
intermingling so that no single voice could be clearly understood.

Another button. "Ed Porter. *Jacksonville Post*. To what extent are the FBI or any other—"Again a push of a button and Ed Porter disappeared. The masked figure spoke softly, as if trying to suggest to his audience that he was a patient, understanding man.

"The thing you must realize, of course, is that none of the people whom I have immortalized knew anything at all about each other before their big moments on camera. They all believed that they were merely playing parts in a drama, and you must admit, they all read their lines beautifully, especially the police chief here. He was really a natural." The masked figure paused for a moment, then used both hands to smooth the mask over his face. "Obviously, all of us are playing roles, all of us are acting our way through a drama we cannot understand. But now I have given us a drama that we can all understand because we can all see ourselves in it. Did you ever think about that? You are watching the greatest mystery, the greatest drama in the world. You are part of the largest audience in the history of the world. It is probably true that more people watched our police chief meet his end here than ever saw Shakespeare performed in person during the last three hundred years." The man's hands moved to his neck and he began to unhook some clasps. "But now, so much for our police chief. So much for my masked friend and lady reporter. And, of course, so much for Tawny. After all, they are really only supporting players. Surely you will want to find out who is the star of the greatest story ever told—the first real-life news and drama series ever created." The clasps were undone now and the man started to roll the mask up over his chin. Slowly, a trim black moustache came into view, and then the mask was pulled quickly up over and free of the man's head, and there he was at last, in full view, for all the world to see. The voice was mature, resonant. The face was familiar to all.

"Good evening, America, this is Roger Tatum."

12

Roger Tatum watched in silent fascination as what appeared to be his own image and likeness stared directly at him from inside the television set. The figure on the screen spoke again. "To date, all of my programing has been video-taped, but I promise all of you that my next appearance will be live. And when I do appear, I will not be in the role of a newscaster or anyone else. I shall appear as myself. Live. Watch for me. And good-night." The voice no longer sounded like Roger Tatum. It was again the voice of a ghost. Slender fingers reached for the trim moustache and started to peel it away from the man's face, and then quite suddenly stopped with the moustache half on and half off. "Looks a little silly, doesn't it?" said the man on the television screen. "But then I thought that about this time we could all use a bit of a laugh." He held the black case up next to his face, pushed another button and the screen went black.

Roger Tatum bounded to his feet in the darkened room and covered the six feet between the sofa and the television set in a single step. He pushed the on/off button and, almost in the same gesture, punched the light switch on the wall. The office of Edmund Laurenson became as bright as the Miami sunshine that had been kept outside by the tightly drawn drapes in back of Edmund Laurenson's swivel chair.

"What kind of nutcake are we dealing with here?" said Roger Tatum, his teeth clenched tightly, his hands locked together in silent struggle.

The swivel chair turned from the drape-covered windows and Edmund Laurenson looked at Roger Tatum almost as if he were looking at the madman in question. "We can't do it, Roger. We can't show this tape. The whole thing has gone too far. The whole country is being turned into a lunatic asylum by one man, and I'm not sure we haven't been helping him."

Roger Tatum sighed, took one step toward Edmund Laurenson's desk and spoke in a voice that was barely more than a whisper. "I don't know, Ed. I'm just not sure what's right anymore." He bent his head slightly and rubbed the bridge of his nose with his right hand, a gesture Edmund Laurenson had seen Roger make in the past when he was under pressure. "I'm tired, Ed. And confused. I feel as if we're damned if we do show the tape, and damned if we don't." Roger took a deep breath, bit his lip and continued talking, as much for himself as for Edmund Laurenson. "If we show the tape, it's like throwing gasoline on a fire. There's already a frenzy out there. And I'm not sure I want to play any part in making our audience more hysterical than it already is."

"I understand how you feel Roger. But you can't hold yourself responsible." Edmund Laurenson managed a weak smile in the manner of a father trying to help a son through a difficult but necessary period.

"I'm not a whore, Ed. You know that. I know that. But who else does? I'm not trying to capitalize on this whole number, although I guess it looks that way to a lot of people." Roger Tatum snapped the fingers on both hands simultaneously as if to punctuate his remarks. "But if we don't show this tape, that nut out there will just keep sending cassettes to television stations all over the country if need be, until someone shows it. And you can bet on one thing, Ed. Sooner or later, someone will show it. And you know that's true just as well as I do. Some station somewhere will show it." Roger Tatum snapped hs fingers again. "Maybe they'll show it simply because it will build ratings and help the station make a profit."

"That's a cynical point of view, Roger, but probably true."

"On the other hand," Roger continued, as if he hadn't heard Edmund Laurenson's comment, "they may show it for the simple reason that it's news. Legitimate news." Roger Tatum looked toward the window if somehow he might find the answer there that he couldn't quite find within himself.

"The truth, Ed, is that I didn't make those tapes. Nor did you. Neither of us killed those people. The fact that the tapes were sent to us is probably nothing more than the luck of the draw. They could have been sent to any other station. But they weren't. They were sent to us. So like it or not, we're part of the biggest news story of the year. If we show the new tape, we'll be accused again of sensationalizing a story, of turning the news into a nightly horror show. Don't show it, and maybe we're actually suppressing the news—or at least avoiding it so we can salvage what's left of our 'Mr. Clean' image."

"So where do you stand, Roger?" Edmund Laurenson said, his voice now as calm as if the two of them were talking about a routine programming decision.

"I guess I stand condemned no matter what I do." Roger Tatum shook his head slowly. "How the hell do you think Cronkite would have handled this if he were a local anchorman my age? I could blow my career simply by doing what I think is the right thing. Only I'm not sure what the right thing is any more."

"You're not going to blow your career, no matter what happens, Roger. Don't you realize that you're already a national figure? I guarantee this episode won't hurt you," said Edmund Laurenson, "no matter what we—or should I say *I*—decide to do."

"If I don't agree with your decision, Ed, I can always walk."

"And I'd respect you for it if I felt you were acting on principle." There was a slight touch of irony in Edmund Laurenson's voice that indicated he wasn't certain whether Roger Tatum would act on principle or self-interest.

"You know Ed, this thing is really getting inside me. I had very mixed emotions when we put the first tape on the air. I know you did, too. It seemed gruesome to me then, it seems gruesome to me now: Letting an insane killer manipulate us, having us show the world his murders for him. Maybe we made a terrible mistake when we showed that first tape. Perhaps if we hadn't shown that first one, the others wouldn't have followed." Roger Tatum stared at Edmund Laurenson who sat motionless, framed by the huge contours of his massive chair, almost as if he, too, were a carefully selected piece of corporate furniture.

Edmund Laurenson spoke, but only his lips moved. His face remained expressionless. "There's no blood on your hands, Roger. Nor on mine. I made an editorial judgement based on what I believed was the right thing to do at the time. As much as a lot of people would like to believe I was interested only in a sensational story, I wasn't. I felt that to censor those tapes, to keep them from the public, would be wrong. My idea was to let the public see and know everything we did. It may have been a mistake, but it was an honest one."

Roger Tatum paced the floor, walking directly in front of Edmund Laurenson, but not seeing him. "Ed, let's both do what we think is right and take the consequences."

"We're already taking the consequences, Roger. And we're both talking like cliches; this is supposed to be real life."

"We started showing the tapes because we felt someone in the viewing audience might hold the key to the murders. Or at least give us a link to the killer." Roger Tatum quickened his pace. "I mean we still don't really even know the sequence of the murders. Tawny may not have been the first tape this guy made. Maybe he started with the schoolteacher, the Sheridan woman. I mean, she's supposedly been missing for years."

Edumund Laurenson looked up at Roger Tatum, but said nothing. He was very weary and suddenly overwhelmed by the incredible chain of events that made such a decision possible in his office. He felt a great sense of unreality, as if he were programmed to listen to Roger Tatum's words and do nothing more.

Edmund Laurenson spoke softly. "He said his next appearance will be live."

"I don't know for sure if he'll ever make that appearance, Ed. Nor do you. And what do we do if he doesn't? Do we hold that tape? Do we turn it over to the police? Because if we do, you can be sure of one thing: A copy of it will somehow leak out and someone else will show it on their news program while we're still debating the right course of action. Like I said before, Ed, we're damned if we do and damned if we don't. And I guess I'd rather be damned for doing."

"I can't blame you for wanting to go with this, Roger. The whole thing has made you a national star, not that you went looking for it. And even though I think you've tried to react professionally and responsibly, the net result is that you stand to benefit enormously the longer this whole thing keeps going."

Roger Tatum nodded. "True enough, but then so does the station. And let's face it Ed, you *are* the station."

"Not to the viewing public, I'm not. To everyone who's been watching this—and that's just about everyone in the country— *you* are the station. And you're also part of what may very well be the biggest story in television news history. God knows what you'll be able to demand come contract time."

"Ed," Roger Tatum spoke softly, slowly. "I hope you're not implying that I want to show this tape because it's in the best interest of my career. Christ, I hope that's not my real motivation."

"You're a professional newscaster, Roger. One of the very best, in my opinion. But you're also a human being. If I were in your shoes, I think I would want to show the tape. It'd be tough for any newscaster to walk away from this kind of story, this kind of an audience. But I'm not in your shoes. And I say we don't show the tape. We've gone as far as we're going."

"If that's what you want, Ed, I'll live with it."

"I always thought you were a class act, Roger. And you are."

Roger Tatum smiled the polite smile of a loser. "I'll live with it, Ed, but honest to God, I'm not sure you're right. I mean, we've both been in this business long enough to know that you can't underestimate the public's appetite for violence and crisis and tragedy. It's ravenous. And the bloodier the better. I've never quite bought the idea that people want good news. They loved Son of Sam. They lapped it up. You know it. You remarked about it then.''

"You're right, of course. But at least I for one am going to stop feeding that appetite.''

"Ed, I hope you're not caving in because of the criticism from the press. Those creeps run sensational banner headlines about the tapes, then sanctimoniously tear us apart for showing them. They're the immoral bastards, Ed, not you.''

"There's a big difference between writing about murders and showing them in living color,'' said Edmund Laurenson, the tone in his voice implying that he hoped the conversation was coming to an end.

"Ed, I grew up here, right at this station. You, more than anyone else, taught me about television news. Remember? 'Show, don't tell.' That was one of your favorites. And, 'If you don't have action footage, give 'em action footage. A building burning. A prisoner slugging a cameraman. A mother screaming for her lost child.' Remember Ed? The emphasis should always be on the picture, the visual side of the story because this is a visual medium. So now you want me to step out there before millions of people and *tell* them what I've seen, rather than *show* them what I've seen. It goes against everything you've ever taught me, and all because you're afraid we're going to get ripped up by the newspapers and a few commentators who want us all to return to a more gentle time. Well, that more gentle time is gone and it's not ever coming back, but if it ever does, I'll be the first one to say let's show it that way. Just show what it is, not what we'd like to be.''

Edmund Laurenson shook his head. "You just don't understand, do you Roger? There's a limit—''

Roger Tatum suddenly pounded Edmund Laurenson's desk so fiercely that Edmund Laurenson was amazed that the desk didn't splinter into several dozen pieces. "C'mon, Ed. Let's be honest with each other. Where was the limit when we showed those Buddhist monks setting themselves ablaze? And what about Vietnam? Every night we got to show napalmed kids and guys getting their brains blown out at close range and kids screaming as they saw their fathers and mothers being butchered. But you can excuse that because that was war and maybe by showing how ugly and horrible it was we could help stop the killing. That was the rationale then, Ed.''

"Go on Roger, I think you're finally getting at your real feelings on this thing."

"Ed, I just think you've always been too straight with me and everyone else to start being something you're not. You're not Eric Severeid. I'm not Edward R. Murrow. So let's not make moral pronouncements. Let's just go back to showing the news as it is. That's the honest thing to do.''

"You know, Roger, I just wonder what our audience would think if they heard us talking like this.''

"I think they'd agree with me, Ed. At least they'd know I was leveling with them. And let them decide for themselves what they should or should not see."

"You're probably right. But someone does have to decide what we're going to show. And in this case, that's me.''

"You know, Ed, you've never pulled rank on me before, never interfered with news content. You were always the one who said, 'Go wherever the camera takes you.' You never pulled up short before. Don't you remember when we had that killer of all those kids—about eight of them and not one more than fourteen years old? Remember when he confessed? We had our camera follow him to the remote areas where he had buried the children. He'd point to a spot on the ground where he thought he remembered digging a grave. And our cameras focused on that spot while the shovels started digging and our audiences sat riveted to their chairs wondering whether they were going to get to see the mutilated and decomposing body of some twelve-year-old who, for all we knew or cared, may have had a mother or father or brother or sister watching the show.'' Roger Tatum smiled sar-castically. ''Excuse me. Did I say 'show'? I meant to say 'news'.''

Roger Tatum turned and walked slowly. ''Of course, the bodies were never found. But that wasn't our fault. Just as it wasn't our fault when we had news specials that let that guy describe in detail how he'd picked the children up, gotten them into his car, and what he'd done to them before he killed each and every one of them while they were screaming for their mothers and God and anyone to please, please help them. Then he said he was sorry for what he'd done and wanted to pay for his crimes. We stretched those interviews, or taped confessions with Rivers, out over five days as I recall, Ed. We showed parts of them every night on the six o'clock news. And again on the ten o'clock news. And the ratings skyrocketed. Remember? And then we patted ourselves on the back and told anyone who'd listen, including ourselves, that we were doing a public service to alert parents to warn their children about going anywhere with strangers. And who knows, maybe we did convince some kids to stay away from strangers. Maybe we saved some lives without knowing it.

''When I saw those tapes of Rivers walking over the ground where he thought he buried those kids, and then our cameras zooming in for closeups of the shovels digging into that ground, I realized that if we ever obtained taped or filmed live murders and could show them to our audiences, that we would, because it makes for powerful television. Because it's drama—and it's visual. But most important—because it's news. When it stops being news, we should stop showing them. But not until then.''

''I'm tired Roger. Terribly tired.'' Edmund Laurenson's voice was detached, as if he could barely concentrate on what was being said. ''I get the feeling that this whole thing isn't really happen-ing. It's all a show and somehow, someone will click off a little switch, and then you and me and this office will fade away and titles will roll across the darkness and this whole sick thing will be over because there's no way it can really be happening.''

''The tape, Ed.'' Roger Tatum's voice took on the character of his on-camera personality. There was a tone of sincerity, a suggestion of quiet respect. "What about the tape, the tape of the police chief? Do we use it or not? We've been sitting on it for six days now. I still can't believe you're not going to let me show it. I think when you think this thing all the way through, you'll realize it's the right way, the only way." The phone buzzed like a persistent fly, interrupting Roger Tatum and causing Edmund Laurenson to move so that his swivel chair swung close to the desk. He picked up the phone.

"Hello," he said softly. There was silence for five or six seconds, then, again softly he said, "Yes, put him on." Roger Tatum retreated to the brown leather sofa and sat down. "Go ahead Chuck, what is it?" said Laurenson, his voice still soft, almost sad. Finally, Laurenson spoke into the receiver. "OK, Chuck. Channel Nine. I'll turn it on right now." He hung up the phone and moved slightly forward in his chair to reach the automatic control on his desk. "That was Chuck Pittman. He says that Channel Nine may have scooped us. At any rate, he said there's a story breaking on the tapes on Channel Nine right now." Edmund Laurenson pushed a button, and the large television screen near the door came immediately alive with color and sound.

Roger Tatum recognized the figure at once, and he felt his stomach squeeze itself tight and a sour taste rise in his mouth. "Oh shit, no," he said softly, as he watched the face of the overweight police chief fill the screen. The two men sat quietly watching the police chief answer questions politely for a few moments until he was joined by a man in a bizarre black-and-white face mask and flowing black cape. In the middle of an exchange of words between the police chief and the man in the mask, a gleaming sword suddenly appeared from beneath the cape, swung forward in a blur of an arc, slicing right through the police chief's blubbery neck, causing the oversize head to look remarkably foolish as the face expressed surprise and shock at finding itself dead.

"Because of the prior showing of the other murder tapes on Channel Eight, we here at Channel Nine had the opportunity to ask ourselves the hypothetical question about how we would have reacted had those tapes been sent to us instead of Channel Eight. We had to conclude that our response would have been the same as Channel Eight's. Like it or not, the tapes are news. To suppress them would, we believe, be tantamount to deceiving our viewers. and, of course, we realized, as Channel Eight did, that there are undoubtedly other copies of the tape. If we didn't show it, it would only be a matter of time before some other station did. Our only real question is: Why was this tape sent to us and not Channel Eight? Or was a copy of it sent to Channel Eight and did they decide not to show it? We sincerely hope not, because to do so would be to break faith with the public and a failure to meet its responsibility to bring all significant news to the public without undue censorship as fully and promptly as possible.''

"You were right, Roger." His voice was a whisper. "And I was wrong. But please don't say I told you so.''

Roger Tatum stood up abruptly, his six foot, one-inch stature looming large in the semi-darkness of the office. "We could get crucified on this," he said. "You try and do what you think is right by holding that tape off the air and now the same people who knocked you for showing those other tapes will beat you to death with this last tape because you didn't show it. We've got to figure some excuse for why we didn't show it this past week.''

"Excuse?" echoed Edmund Laurenson. "There is no excuse. We didn't show it because I said don't show it. This is still a privately-owned station. No one can tell me I have to show something that I believe works against the public interest." He placed his hands on his desk and with a slight push raised himself from the swivel chair. He stepped in back of the chair and began to draw the black drapes, letting the mellow orange of a late Miami afternoon into his office.

"I've got it," said Roger Tatum.

"You've got what?"

Tatum started walking slowly toward the sunlight, speaking with urgency as he did. "I go on with my news show, and I acknowledge that, yes, we did have the tape a week before Channel Nine received the dupe. But we weren't trying to suppress or hide anything. We had simply decided to take a chance, to lure whoever is responsible for these tapes out of hiding. We figured that if we didn't show this last tape he sent us, he might get frustrated and try to contact us. We were hoping we might get him to phone us or write us or reach us by some other method.'' Roger Tatum turned suddenly and began retracing his steps. ''Oh yeah,'' he continued, ''this could even work to our advantage. I think it could get both of us off the hook. All I do is say that we realized our plan might not work, that the person responsible for these tapes might simply start mailing them to other stations. But damn it, we had to take that risk. We had to try to get him to contact us. Why? I'll tell you why. Because the people in our news department and the executive leadership of this station are far more interested in helping to protect the citizens of this community than we are in beating the rest of the world to a big news story or boosting our ratings.''

''You don't think anyone's going to believe that, do you?'' said Edmund Laurenson.

''I guarantee it. We've got to take the initiative. We can't just sit back and take all the flak. We're the ones—I'm the one, really—who received all the tapes. There must be a reason why. Why our television station, in the first place? Maybe that should be part of our story. Why this station? Why Roger Tatum?''

''Maybe,'' Edmund Laurenson answered, ''because the person responsible for the tapes is a fan of yours. Maybe you should invite him to appear with you on the show. You know, on the news tonight you appeal directly to him, talk directly to him. Tell him why you didn't play his tape.''

''Put ourselves right back in the middle of the picture, right?'' interrupted Roger Tatum.

''Right,'' answered Edmund Laurenson.

''You know Ed, for a minute there I thought you had lost touch.''

''I have lost touch, Roger. So have you. All of us have. Because you see, none of this is real. It can't be.''

13

Gavin Risen awoke. His eyes immediately focused on the electronic red figures in the digital clock atop the nearby night table: 5:11, then in a second, 5:12. Was that a noise outside? Or was someone in the room with him? Something had caused Gavin to come wide awake in an instant. He lay perfectly still so that if someone were in the room with him, or was looking at him through a window, he'd think he was still asleep. He lay there in the darkness listening intently for any sound; muffled breathing from a closet, an animal ransacking the garbage, soft footsteps crushing leaves and twigs outside the house. Without moving his head, Gavin opened his eyes as wide as he could, and let them travel freely around the darkened room like two minicameras doing a slow pan of a deserted set. Occasionally, when he spotted an object he did not recognize immediately, he would use his unique gift for zooming his vision in tight for extreme close-ups. What at first appeared to be the silhouette of a crouching dog was the portable heater he had set up only two nights before in anticipation of a cold spell that had never materialized. The coiled snake at the edge of the closet was merely a long strand of rope that had been wrapped around the box containing his two weeks' supply of groceries, which were delivered the day before. How did it get there, on the floor? Gavin couldn't remember, but it really didn't matter. He could clearly see it was nothing more than a strand of rope, nothing to fear, nothing that could harm him. Gavin closed his eyes for a moment and tried to recall what it was that had caused him to come awake so suddenly.

Even before he opened his eyes he saw it. A hot bright light a hundred times more brilliant than anything Gavin had ever seen, pouring in through every window like frozen fire and filling the room with an incredible power that caused Gavin to shield his eyes with his arm lest he lose his sight forever. Simultaneous with the appearance of the light came an unearthly high-pitched whining sound that strained higher and higher, totally disorienting the slender man lying on the bed, an arm covering his eyes, his free hand holding one ear while he pushed the other side of his head hard into the mattresses in a vain attempt to block out the noise. And then, as suddenly as it had started, it stopped. The searing light was gone, the room was in darkness. The screaming sounds had stopped, leaving a menacing silence that now moaned in Gavin Risen's ears. Slowly he moved his arm away from his eyes and lifted his hand away from his ear. He lay in the blackness, and only the figures on the digital clock reminded him that he was alive. But when he looked at the figures on the digital clock he began to wonder why they read 5:08, when only moments before they had read 5:12. Maybe the incredible light and sound had caused the clock to malfunction. Or maybe, just maybe, he was moving back in time. He stared at the clock for what seemed like forever before the final digit on the right rearranged itself to form a 7. He kept his eyes fixed on the clock until the 5:07 became a 5:06.

Gavin lay in bed and tried to think of a logical reason why time had always moved forward instead of backwards. He couldn't. It was too much for him. And then suddenly he thought he knew what might be going on, the reason for the blinding lights and the deafening noise. It was one of two things. Either the lights were police search lights blazing through his window, and the noise was a type of sound device police use to disorient people to destroy resistance to capture. He had seen the police use such techniques dozens of times on television. Or maybe the light and sounds were simply signals that the message Gavin had been waiting for all these years had finally arrived.

If it were the police, he would know soon enough. The lights and the sounds would be coming at him again full blast in a matter of minutes, maybe seconds. He looked up at the clock. 5:03. And then he looked up over the clock to the four-paneled window that faced out toward the main house, and he saw it. In the lower right-hand frame, for only a fraction of a second. A face seemingly suspended in space, as if the window frame had become a television screen. The face was gone in a flash, before Gavin could recognize who it was or even what sex it was. And then, another face flashed on for a fraction of a second in the top right panel of the window frame, but it too was gone before Gavin could tell if it was the same face that had appeared an instant before. Then, simultaneously, all four frames were filled with a face, the same face, and Gavin recognized it at once. Four sets of lips moved and four identical voices spoke the same message. "It is time," they said, "it is time to do it." Then the faces disappeared so quickly and completely, it was as if they had never been there. Gavin remained motionless in bed, unsure of what to do. Should he simply lie there and wait for further instructions or some other sign. Or should he set into motion the final stages of a plan that had been materializing in his mind for years. Gavin's body was rigid, his senses acutely alert. He began to move, rising from the bed as slowly as a man twice his age might do. His eyes penetrated the darkness, his ears could hear even the fluttering of birds' wings in the hundreds of trees that surrounded the estate. He moved through the blackness of the room until he reached the large console television set against the wall. His fingers moved softly across the screen and over the panel of dials until he touched the on/off button. He pressed it. Almost at once a soft glow formed in the center of the screen and began to spread its light throughout the room. Out of the glowing light, a face formed on the screen. It was the same face that Gavin had seen on the window panels. A face he had seen many times before. It was a long, narrow face, with damp straight black hair moving down across the forehead. The nose was sharp, the cheekbones angular, the ears pointed. It was a face that Gavin knew and trusted. And then the lips on the face parted and they spoke. "Good morning, Gavin. It's time."

Gavin stared at the face on the screen and said "Good morning, Mr. Spock. I've been waiting for you. I've been waiting for you for so long."

Mr. Spock's features remained expressionless but he stared at Gavin long and hard, as if he were looking directly into the man's mind. "You're not like other humans, are you Gavin?" he began. "You're more like me. Your mind is precise. Your thinking isn't muddled by the weakness of emotions. You know what is important and what isn't. And you have respect for the future. That is vital, having respect for the future, isn't it?"

Gavin nodded, his eyes fixed on the clear depths of Mr. Spock's eyes. "I'm ready," said Gavin softly. "I'm ready to do my work."

Mr. Spock's thin lips seemed almost ready to form a smile, but instead they merely parted over strong-looking white teeth. And then he motioned for Gavin to move closer to him as he spoke. "Perhaps you'd like to come in here for a while before you do your work. To see what it's really like and how it's going to be for you."

Gavin edged closer to the large TV picture and spoke respectfully to the large image of Mr. Spock in front of him. "Do you mean it? Can I come inside? I've always wanted to, but I never knew how."

"Come on, Gavin," urged Mr. Spock, his voice a flat monotone, "there's nothing to it." And then Mr. Spock moved and his arm reached out through time and space and the television set until his long slender fingers touched Gavin Risen's face. An irresistible thrill roared through Gavin's body, generating a greater sense of pure physical excitement than he had ever known. It was nothing at all like when a human being in the outside world had touched Gavin in the past, not like when his mother kissed him or someone bumped against him on the subway or in a store, or when he was forced to shake hands with someone during a job interview. The feeling of human flesh making contact with his own had always been repulsive to Gavin. But this was different. It was like touching a pure stream of electronic power and coming in contact with the energy locked inside a meteor or a moonbeam.

Mr. Spock's fingers moved from Gavin's face to his arm and wound slowly around Gavin's wrist and urged him gently toward the television screen. "Don't be worried," said Mr. Spock in a calm but authoritative tone. "You are simply going to move from one medium to another, to leave one state of existence and enter another."

Gavin's mind was racing, and he began making closer and closer contact with the television screen itself. "I'm not worried," he said aloud. "This is what I've been waiting for." And then his face was pressed up against the glass of the television screen and he could feel a billion gentle vibrations breaking down each molecule of his face so that it could pass through the barriers of time and space and move inside the television set to be with Mr. Spock. He felt his features and body being absorbed into a beam of pure light and his ears buzzed with the sound of a thousand voices blending together in a steady drone that seemed to surround him now completely. He felt his body fall apart and float freely so that he could see each piece of it inside and out from every possible angle all at the same instant. And then he could see his eyes looking at themselves, seeing themselves and seeing through themselves. There was an explosion of vibrant light not unlike the powerful beam that had blasted through his window only moments—or was it years—before. And now the light broke up into amazingly intricate patterns, like electric cobwebs spiraling off into space and Gavin Risen raced after them, his entire being filled with a surge of elation. His body and mind became one constantly changing sensation that throbbed with a rhythm linking his every cell with a cascading explosion of electrons and neutrons all about him. The center of his being was an avalanche of colors moving in an incredibly complex kaleidoscope, and then suddenly he was through it, floating free in space with Mr. Spock by his side.

"You've done it, Gavin," said Mr. Spock. "You have become one with your image and there is no greater accomplishment in this universe or any other because you have shed the physical limitations of human life."

And then Gavin saw them all around him, all the friends he had loved and lived for all these years. He could not look anywhere without seeing someone he loved. There was Rod Serling. He nodded at Gavin and smiled. Molly Goldberg winked. Dan Rather looked up from a desk. Dinah Shore and Merv Griffin and Anwar Sadat were talking to each other and smiling. Jack Benny was listening to John F. Kennedy, and Frank Blair was dancing with Bess Myerson while Hugh Downs played the piano. There was Jack Lescoulie, and he hadn't changed one bit in all these years. Nor had Les Crane nor Perry Como nor Giselle McKenzie.

"So this is what it's like," thought Gavin. "This is where they all come. This is where they all live forever."

"Don't misunderstand," said Mr. Spock. "This is temporary for you, Gavin. It's only a visit. You can't come here to stay forever until you've done your work."

"I know," said Gavin. "And I know what I must do to deserve this." He looked about him and saw the very familiar face of a girl who had danced in the chorus of a thousand different shows but whose name was never listed on the credits.

"Who is she?" asked Gavin.

"Oh, I don't know," answered Mr. Spock. "We must have thousands like her here. Both male and female. But no one knows their names because their names never became well known. Just their faces. Of course, they've every bit as much right to be here as a lot of us because their images were seen by as many eyes and probably as many times as the big-name stars."

Gavin looked at Mr. Spock and his voice was very serious

when he spoke. "I want so much to be a part of all this. I'm so happy you came for me. This is all so much more real than the outside world."

"Hi, Gavin, how the hell are you?" It was Joe Tawny dressed in the same clothes he had worn when Gavin had fired a bullet into his brain, only now there were no traces of the bullet wound. Tawny's forehead was smooth and clear and framed by strings of dirty blond hair.

"So you are here," said Gavin, his voice rising in a sense of wonder. "And I'm the one who made it possible. Aren't you glad now? Isn't this better than being on the outside?"

Tawny smiled and blew Gavin a kiss. "I'll tell you, I'll never know how to thank you. I mean you made my image mean something. I was really no one, no one at all until you came along. So many people die alone and the world never notices them and they leave no image behind. But me, I'm really and truly immortal because so many people shared my death."

Mr. Spock looked on in stately silence as the dialogue between Gavin and Tawny continued. "Are the others here? Did they all make it?" asked Gavin. "Look over there," said Tawny, not pointing in any direction or otherwise indicating where Gavin should look, but he somehow sensed the right direction and there they were: the police chief, his head once again situated firmly atop his blubbery neck, Camille Sheridan looking quite professional and knowledgeable, and, of course, the masked figure. "Hi!" they chorused and they waved to Gavin.

"Watch this one," said the police chief as he bent forward and his head fell off and was caught between his hands as a geyser of blood gushed out and over the hollow stump of his neck. After a second or two the stubby hands placed the head back atop the fat neck and with an almost comic gesture patted it firmly into place.

Camille Sheridan smiled. "We owe it all to you."

"Who loves you Gavin baby?" Gavin heard the familiar voice and turned quickly, and there he was, Kojak, standing in front of Gavin, lollipop in mouth, the lenses of his glasses gleaming with reflected light, his bald head a rounded bullet of hardened flesh.

Then Gavin heard another familiar voice coming from still another direction. "And you can take that to the bank Gavin, you weirdo." The stocky figure in the sweatshirt with the cut-off sleeves moved toward Gavin, a huge happy smile moving across the swarthy features. But before Barretta moved more than two or three steps toward Gavin another voice could be heard, soft spoken and nasal and familiar to Gavin for years: "Just give us the facts, please Gavin. All we want are the facts." Sergeant Joe Friday's face was expressionless.

And so it went. Everywhere Gavin turned, he was face to face with famous images he had seen over the years, only now they were all talking to him, they were paying attention to him, Gavin Risen, and treating him as if he were one of their own. There was John Cameron Swayze smiling hello and pointing to the watch on his wrist. Richard Nixon actually patted Gavin on the back and Idi Amin did a little dance. There were boxers and ballplayers and singers and ventriloquists and news commentators and quiz show panelists. There were dancers and weight lifters, musicians and magicians, diplomats and convicted killers and ice skaters and gymnasts and weathermen and sportscasters and congressmen and kings and queens and victims of floods and fires. There were doctors and lawyers, housewives and soldiers and private investigators. They had all managed to pass through the barrier of reality and enter the eternity of illusion, and Gavin wanted to be with them so much now and forever because he knew them so much better and more fully than he did people on the outside. And then he realized that it must be true for others, too. How many millions of eyes and minds knew the people he saw parading before him now better than they did anyone on earth. How many knew the Hollywood Squares better than they knew their neighbors. How many knew Andy Griffith better than their mailman or their grocer. And trusted him more fully. Or was Gavin the only one?

Still the parade continued. Lawrence Welk and John Dean and Eileen Wilson and Joseph Welch and Warren Hull and Elvis Presley and Kay Starr and Joe McCarthy. And then there was Charles Manson and Carol Lawrence and John Chancellor and

Ethel Mertz. Sirhan Sirhan was laughing and Perry Mason was reading and Fabian was singing and David Berkowitz was writing a letter.

"How do you like it here, Gavin." The voice was Mr. Spock's, ever calm and in absolute control.

"Everyone here is so real, not like in the outside world. I could stay here forever," answered Gavin as his eyes kept trying to take in all the faces that flashed before him.

"You can stay here forever, Gavin. You do understand that, don't you. You can become immortal. You can become timeless. But you know the qualifications."

There was a loud roar and a sudden flashing of lights and the Starship *Enterprise* came into view, hurtling through galaxies in fractions of seconds until it hovered directly over Gavin and Mr. Spock and a laser beam descended from the bottom of the ship and froze into a solid staircase, which Mr. Spock began to ascend immediately, motioning Gavin to follow him as he covered two and three steps with each stride. Gavin followed Mr. Spock rapidly as he moved up the staircase of light. Each step he climbed immediately disappeared behind him so that he had no choice but to continue until he had actually boarded the Starship *Enterprise*.

"Captain Kirk, may I present Gavin Risen." Mr. Spock's voice echoed through the large ship, but Gavin barely heard it, his eyes were so busy exploring the flashing technological apparatus, as well as the familiar faces all about him. There was Doc over by a blinking control panel. And Scotty was busying himself with some charts. The rest of the crew were appropriately active. Captain Kirk sat in the captain's chair, taking his eyes off a video screen charting the starship's progress only long enough to acknowledge Gavin's presence.

"Where are we going?" whispered Gavin to Mr. Spock. There was a pause before Spock's answer, as if he had to calculate factors like speed and course direction in his mind. "We're going anywhere and everywhere," he said. "There is no place in space we cannot reach, no corner of the universe we cannot penetrate, no area of any man's mind we cannot enter." There was a sudden surge as if the starship had shifted into high gear and broken through some invisible shield that held its speed in check, because now there was a tremendous sense of freedom and Gavin felt himself hurtling toward forever and the unknown, but there was no fear within him because he knew his companions and trusted them well, and if one was going to journey through infinity, what better way to travel than with Captain Kirk and Mr. Spock at his side?

Through the huge windows of the starship Gavin could see the universe gliding past his eyes. The moon was a vanilla cough drop. Meteors moved through the blackness like corks launched from hundreds of giant bottles of champagne. Great cosmic clouds drifted by, and when they cleared, Gavin could see it directly below and to the left. A small blue and white circle of light seemingly lost in space. Again, he heard Spock's voice, but he knew immediately from the tone that the remarks were not directed to him.

"Are we heading for Earth?"

Captain Kirk's answer was quick, precise. "Yes. We're on course for Earth and should be within her atmosphere in about forty-eight seconds. My instructions say that our passenger is to disembark there for the completion of an important mission."

"Did you hear that, Gavin?" Mr. Spock's voice, as always was firm, calm. Gavin merely nodded, but in his mind he was smiling with anticipation as the earth seemed to float closer and closer, until he heard Captain Kirk give the command. "Prepare to launch passenger through space and time for immediate reentry into reality." Members of the crew guided Gavin to a sleek chamber at the front of the ship. A hatch was opened and without being told what to do, Gavin climbed inside, realizing that he had become a human missile that would soon be fired toward Earth. Gavin closed his eyes and his body tensed in anticipation of the blast-off. He began a silent countdown in his mind.

The firing was a smooth, painless process, and Gavin once again found himself floating weightlessly through space, the rapidly approaching planet called Earth growing larger each second. And then he felt as if his face and body had burst into flames as he penetrated the earth's atmosphere and the pull of gravity grabbed at him with enormous power and he was drawn down to a destination and a destiny over which he had no control. Below, he could see a long thin needle jutting up through the clouds and it seemed as if invisible beams emanating from the tip of the giant pin were guiding Gavin directly to it, and then he could see that the giant pin looming up over the earth was a television transmission tower and then his body entered the head of the pin at the speed of light and once again he could feel his being breaking down into a billion separate molecules and then instantly coming together again as a cylinder of pure energy that moved through time and space simultaneously, and then there was an eruption of colors and sounds coming together in a blinding, deafening outburst followed by a deep, still darkness and total silence. Gavin Risen opened his eyes. He was seated on a plain brown wooden chair in his bedroom, facing the television set. The set was on, but the screen was empty, save for what appeared to be an explosion of black and white dots flickering and bouncing off each other in meaningless confusion before the start of the day's programming. But to Gavin Risen, the black and white dots were communicating a most important message. He stared at the otherwise empty screen for a full five mintues before he rose to his feet and said quietly over the soft drone of static, "I understand."

Gavin Risen walked slowly to his bedroom closet, stepping over discarded packages of crackers and small, empty milk containers. As he reached the closet door, he turned and stared again at the television screen and the billions of black and white dots. He nodded slowly, then turned and opened the closet door. The first piece of equipment he saw was the submachine gun, black and sleek and hanging from its strap on a hook Gavin had hammered into the closet wall within days after he had moved into the estate as caretaker. Gavin's hand reached for the strap and within a second the firm, solid feel of the stock pressed against his side. The metallic touch of the trigger was cool on his fingers and he raised the short barrel and brought it softly to his lip. He had never fired the gun, but he had seen it perform successfully many times in gang wars on shows like "The Untouchables." He knew it was a terrifying weapon, that with it one person, acting alone, could kill dozens, perhaps even hundreds of people before he could be stopped. He knew it could fire four hundred fifty rounds per minute, each round a potential killer. But he also had heard police experts talk about this particular weapon on a television documentary about guns in America, and he knew that it was not a particularly accurate weapon. Anyway, it wasn't right for his purposes. It was dramatic, all right. But it wasn't what he needed. He placed the thick leather strap over the hook and guided the machine gun softly back to its resting place, taking special care that it did not hit up against the wall. Gavin's eyes had become accustomed to the semidarkness of the closet, but he moved his hand to the light switch, so that he could see more clearly the arsenal he had been building up bit by bit, even during the years when he was working at Reinhart's Tavern. His eyes focused immediately on the holster hanging next to the submachine gun. The plastic handle of a Colt Python was visible beneath the leather flap of the holster. Gavin quickly removed the Colt Python from the holster and moved his fingers softly over the four-inch barrel, lingering for a long second at the sighting pin. There was a gun belt and gun pouch near the hook where the Colt had hung, and Gavin checked the pouch, finding it filled with fifteen cartridges. His hand moved to the lever at the side of the Colt and pressed it hard. The bullet cylinder swung out and Gavin could see that the Colt was fully loaded. He replaced the Colt in the holster, then in a moment, his hands supremely steady and sure, he had placed the gun belt through the loops of the holster and cartridge pouch and buckled it around his waist. This one would do nicely, he thought. But it would not be enough, not for what he wanted to accomplish.

His eyes moved to the olive-green satchel lying on the floor in the rear of the closet directly in back of a sawed-off shotgun. Gavin bent carefully and lifted the satchel, holding it by the broad canvas strap designed to be carried over the shoulder. He opened the flap and looked inside. There they were, sitting there quietly, just as Gavin had remembered them. Eleven hand grenades, Vietnam vintage, pins all picturesquely in place, dozing silently in the soft canvas pouch that had been their home for years. Gavin lifted the strap and placed it over his neck so that the satchel itself hung down at his left hip opposite the Colt Python. He reached into the sack and his fingers wound sensuously around the distinctive shape of a grenade. He pressed it gently into his palm, then lifted his hand from the bag so that his eyes might examine his small but powerful ally more carefully. For a moment or two, Gavin was tempted to pull the strange looking pin from the missile to see if it would unleash the same explosive force he had witnessed on "Combat" and countless war movies. Instead, he simply cupped his hands together and cradled the grenade for a moment before placing it back in the pouch. Then he bent and his hands gripped a solid, rectangular black box with three raised white buttons on the surface. He paused for a moment, concentrating on numbers he had committed to memory. And then his fingers moved swiftly over the buttons, pressing them like piano keys in a sequence that had significance only for him. Then he placed the box in the pouch alongside the grenades.

He realized that he was nearly ready but that he still lacked one very essential piece of equipment. Where had he put them? Gavin's eyes roamed over the contents of the closet, zooming in for extreme close-ups whenever they encountered a shape which they didn't immediately recognize. And then he remembered. Up there. On the ledge at the top of the closet. In the old steel footlocker. He stretched as far as he could and extended his arms as far as they would reach and then at the ends of his fingers he could feel the thin steel handles on either side of the footlocker. The weight of the locker strained his fingers sorely as he pulled it forward with painful grunts until it stood balanced on the very edge of the ledge. Then slowly and carefully, he tipped the locker on one end until it glided easily onto his shoulder. From there, he lowered it quickly to the floor, where he quickly flipped the latch and opened the lid, and there they were, bright and gleaming atop an assorted selection of knives, masks, hatchets, trenching tools, and bayonets. Two sets. Smooth, shiny steel circles linked to each other like identical twins. Handcuffs. Two sets of them. Keys protruding from the locks of each set. Gavin bent and fondled them slowly, tracing the circles with the index fingers of both hands as if he were performing a sexual rite.

Gavin lifted both sets of handcuffs from the trunk. He placed one set inside the pouch next to the grenades. Then he took the other set, turned the key, and snapped open the cuffs. He placed one open cuff around his left wrist, then snapped it shut leaving the other cuff dangling loose. He dropped the key in the open footlocker, then slammed the lid shut with his foot. He stepped back out of the closet, clicked off the light switch, and turned to look at himself in the long mirror on the back of the bedroom door. The Colt Python and cartridge pouch hung neatly on the gun belt around his waist. The olive green pouch hung harmlessly at his side like an innocent mail bag. One handcuff encircled his left wrist, with another, open, dangling just a few inches below. The steel was cool and hard against Gavin's skin. He had everything, he thought. He was ready.

He moved quickly and quietly across the room until he reached another closet. He opened the door and entered a large walk-in area lined with assorted costumes and cloaks and work clothes. He selected an oversized blue raincoat that reached past his knees. He put the raincoat on, concealing the Colt Python and the pouch with the grenades and black box. Only the dangling handcuff was visible; but Gavin knew he could conceal that merely by keeping his hand in his pocket. Just before he left the large walk-in closet, Gavin picked up a small black attaché case. He didn't bother to open the case because he already knew what was inside. And he knew it was in perfect working order. He stepped back out of the closet and closed the door. And then he looked at the television screen. The billions of black and white dots had disappeared. There were two images on the screen. The faces of two men. Gavin recognized both of the men at once. He walked slowly across the room until he was standing within eight or ten inches of the set. The two faces on the screen were about the same height as the Colt Python hanging in the holster on Gavin's hip inside Gavin's raincoat. Gavin's hand reached through a slit in the raincoat's pocket and flipped up the top of the holster. He wrapped his hand around the hard plastic butt of the gun and lifted the Colt Python out of the holster and through the raincoat pocket until it was pointed directly at the face of the man on the left of the screen, the distinguished looking dark-haired man with the moustache who was speaking, totally unaware that Gavin's finger was tightening slowly on the trigger.

"Hello," the man said, "my name is Roger Tatum."

"Bang-bang," answered Gavin Risen, "you're dead." Gavin lowered the Colt Python from in front of the screen and placed it back through the torn-out pocket of the raincoat into the concealed holster on his hip. Gavin listened as Roger Tatum introduced Dr. Dukoff to the viewing audience, noting that Dr. Dukoff would be making regular appearances on the Roger Tatum News Report until such time as there was a major break in the videotape murders.

"I think it's time I made a guest appearance on one of your Special News Reports, Roger," Gavin said to the television set. "Perhaps the next time you interview Dr. Dukoff, I'll just drop in. I'd really love to be there. In fact, I will be there. You can count on it."

14

Gavin stood silently, his mouth dry, his body aching with a sweet expectancy he had not experienced since his sword had made contact with the rolling flesh of the police chief's neck. His finger tensed on the trigger, then relaxed. The cameras were on the other men. But soon they would be on Gavin. The bright lights on the set made it easy for him to see the two men, but impossible for them to see him.

"I think perhaps the most amazing thing about these tapes," said Dr. Dukoff, "is just how quickly we've gotten over our initial shock and have come to regard them as simply another sensational news story." Dr. Dukoff arched his bushy black eyebrows as he looked directly at Roger Tatum to see if the newscaster agreed with him.

"Your point is well taken, doctor," nodded Roger Tatum. "I think perhaps that ever since the Kennedy assassination and the subsequent shooting of Lee Harvey Oswald on live television, we have found it increasingly easy to accept what previously had been unacceptable, to adapt to shocking events with remarkable speed."

"Take the skyjackings," interrupted Dr. Dukoff, nervous, slender fingers forming a shaky bridge in front of his chest. "I mean the first time someone skyjacked a plane it was an event of monumental, earthshaking proportions. People couldn't believe it had actually happened. Their initial reaction was that it was something straight out of a Hollywood movie.'' He paused to give Roger Tatum a chance to comment on the subject.

''Of course,'' answered the newscaster. ''Before long, sky-jackings became incredibly commonplace. Emotionally disturbed individuals. Terrorists. Practically anyone with an ax to grind—real or imaginary—began to make off with a seven-forty-seven and its passengers or whatever, whenever the mood hit them.''

''Ah, yes,'' intoned a suddenly aggressive Dr. Dukoff. ''But the major point is how quickly we adjusted to it all. From page-one banner headlines, and around-the-clock TV coverage, skyjackings soon lost their dramatic fascination for the public. Or should I say 'audience.' Because these events, like it or not, have in fact become dramas that viewers and readers follow with the same kind of intensity they might previously have saved for a favorite dramatic program or film or novel. Real life and fiction have become almost inseparable. In fact, in a great many minds, they are already inseparable.'' Dr. Dukoff paused, his thin fingers pushed at wire-rim glasses, and for a second or two he seemed to lose his train of thought. ''Ah, but I didn't follow my thought through to the end. The point I wanted to make is that after capturing the world's total attention, skyjackings slipped to the point in media coverage where they became a second, third, or even fourth story on the nightly news. They even dropped off the front pages. It was as if, during the course of a season, skyjackings had slipped badly in the ratings, and news directors started searching for something fresh, something new. Or as I've heard people in television say, something that's 'now'!''

Roger Tatum waved his hand in Doctor Dukoff's direction. ''I'm not so certain the news directors of this station or any other television station would agree with you, doctor. Frankly, we're a little tired of the cliché that we make the news rather than just report it, which is all that we really do.'' Roger Tatum smiled nervously and continued. ''But please, doctor, let's not get sidetracked into a discussion on the role of television news in today's society. Perhaps another time. But for now, let's keep the discussion centered on what's important to our viewers right now.''

Gavin Risen stood motionless, except for his right arm and hand, which now began to move the Colt Python so that it was no longer pointing at Roger Tatum. It was now aimed at Dr. Dukoff.

''I really did not mean to attack this station or any other television station,'' said Dr. Dukoff in a tone that was conciliatory but not apologetic. ''I'm simply trying to underscore that as we, as a society, become more and more exposed to acts that are aberrations—whether these are planned to attract television coverage or simply attract it in an incidental fashion—the more passive and adjusted to them we become. The television murder tapes are perhaps our most shocking media event to date. But we are getting used to them. They are not quite as sensational today as they were a few weeks ago. They are, in fact, already on their way to becoming old news.''

''Unless,'' Roger Tatum interrupted, ''we should receive another tape.''

''Or,'' said Dr. Dukoff, obviously continuing Roger Tatum's thought, ''unless we witness some kind of live appearance on television by the creator of those tapes as we were promised.''

''Do you personally think he'll try to do it?''

''Yes.''

''Why?''

Dr. Dukoff examined the nails on the back of his right hand. When he spoke, his tone was matter-of-fact, academic. ''For one thing, because he said so. And for another, because he has our attention. He knows that the entire world is watching. That everyone is waiting. That the world will listen to whatever it is he has to say.'' Roger Tatum looked at Dr. Dukoff intently.

Small beads of perspiration began to form on Gavin Risen's forehead. His hand, holding the Colt Python, began to feel uncomfortably warm, almost slimy.

"God only knows," began Dr. Dukoff. "As I mentioned during our last interview, there's a very formidable school of thought that these tapes have been created by a group of unidentified terrorists." He pushed his wire-rim glasses back further on his prominent nose. "The only trouble with that theory, of course, is that a group of terrorists or political activists could hardly expect to win any sympathy whatsoever for their cause through these tapes, which, by the way, have been condemned by every, and I emphasize *every*, nation on earth."

Roger Tatum nodded, indicating he wished Dr. Dukoff to continue.

"The other side of the coin, then, is that these are terrorists without a cause. Terrorists whose only raison d'être is to terrorize. Not for any cause. Not for any purpose. For no other reason than to strike terror in as many hearts and minds as possible."

"Again, you are saying 'they.' Does that mean you still believe that the tapes were created by a group rather than one individual acting alone?" Roger Tatum's manner of interrogation was, as always, calm and professional.

"I don't know," said Dr. Dukoff, an expression of doubt creasing his earnest features. "It seems logical enough, of course, to assume that an undertaking of this scope could obviously be handled better by a group than by an individual. But then, nothing about this entire situation has been logical."

Roger Tatum's silence could only be interpreted as a cue to continue.

"I mean, Roger, after all, there's nothing more illogical than you and I sitting here calmly discussing the reasons behind the most remarkable murders in modern times. I mean, if someone five years ago had told me that we would be sitting around now watching murders especially programmed for television, and that you and I would be dissecting those murders in the manner presidential speeches are analyzed, I would have told that person that he or she had better see a doctor or something."

"Of course," said Roger Tatum nodding, "so would I."

Gavin Risen realized that he, too, had nodded involuntarily.

"But then, whoever would have believed the Black Saturday terrorists' murder of the Olympic athletes at Munich after playing out their drama on television, complete with masks and all the trappings of a made-for-TV movie." Roger Tatum held up his hand in a quick gesture seeking permission to interrupt but not waiting for the permission to be granted.

"It was a made-for-TV movie, doctor, starring William Holden, if I remember correctly."

"Yes," Doctor Dukoff answered, "but the movie was made *after* the event. Had it been made before the murders at Munich, I daresay most of the viewing audience would have thought it a quite improbable plot. We no longer think that way. Today, we know that the strangest things we can imagine do really happen. In fact, things that are weirder than we could have imagined ten years ago now take place on an almost routine basis. I can almost guarantee that years from now many people will swear that they saw doctors operating to save President Reagan after he was shot by John Hinkley, Jr. And in a sense they'd be right. Because, one year after Reagan was shot, the doctors and nurses who actually worked over him at Georgetown Hospital appeared in a television dramatization of the event. So here we had the people who participated in the operation playing themselves in a production where an actor played the President and yet the President also appeared as himself. And, in this case, incredible as it may seem, the President had previously been an actor. So we had an actor playing a President who had been an actor."

"Let's get back to specifics, doctor. You mentioned a moment or two ago that the tapes could have been created by a new breed of terrorists who terrorize for no other particular reason than, well . . . to terrorize. Could you carry that thought a little further please."

Gavin Risen began to feel a surge of impatience. Why were they talking about terrorists?

Dr. Dukoff averted his eyes from the camera for a moment,

glancing upwards as if he might find the answer he was looking for floating six feet above his head.

"You remember Leopold and Loeb?" he asked.

"Well I don't remember the case when it happened, naturally," said Roger Tatum, "I'm not sure I was even born then. But I saw the movie."

"Where did you see the movie?"

"On television, I think, about six years ago."

Dr. Dukoff flashed an ironic smile and again studied the back of his nails before speaking. "That was, of course, the classic case of a thrill killing, killing for the sheer excitement and adventure of it. Killing for the perverted thrill of the actual act itself, but also killing for the exhilaration of watching everyone hunt for the killers, when you alone know who the killers are. It's so simple, yet so dramatic. Everyone in the world wants to find the killers, but the only people who know who the killers are are the killers. It can provide an enormous feeling of power, of omnipotence, if you will, for the killers. At least until they're caught."

"I thought you were talking about terrorism, not thrill killing." Roger Tatum's index finger smoothed the side of his moustache, a sign that he might be getting irritated with the manner in which his guest eluded direct questions and drifted off onto tangents.

Roger Tatum was not the only one annoyed at Dr. Dukoff's evasiveness. Gavin Risen's face remained expressionless, but his eyes moved away from the men's faces to his hand, which was holding the Colt Python. The hand did not seem to belong to the rest of Gavin's body. He studied his hand intently for a moment and concluded that it seemed to belong to the gun; they appeared to have become one. Gavin heard Dr. Dukoff's voice now as if he were speaking at the entrance of a long tunnel and Gavin was listening at the other end. His eyes moved back to the man's face.

"Look Roger, I think it's only fair to remind our audience that I am not Solomon, nor am I a psychic. I'm a criminal psychologist, which, I assume, qualifies me to make some educated guesses as to the motives behind these tapes, but it does not necessarily mean that I am closer to the truth of the matter than any of our viewers.'' Roger Tatum moved forward in his chair. The expression on his face indicated that he was about to apologize, but Dr. Dukoff continued speaking.

''It seems to me that terrorism and thrill killing need not be mutually exclusive. By that I mean that in this case, the major thrill may be in terrorizing an enormous audience. If Leopold and Loeb felt great exhilaration because there were so many people looking for them, imagine the kind of sensation our killers must feel in knowing that the entire nation—make that the entire world—has been watching their acts of violence, and wondering who they are.''

''Again, doctor, you keep saying 'they.' ''

Dr. Dukoff smiled grudgingly. ''Okay, it could be a 'he' or a 'she', but I rather doubt it. I still suspect it's a 'they.' ''

''If you believe,'' said Roger Tatum, ''that he, she, or they receive some kind of perverted thrill from these actions, then what do you think will be the type of telecast or event or what have you where we can anticipate that they might try to make a live appearance?''

Gavin Risen didn't really want to hear Dr. Dukoff's answer. The man was wrong about so many things. He just didn't have the mind to appreciate the scope of what Gavin had been doing and what he was going to do. Gavin was tired of Dr. Dukoff, and he decided that he would do something about him very soon. But he would let him continue for a little while longer. Just a little while.

''It will be something spectacular, I think. A sporting event. Perhaps the Super Bowl. A presidential speech. Maybe, God forbid,'' said Dr. Dukoff smiling, ''even a live newscast.''

The smile was still on Dr. Dukoff's face when the bullet burst through the left lens of his glasses and entered his eye with such force that it passed cleanly through his brain and out the back of his head before Roger Tatum could completely stifle the question he had started to ask.

"If these, doctor—oh Jesus." Roger Tatum's own eyes seemed to increase enormously in size as the horror of the instant seized him.

Dr. Dukoff's neck snapped forward so that his chin was resting on his chest, giving the appearance that he had been sent into an immediate deep sleep on a hypnotist's command. He could indeed have been sleeping, except for the torrent of blood that rushed out from the empty socket of his left eye and gushed down his jacket and shirt.

Gavin Risen felt the pistol jump in his hand and saw the force of impact when the bullet stopped Dr. Dukoff's speech in midsentence. No sooner had Gavin seen Dr. Dukoff's head start to move forward than his eyes, as if to confirm the evidence, glanced quickly at the nearby monitor, where he saw Roger Tatum staring in shock at the bloody figure seated next to him.

It took Roger Tatum the better part of three seconds to realize that his own life was in danger, but even before he could move, or before any of the cameramen or technical crew could react, Gavin was racing toward the elevated desk where the cameras were trained, shouting, "Keep those cameras on! Keep those cameras on, I'm coming! I'm coming! Keep those cameras on!"

Roger Tatum was frozen to his chair. Although he commented nightly on events of astounding violence, this was the first time that a gun was actually pointed at him; that his own life was threatened.

One of the cameramen, reacting instinctively, made a desperate attempt to tackle Gavin as he raced toward the news desk. The barrel of the Colt Python cracked down hard on the cameraman's skull, and even before he realized that the figure moving past him was armed, the cameraman lost consciousness.

Now Gavin was at the desk, the muzzle of the barrel pressed hard into the side of Roger Tatum's forehead. Roger Tatum's eyes closed in silent anticipation of a sudden explosion. Before he could open his eyes, Gavin had moved the gun away from the newscaster's forehead, seized the man's right wrist, and snapped a handcuff shut around it. He was now locked to Roger Tatum who opened his eyes and looked up at Gavin. Again, Gavin placed the gun next to the newscaster's forehead. Roger Tatum tried to speak, but the only sound that came from his lips was a cross between a hoarse cough and a cry of pain.

"Keep those cameras on me," Gavin yelled. "Keep those cameras on me. The second they are off me, I'll put a bullet through his head." Gavin turned his body to the right and with his right shoulder pushed the dead Dr. Dukoff off the chair to the floor. He then sat down quickly in the chair himself, taking his place as the next guest on the special "Roger Tatum Report." Gavin glanced quickly at a monitor on a table a few feet away, out of camera range, so that Roger Tatum and his guest could check their own appearance from time to time. He could see himself and Roger Tatum, lips clenched tight, eyes screaming. The cameras were indeed still on. Gavin looked around the room, his eyes adjusted to the hard bright lights that blazed down at him from above. To his left he could see the small red light atop the camera, signaling that it was rolling. He could sense as well as see everyone in the room—one cameraman behind the lit camera; another to his right, moaning softly and holding on to the dolly beneath his camera as he tried to lift himself back to his feet; a soundman about twenty feet behind the fallen cameraman; the director, a woman about thirty-six years old, dressed in black sweater and slacks and wearing a headset. She stood motionless in the center of the room holding a clipboard. Because of the intense light, Gavin could not see her eyes, but he knew she was staring at him. Maybe he should kill her. But there was no hurry. And, of course, there was Roger Tatum, the side of his forehead seemingly cemented to the muzzle of the Colt Python. Gavin looked at him. The man's face had rapidly acquired the pale yellow-green and gray texture skin generally assumed when someone is getting ready to vomit or faint. Little bubbles of sweat slid across Roger Tatum's brow and down the slopes of his face along either side of his aquiline nose. His moustache seemed to quiver slightly. He did not move.

Gavin Risen realized that this was the moment he had lived for, that he was beginning to set in motion an event that would live in the minds of men for all time. He continued to look back and forth between the monitor and the small red light atop the camera to his left, to make certain that he was indeed being televised. When he spoke again his voice was quite even, with a sense of confidence and control.

"Please listen to me. And listen to me very carefully. I am talking to the people here at the studio and to the people at the network, and in the viewing audience, and especially to the police." Gavin's face remained expressionless, and the hand holding the Colt Python to Roger Tatum's forehead was steady. "If you want this man to live"—he nodded toward Roger Tatum while keeping his eyes focused on the camera—"you must do exactly as I tell you. Not only is the gun in my hand loaded, but I am armed in another, far more powerful, way." He placed the revolver on the chair in front of him. He slipped his free hand inside the raincoat and, after a second or two, brought it back into full view of his audience. Only now the hand was holding a grenade. He held the grenade up for everyone to see and then spoke to the cameraman on his left. "Please move in for a tight shot so that everyone can clearly see what I'm holding in my hand." Gavin glanced at the monitor and was pleased to see that his instructions were being followed so swiftly. He smiled in his mind as the monitor showed the grenade resting in his hand in vivid detail. With the camera still tight on his hand and the grenade, Gavin spoke again, his off-camera voice communicating the same detached sense of control that various lecturers on the educational stations seem to possess when they are explaining solutions to academic problems.

"This," said Gavin, "is a live grenade. I have more than a dozen such grenades on my body at this moment, and if anybody fails to follow my instructions completely I will not hesitate to explode them immediately, in which case not only will this man on my right be blown apart, along with myself—all the other people in this room and perhaps more throughout the building will quickly become flying pieces of flesh, brought to you in living color.'' Gavin's voice remained distant. The pace at which he spoke was neither fast nor slow, and someone just turning on a television set at that precise instant might have thought that the man with the grenade in his hand was merely reenacting a violent scene with a fellow newscaster to show viewers how a particular crime might have taken place. There was nothing in Gavin Risen's tone to communicate that anything was out of order. But after a moment of looking at Roger Tatum, anyone could see that the terror in his eyes spoke far more loudly than Gavin Risen's monotone. Gavin quickly placed the grenade back inside his raincoat and patted his hand against the pouch so that he could feel the hard shape of the black box with the three raised white buttons.

"Before we continue," he said, "I think it is only fair to mention that the grenades represent only a fraction of the explosive power on my body." His hand moved from inside the raincoat, and he held the black box up for his audience to see. "This box contains enough destructive force to destroy this building. But that is not the real beauty of it. The real beauty lies in these three buttons. I have arranged the detonation device in such a way that only someone who knows the proper sequence in which the buttons are to be pressed can disarm the bomb. And I am the only person who knows that sequence. So if a sniper, or someone else, should succeed in killing me before I set off the grenades, which in turn will set off the bomb, the bomb itself will go off before anyone can defuse it." Gavin placed the innocent-looking black box back inside his raincoat and into the pouch.

"Of course," he said, "I may be bluffing. It may be an automated bomb. But then again it may be nothing more than a black box with buttons on it. But, that's the beauty of it. You can't tell if it's fake or real." Gavin turned again toward Roger Tatum. "Now," continued Gavin, "for my instructions. They are simple. A live camera is to be kept on me at all times. All times. The moment I do not see myself on the monitor over here is the moment I shall explode the grenades. There can be no exception to this. The camera must be kept on me at all times. That is my first insruction." Gavin Risen pulled the Colt Python away from Roger Tatum's face and instead pointed it toward his own body. "If my instructions are not obeyed, it will not be necessary to put a bullet through Mr. Tatum's head. One bullet fired into my grenades will have a far more dramatic effect." Gavin Risen turned toward Roger Tatum, who seemed somewhat relieved that the cold steel circle of the Colt Python's barrel was no longer pressing against his head.

"Would you care to comment on this news event, Mr. Tatum?" said Gavin. "It's certain to be one of the big news stories of this year. Maybe the biggest news story of any year. And you not only get to report this news story and comment on it Mr. Tatum, you *are* this news story. You, and what happens to you, that's the news tonight. What do you have to say about that, Roger Tatum?"

Roger Tatum's throat had never felt tighter, nor his mouth dryer, nor had his heart ever pounded quite so loudly. For just an instant he looked quickly at the dead Dr. Dukoff seated next to him and his mind collided with all the orderly events of his lifetime and the insanity of the last few moments. He was certain that he would not be able to speak when he tried, but he tried nonetheless, not having the vaguest idea of what the words meant that formed on his lips and actually managed to become audible.

"Where did you come from?" he heard his voice say, and he wondered why he had never really heard his voice before. Did he sound that way to everyone? And why did he feel as if he wanted to urinate so badly? "How did you get in here?" he asked abstractedly, "how did you get in?"

Gavin's answer was given without hesitation. "What difference does it make how I got in? Do you think our viewers care how I got here?" Roger Tatum nodded silently as if to indicate agreement. Gavin continued. "Let's just say that I got here either by walking in or by means of satellite. What difference?" Gavin moved his eyes away from direct contact with the camera and looked at the monitor. He moved his head quickly from side to side and was delighted when the image on the screen that looked so much like him did exactly the same. They weren't trying to trick him, he realized. He was in control. Complete control. Unless, of course, they were merely showing closed-circuit on the monitor. They could, after all, have cut Gavin's image off the air within seconds after he had shot Dr. Dukoff and joined Roger Tatum at the nightly news desk. All they would have had to do is just keep showing Gavin his own image on the monitor while they substituted something else for transmission to their viewers. This way, they could keep Gavin from communicating with all the people he wanted to reach, while the police and network people stalled for time until they could figure out a way to capture Gavin while minimizing the risk of injury or death to Roger Tatum and the other people present in the studio. They could do it, of course, Gavin realized—if they dared. But they would never get away with it. Gavin would see to that.

"Lest there be some chance that a foolish network executive might try to trick me into thinking that I'm actually on commercial television when I'm merely being shown on a monitor in this studio, let me be quite direct. If you try to fool me I will know it immediately, and Roger Tatum will be dead within a second. I repeat: keep a live camera on me at all times." With that Gavin Risen again placed the Colt Python on the desk in front of him, to his right, so that Roger Tatum could not reach it, but so that Gavin could do so within a split second. Then Gavin Risen bent slightly and with one hand reached beneath the desk. He placed on the desk the small black attaché case he had carried with him into the studio. Quickly, he flipped the steel latches and opened the case. He reached into the case and removed what appeared to be another small black case. "Bring the camera in tight on this," said Gavin. The cameraman obeyed immediately and Gavin sat staring down at the small black case, and then he turned the case so that everyone in his viewing audience could see the front part of the small black case, and when they did they realized that it was a small, slim portable TV set—the smallest and slimmest man-ufactured, with a three-inch screen and a total thickness of one and one-half inches.

"All right," said Gavin, "pull back a little now to include me in the picture." He turned the small portable television set back toward himself so that the screen was facing him at the desk. And then he saw what he wanted to see in black and white, the picture clear, precise. It was a picture of Gavin looking down at a small black case. He kept his gaze fixed on his own image as his hands tightened on the miniature portable TV set. He spoke directly to the screen. "So far, so good," he said. "But remember. Keep the camera on me at all times. Do not take it off me for even an instant." Gavin looked up at the camera and spoke directly to it, his voice still totally calm and mechanical. "All right," he said, "pull back now for a shot that includes both Roger Tatum and myself. Our real telecast is about to begin." The faces of Roger Tatum and Gavin Risen filled the tiny screen on the desk in front of Gavin.

"Well, Roger," began Gavin methodically, "you've had a moment or two to gather your thoughts now, and I thought you might like to ask me a few questions. You know, a person-to-person kind of interview. Because it looks as if Dr. Dukoff will not be answering any more questions. At least on this program." Roger Tatum's lips were tight. It looked as if he were biting into his own moustache. "Go ahead," said Gavin. "Say something. Anything. Because we're probably going to be on the air for a long time, you and I."

Roger Tatum's voice was professional. "How long are we going to be on the air?"

"Oh, I'm not sure yet," answered Gavin. "It all depends on how long it takes to build the audience to the size it should be."

"And what size is that?" asked Roger Tatum keeping an appearance of composure that was betrayed by a sudden twitching of his left upper lip beneath the moustache. Gavin stared into the camera.

"Well, I'm not certain exactly. But I do think it would be nice if everyone in the world who owns a television set or who has access to one were watching me.'' Roger Tatum began to sense that the more he talked to the madman chained to him the greater his own chances for survival would become.

''You want everyone in the world watching you?''

''It would be nice.''

''May I ask what your name is please.''

''Of course. My name is Gavin Risen.''

''Are you the person who created the series of television tapes that we've been talking about?''

''Yes,'' Gavin nodded as he answered. ''I'm the person responsible for the tapes. Apart from their content, how did you like their quality?''

Sensing that it would be a mistake to antagonize Gavin Risen, Roger Tatum gave the answer he assumed was expected of him. ''Actually, they were quite good technically. Everyone connected with the investigation of the case felt certain the person who taped them had professional experience. It was never said publicly, but nonetheless that was the feeling. I can assure you of that.''

''Thank you,'' said Gavin politely. ''It is always nice to be recognized by one's peers. But let me turn the tables on you for a minute, Mr. Tatum. How does it feel to actually be the news, to actually be the biggest story in America instead of just reporting it? There's quite a difference isn't there?''

Roger Tatum swallowed hard and hoped the light-headed feeling he was experiencing would not cause him to faint or make a spectacular fool of himself in front of millions of viewers. If he ever survived this incident his career would hinge largely on how he handled himself now. If ever a television news commentator had been put in a crisis position, this was it. He clenched his hands into two separate fists and spoke softly, surprising himself that his voice did not sound shaky.

''Frankly, Mr. Risen,'' Roger Tatum began, ''I'm frightened. First, for my own life and the lives of everyone here in the studio with us. And second, because I don't understand what's going on.

I don't understand what you want.'' Roger Tatum paused, waiting for Gavin Risen to answer, but Gavin sat quietly staring at his own image on the miniature television set on the desk in front of him. Roger Tatum's head began to feel like a separate entity, floating freely above his body and looking down on the bizarre news report. He felt as if consciousness could slip away at any second, and with it, perhaps, his own life, because if he lost consciousness he would not be awake when the calm young madman seated next to him sent a bullet into his skull at point blank range or pulled the pin from a grenade and set off an explosion that would excite television viewers who had never actually seen a man's body blown apart, the head hurtling in one direction, while bits of fingers and ribs and legs and intestines flew off frantically in all directions at once like a flock of feeding birds frightened by a sudden noise. Roger Tatum fought to keep his composure, because if this was to be the end, the time he had wondered and worried about every day since his fortieth birthday, he wanted to be in control when it happened, he wanted to know, at least, if there was an instant, even a fraction of a second when one is aware that one is dead. Or would it come so quickly that he would never know? And then a tiny speck of a thought started somewhere in his head and he tried to locate it and then he did find it, a little blur of an idea that seemed to want to slide out of his head through his ears, but he brought his free hand up to the side of his face to cover his ear and seal in the idea until he could understand it. And then he knew what the idea was trying to tell him, because it spoke to him in his own voice, but in a whisper, so that not the man chained to him, nor even the television viewers, could hear it. The secret voice said, ''Stall for time. Keep talking and stall for time. The police are probably surrounding the studio right now.''

And then Roger Tatum felt his head again become one with his body and he realized that he was not going to faint or humiliate himself or for that matter die with anything less than honor, because he had listened to the voice in his head, and he was going to do in the moment of the greatest crisis of his life, what he knew how to do best—cover a news story. He was not going to give in to the fears of Roger Tatum, forty-eight-year-old divorced father of two teenage daughters. A man who got nervous on airplanes and slept with the lights on, and always rode with his car doors locked. He was going to perform instead as the television personality he had become over the years—as a newscaster of integrity and courage who was not going to cower before some crazy fiend. "Hell no," he thought, "I'm not going to die. If I hold up now, I'll be a national hero."

"You never really answered my question, Mr. Tatum. How does it feel to be the news rather than just reporting it? Does it make you feel any more important?" As Gavin Risen spoke, he glanced back and forth between Roger Tatum and the image of Roger Tatum on the nearby monitor and to the image of Roger Tatum on the small screen directly in front of him.

"I think, Mr. Risen," Tatum began, "if that is your name, that I can, for the first time, begin to understand the feelings of people who were held as hostages by other terrorists."

The Colt Python suddenly appeared on camera again, pointed directly at Roger Tatum. "Why do you say 'other terrorists,' Mr. Tatum, implying that I am a terrorist? I am nothing of the sort. Just because this Dr. Dukoff here thought I might be a terrorist doesn't make me one."

Roger Tatum spoke softly, almost respectfully, his eyes fixed on the barrel of the Colt Python rather than Gavin Risen's face. "Then what are you?"

"I am," said Gavin, "an entertainer. And also an artist. And also, I am the future."

"I don't understand anything you're talking about, Mr. Risen. Don't you realize that you just killed someone, that you have murdered a human being in full view of our audience. Don't you realize that the authorities will take action, that you are not going to get out of this." No sooner had the words raced from his mouth than Roger Tatum realized he had said the wrong things. Certainly he didn't want to irritate the man, to spur any sudden action. Roger Tatum was greatly relieved when he realized that his words had not angered the person who could, merely by tightening his index finger for a fraction of a second, cancel Roger Tatum out forever.

Gavin Risen moved his unchained hand to the miniature black portable television set in front of him on the desk. There was a barely audible click-click. He studied the small screen, and while his expression never changed, the hardness in his eyes clearly communicated that he was not pleased with what he saw on the screen. "Mr. Tatum," said Gavin, matter-of-factly, "are you aware that even at this very moment, your life's being in immediate danger is not considered a newsworthy event on Channel Four. Here, look. See what we're competing against."

Gavin held the small television set up next to his face so that the miniature screen could be picked up by the studio cameras. He looked at the monitor and could see his own face like some great gigantic genie looming over three extremely small people seated in tiny living room chairs. "Merv Griffin," said Gavin Risen. "A Merv Griffin rerun. Channel Four thinks a Merv Griffin rerun with Charo is more important than your life, Mr. Tatum, more important than the biggest news story of modern times."

Gavin's voice remained even. "Let's see what the other channels have on at this time," he said, turning the tiny channel-selector knob on the miniature set. Click-click, click-click. He moved the small set away from the side of his face and held it in front of his eyes for a brief moment before turning it again toward the camera. "Things are looking better on Nine," he continued. "Channel Nine has picked up our transmission and is showing it to their viewers." The small television screen was a microcosm of the larger picture that Gavin could see on the monitor. A world inside a world. "Well, what do you think of that, Mr. Tatum? Here I've been a guest on your show for only about five or ten minutes and already I've won over all of Channel Nine's viewers. Can you imagine how you've just gone up in the ratings?"

Gavin looked again at the monitor and there was a sudden scrambling of the picture, thick black horizontal lines bouncing across the screen and blacking out both his and Roger Tatum's faces. His hand instinctively tightened on the Colt Python, his arm extended and stiffened until the gun again was pointed at Roger Tatum. There was a deafening explosion as Gavin's hand jumped in unison with the gun and a thin sliver of smoke slid out of the barrel and Roger Tatum's eyes bounced in their sockets and he knew he was dead.

"The next one goes through his head," announced Gavin. "Do you hear me? Fix that picture in one minute or I'll put a bullet right through his head. Fix that picture at once or everyone in this room is dead. You have one minute, starting now."

Roger Tatum opened his eyes and realized that he was not yet dead. He saw that Gavin's eyes were focused on the flickering images in the monitor and for less than a half second he entertained the idea of attacking Gavin, seizing the hand with the gun, and holding on till the others in the studio could help him overpower their captor. But even before his muscles could tense in anticipation of action, the screen on the monitor suddenly cleared and solidified and he could see himself on the screen next to Gavin Risen and he knew that if he moved, this time the bullet would not miss his face by inches.

"All right, all right," said Gavin. "That's more like it." He looked up at the camera on his right, which had now dollied in close, its red light informing Gavin that it was live. "Take a shot of this, will you," he said to the camera.

Gavin never had an opportunity to explain what it was that he wanted a shot of because a metallic voice interrupted before he could finish his instructions.

"Mr. Risen," the voice began, "I believe that is your name, isn't it, Mr. Risen?" Gavin's outward expression remained calm, but his eyes raced around the studio trying to locate where the voice was coming from. "You can't see me, Mr. Risen," the voice continued. "I'm in the control room. But I can see you. And not just on television. I can look out and see you sitting there with Mr. Tatum."

Gavin took a quick glance at Roger Tatum still sitting next to him in icy-eyed silence and then stared straight ahead at the live camera as if to ignore the invisible voice. "Surely, Mr. Risen," the voice droned on, "you realize that it is just a matter of time until this dramatic episode ends. Even now as I speak to you, the studio is being sealed off. If we wish, we can have sharpshooters, unseen by you, take aim at your head, and you would be dead before you realized anyone had even squeezed a trigger." The voice was bluffing and Gavin knew it. They couldn't take a chance on a bad shot that might hit the grenades and blow up all of them, the invisible voice included, into unconnected chunks of unintelligent flesh. And they couldn't take a chance that the black box with buttons on it wasn't really a bomb. If it was, and Gavin was the only one who could defuse it, they wouldn't dare try to kill him, would they? "But we don't want to do that," the voice continued, soothing and smooth. Gavin could not recognize the voice, but he could place the manner of delivery. He had heard the same soft kind of delivery by a psychiatrist on "Lou Grant" who was trying to talk an armed terrorist into releasing hostages, so Gavin knew precisely what to expect. "What we would like to do, Mr. Risen, is talk to you. We'd like to hear from you in your own words, what it is that's bothering you, and if there is anything we can do to help. We do not want you to be hurt, Mr. Risen. We do not want anyone to be hurt."

Gavin wondered exactly whom the invisible voice belonged to. Probably the news director sitting in the control room by himself, trying to distract Gavin or at least engage him in conversation until such time as the police could take appropriate action. Gavin smiled in his mind. Maybe the news director had seen that particular Lou Grant show too. It was amazing, thought Gavin, how much we have all learned from watching television. By now even a fifteen-year-old high school kid realized that the first thing you did with a terrorist who held hostages was try to engage him in dialogue, try to draw him out of himself and get him to the point where he could, to some degree, trust and identify with the person who was speaking with him. Gavin remained silent for a few seconds, debating whether to answer the invisible voice or simply pretend it did not exist. He looked again at the monitor and was pleased to see his own image and that of Roger Tatum's. His mind traveled into a million homes and he could see all sorts of faces—young, old, black, white—staring at the very same image he could see on the monitor and his own small portable television set. How many people were looking at him, he wondered. Millions, no doubt. How many millions? But it really didn't matter, yet, because this was only the beginning. Gavin knew he was on his way to becoming immortal. And then his mind made a leap far into the future, and he could see that he was at the filming of a motion picture created to capture the events that he had set in motion today. He wondered who would play Gavin Risen, and he wondered how faithfully they would portray him. Would they try to picture him as a terrorist or someone insane? And why would they need to make a movie and have an actor play the part of Gavin when everything that was happening today was being recorded on videotape anyway? There could be no more accurate record than what was really happening. But Gavin knew that one day the film would be made anyway. And probably one day soon. Hadn't they made movies already about Munich and the Cuban missile crisis, the life of Lee Harvey Oswald and the death of Martin Luther King? And he knew that they would "interpret" Gavin Risen any way they wanted to when they made the film. And that's why it was so important that he not be misunderstood today, that he get his message across clearly and leave an accurate record of who he was and what he was on videotape, so that no matter what some scriptwriter wrote and no matter how some actor performed a few years from now, the world would always remember Gavin Risen as he was.

"Mr. Risen. Are you going to talk to us. Are you going to tell us what you want?" The moment's silence was broken and now Gavin dismissed the idea of a future film from his mind so he could concentrate fully on the drama that was now unfolding live for millions of viewers.

"Please do not think me so stupid," Gavin began, "that you believe I do not understand your intentions by talking to me like this. But I think you must face facts. I have Roger Tatum here.

And your other people, of course. If you wish to sacrifice them on live television you can get me. If you wish them to live you will do exactly what I say without any tricks. Do you understand?'' Gavin again pressed the barrel of the pistol against the side of Roger Tatum's head. Roger Tatum sat motionless, eyes straight ahead like a dead man staring into eternity. There was silence for ten seconds.

"We understand," said the invisible voice. "And we will cooperate without any tricks. You have our word."

Gavin Risen spoke directly into the camera again. "All right," he began. "The first thing you must do as of this moment is remain silent. I do not wish to hear your voice again, except to answer 'yes' or 'no.' Do you understand?"

"Yes."

"From this point on, the only other person to speak besides me will be Mr. Tatum. He is, after all, a noted interviewer, and I think together we can give our audience the greatest interview in television history. Isn't that right, Roger?" Gavin again removed the pistol from the side of Roger Tatum's head and placed it on the desk to his right. "What's that, Roger? I didn't hear your answer."

"Yes," said Roger Tatum, his voice a whisper.

Gavin's eyes again scanned the studio to make certain that no one had moved. Everyone was where they should be. Gavin's tongue played with the edge of his upper teeth for a second, sliding back and forth over the sharp edges before disappearing back into his mouth. "Here is my next instruction. Please see that it is carried out at once." He paused and lowered his gaze for an instant, and then raised his head and glared directly into the camera as if challenging it to stand up to the intensity of his eyes. "Within fifteen minutes, all television stations in this area will carry this telecast. I want to see my face on every channel. There will be no Merv Griffin reruns. No *Sea Patrol* or Mary Tyler Moore. There will be only me. Do you understand? Only me and Roger Tatum on every channel. If this is not achieved within fifteen minutes, Mr. Tatum and the others present in this studio with me will be sacrificed. Do you understand?" Gavin listened through a long silence and then the invisible voice gave the answer he was waiting for. "Yes, we understand. But what if—?"

"What if nothing!" Gavin shouted at the camera. "I told you to keep your answer to a simple yes or no. I do not want your comments. I want your obedience." Although his expression never changed, it was obvious from the speed of his words and the sharpness of his tone that Gavin was angered. "I'm telling you" he went on, "there will be no what ifs for you to worry about. Either my face is on every channel in this area in fifteen minutes or Roger Tatum is a dead man. Now do it. Don't say anything more, just do it."

Roger Tatum began to fantasize. He could see himself seated at his nightly news desk with the President of the United States beside him, the first time in history that a chief executive had granted an exclusive interview to one commentator. "Before I answer any questions, Mr. Tatum," the President began, "I just want to say how happy all of us here in America and I'm sure I speak for people in other nations, as well, how happy we all are to have you back alive and well." Roger Tatum nodded toward the President in a graceful gesture of humble gratitude. "Your courage," the President went on, "your courage under extreme pressure will be an example for all of us to stand up to the terrorists who would threaten the stability of our national life."

"Go ahead, Mr. Tatum, ask me anything you like." It was Gavin Risen's cold and monotonous voice bringing Roger Tatum back to painful reality. "You have with you, perhaps the major news story of our time. Ask me anything you want. And if it's within reason, I'll answer it as best I can. We have about fourteen minutes left before my deadline for complete coverage. But I'm sure they'll comply. I mean, after all, Mr. Tatum, they're not going to let me kill you in full view of all your fans out there."

15

"Good evening. This is Danton Morris from New York with the seven P.M. news and a major break in the videotape murders. At this very moment, in Miami, a man named Gavin Risen is holding Roger Tatum, our network affiliate news anchorman from Miami, and two cameramen, a sound technician, and an assistant news director as hostages in the news studio of WCQM, Channel Eight in Miami. They have been held there since early this morning, when a special update report by Roger Tatum on the videotape murders was interrupted by a gunshot that killed the program's guest, Dr. David Dukoff, a noted criminal psychologist. After shooting Dr. Dukoff, a man who identified himself as a Gavin Risen immediately raced to the news desk, where he handcuffed himself to Roger Tatum and then announced that he wanted a live camera kept on him at all times or he would shoot Mr. Tatum as well. The terrorist—if that's what he is—also revealed a hand grenade, which he claims is live, and he said that he has other hand grenades on his body. He also has a black box with buttons on it, which he claims is a powerful explosive which only he can defuse, so that he will be more valuable to the authorities alive than dead. He subsequently announced that he would have no communication with outside sources, and he insisted that all channels in the Miami–Fort Lauderdale area televise coverage of his takeover of the Channel Eight news.

Shortly after eleven this morning, he gave a fifteen-minute deadline for all South Florida stations to pick up coverage of the event, restating his intention of killing Roger Tatum at once if his instructions were not followed completely. Within nine minutes of the time he issued the ultimatum every station in South Florida —network, independent, and educational—were all carrying identical coverage of the event, with no breaks allowed for any purpose whatsoever.''

Danton Morris covered a cough with the side of a fist. ''And so, since approximately eleven-thirteen this morning, all the television stations in South Florida have been carrying one of the most dramatic and bizarre events in television history. And we shall be joining that coverage for a few moments when we return.''

The commercial that followed emphasized the incredible value of a video television recorder, the marvelous machine that recorded television programs you might not be able to see during their regularly scheduled time, but which you could enjoy anytime at your convenience once they had been taped by Vitamax. ''Just think,'' the voice-over said, ''your favorite programs, your favorite films, your favorite sporting events, your favorite news stories, yours to keep for all time—to become a part of your life forever—through the combined miracles of television and Vitamax, the machine that lets today last forever.''

There were two other commercials—one for Excedrin and one for American Express, followed by a thirty-second promotional spot for a special program to be telecast later in the week for a mammoth superstar party in honor of the network's forty-fifth anniversary in television broadcasting.

When Danton Morris returned to the screen, he did not occupy it alone. Behind him, almost life-size, were the images of Gavin Risen and Roger Tatum. ''What you see behind me now is what viewers in South Florida have been looking at all day. Two men—Gavin Risen on the left, and the anchorman for Channel Eight in Miami, Roger Tatum. As we mentioned a moment ago, Gavin Risen has claimed responsibility for the videotape murders. Earlier this morning, he surprised a Miami *News Report* telecast, shooting a guest fatally and taking over the program. He has been on the air live since that time, insisting that the moment the cameras go off him for any reason, he will kill Roger Tatum.'' Danton Morris turned in his seat to view the images behind him. ''What you see going on behind me is happening live in Miami, at this very moment. Listen.''

Danton Morris's image dissolved in the center of the screen and now there was only Gavin Risen and Roger Tatum. Gavin Risen was speaking.

'' . . . have tried to attribute motives to me that are totally untrue. That have no basis in fact. I am simply the first person of the future. The first one to understand where everything is headed. We must be aware that we are moving past the time when fact and fiction and image and reality are considered separate entities or even opposites. The only reality that exists is an image, a reflection of itself.'' Roger Tatum by now appeared relaxed, as if he were merely interviewing another routine guest on another ''News Report'' interview. He spoke.

''What about your personal life, Mr. Risen? In all the hours we've been here, you've told us only about your beliefs, nothing really about yourself. Where you live. Your family life. Education. Career. That sort of thing. Surely, our viewers would be most interested in hearing about your life. About what has led you to take the actions you've taken today.''

Even before Gavin started to answer, white type started to roll across the bottom of the screen, drawing Gavin's gaze away from the camera and over to the monitor. The words rolled across the bottom of the screen, beneath his own face and that of Roger Tatum. They read: MR. RISEN, PLEASE EXCUSE THIS INTERRUPTION, BUT IT WAS THE ONLY WAY WE COULD REACH YOU WITHOUT SPEAKING. The phrase rolled across the screen from left to right three times. Then, assured of Gavin's attention, new words rolled across the screen. THE PRESIDENT OF THE UNITED STATES WOULD LIKE TO SPEAK WITH YOU, MR. RISEN. This time the phrase rolled across the screen only twice before Gavin raised his right hand as if to signal "enough." Gavin waved his hand from left to right, in front of the camera, then stopped and dropped it to his side.

"If the President of the United States wishes to speak to me, he may do so," Gavin said without any sign of emotion or indication that he was impressed with the idea. "But only for five minutes. And only on the following conditions." Gavin paused momentarily to collect his thoughts, then proceeded with his instructions. "First," Gavin said calmly, "I must be able to see him when he is speaking. I have no intention of sitting here wasting my time and the time of millions of viewers listening to someone do an imitation of the President." Gavin paused to let his words sink in, then continued, "Second," he said, "this is to be done without taking my face off the screen. What you will do," said Gavin, "is work with a split screen. I will be on one side of the screen. The President will be on the other. Is that clear?"

"Yes, it is clear," the invisible voice answered.

"Third," said Gavin, "and this is most important. I will talk to the President exactly one hour from now only on the condition he gives me his word that our telecast will be carried by all the networks, and as far as he has control, every television station in the country."

Again there was silence, but this time the silence extended for a full thirty seconds before Gavin spoke again. "What are you waiting for? Does the President agree or not agree to those conditions?"

Ten more seconds of silence passed, then: "The President agrees. One hour from now. He can only give his word about the networks. He can't guarantee what the independent stations will do."

"That's all right," said Gavin, "they'll be watching us, too. Everyone will be watching us."

Once again, Danton Morris appeared in the center of the screen, blocking out part of Gavin Risen's face. As he spoke, Gavin Risen's voice died down under his own and Gavin Risen's image grew smaller and smaller until he disappeared completely behind Danton Morris, who was seated at his news desk.

"You heard it exactly the way I heard it, at exactly the same time I did. If ever there was instant national news coverage, this is it. You saw the news being made exactly when it was being made. And from what I can gather, we'll all be going back to that television studio in Miami in one hour for a live telecast of the conversation between Gavin Risen and the President."

Danton Morris cleared his throat. A huge airplane suddenly appeared behind him. "Meanwhile, elsewhere in the news, congress today voted to stop production of the controversial B-four-V. . . ."

Gavin Risen's mouth was extremely dry. He had been on the air talking now for over nine hours, and his tongue had begun to taste like dry, hot rubber. There was the start of an angle of pain, sliding down his left arm, reaching to the wire-thin wrist encircled by a bracelet of steel that locked him to Roger Tatum. There were other aches in his body, too. A dull but hard tightness in his bowels, a stiffness in his knees that he tried to alleviate by rubbing them gently against each other. And, of course, his eyes. They had begun to sting under the hot lights as if little slivers of solid heat had been forced into them gradually over a period of hours. He moved his tongue around inside his mouth in search of any sign of moisture, but there was none. He knew fatigue was beginning to invade his mind and body like an unseen enemy gas that one inhales with a smile, breathing in fatal fumes that enter the lungs as innocently as air. He knew that soon he would have to have food and water and move about or his senses would be dulled when they burst through a door or dropped down on him from the ceiling and grabbed his arm before he could put a bullet in the pouch of grenades he felt resting against his hip. He looked at the monitor and could see that Roger Tatum looked far more tired than he, a dark circle of whiskers spreading on his cheeks on either side of the moustache. "He's no danger to me," thought

Gavin. "He'll sit there obediently until he dies or they take him away from me." Gavin looked into the camera, but his mind drifted before he could speak and he bit his lower lip sharply, the pain causing his consciousness to come more sharply awake. He told himself that after he spoke to the President in fifteen minutes or so, he would make arrangements for food and water, and for transportation, of course, to complete the final phase of his plan.

He spoke to his audience for the next fifteen minutes in the incoherent fashion of someone who appears sober but whose speech clearly indicates he has had sufficient amounts of alcohol or drugs to cloud his thoughts. And then, suddenly, the clouds evaporated from his mind and he saw the type rolling across the bottom of the screen. THE PRESIDENT IS STANDING BY. YOU WILL BE ON THE AIR, LIVE, ACROSS THE NATION IN TWO MINUTES.

The pain in his shoulder disappeared, the uncomfortable strain in his bowels subsided. His senses came alive and, miraculously, his mouth was no longer dry: in fact he slid his tongue along his lips to moisten them. And then he saw on the monitor that his own image was being pulled over to the left-hand side of the screen. A narrow black line ran down the center of the screen from top to bottom—and there he was, on the right-hand corner of the screen, the President of the United States.

Gavin felt a quiver of excitement as he compared his own face to that of the President. There they were. Live. For the entire nation to see. "Isn't this something," said Gavin, before the President could speak, "appearing at the same time, the two most powerful people on earth."

16

The President's face remained as passive as a wax mask, letting everyone know immediately that his performance tonight would be low key; that he would react with neither pleasure nor anger at any remark by this crazy man who had interrupted more than half of America's after-dinner plans.

The President had been in office less than eighteen months, but he had already demonstrated a far more daring and creative imagination in his use of television than any of his predecessors, appearing with a frequency and flair that frustrated the opposition party but nonetheless caused them to express professional political admiration for his ability to influence public opinion by bringing his case on vital and controversial issues to the American people as quickly and dramatically as possible. "He plays to the country like Donny and Marie play to a studio audience," one Colorado senator noted on a recent *Issue and Answers* program that Gavin recalled quite vividly.

Now, seeing the President's full and fleshy features alongside the angles and valleys of his own face, Gavin realized that Central Casting had done quite a job. Clearly, they looked as though they could make great running mates. The President, a plainly honest and open political face, with lines of experience and painful compassion crisscrossing near the corners of his eyes; the vice-presidential nominee, Gavin Risen, lean esthetic, clear-eyed, with a sense of the visionary about him; a man accepting the call to high public office reluctantly, but aware that his country's need outweighed his sacrifice. Finally, the President spoke, and the casualness of his tone almost convinced Gavin to keep alive the fantasy that they were both appearing on the same podium at their party's national convention.

"My fellow Americans, and, of course that includes you, too, Mr. Risen, this is one time I appear before you when, obviously, I would prefer not to."

Gavin admired the smooth self-confidence combined with an almost spiritual sense of humility in the President's delivery. The guy was a real pro. If he played his cards right tonight, Gavin thought, he could doubtless improve his position in the polls. Gavin leaned forward slightly, almost impatient to find out if the President would try for some political points first, or deal directly and forcefully with the crisis confronting him now in full view of most of the 49.6 million people who had elected him—and most of the 46.3 million who had voted against him and were now perhaps secretly praying that he would fall flat on his face. This was what television was really supposed to be all about. Gavin realized that the surface of his skin had become galvanized and he could feel an erection growing almost painfully inside the tight pull of his pants. It was a thrilling moment, yet he knew that he must not forget about Roger Tatum or any of the others in the studio with him. That could be fatal.

"Let me begin by saying quite clearly and as plainly as possible that the American people will not tolerate terrorism. There is no place for it in their country, or in any civilized country on earth. The fact that I am speaking to you—and the American people— live on television tonight should in no way be construed as a victory for whatever cause you represent. Because it is my purpose to state clearly and unequivocally, that no cause—no cause at all—justifies the unlawful seizure of the property of the American people, be that property a plane, a building, or public or private means of communication."

Gavin, not disrespectfully but almost ceremoniously, stifled a yawn. Somehow the taste of metal had etched its way into his gums and across the roof of his mouth and coated his tongue like a dried-out layer of aluminum. God, he needed water, a Coke, anything liquid, preferably icy-cold. When the President and he were finished with their telecast, he would have some Big Macs and oversize Cokes sent in. He smiled in his mind and wondered how much a plug like that would be worth to McDonald's. Plenty, he'd bet. Let's see, they got $300,000 for thirty-second commercials on the Super Bowl. He had heard that on the news. He should be able to get at least that, maybe more, because this had to be bigger even than the Super Bowl.

Gavin realized that his mind had begun to drift into a series of slow dissolves and sound fade-outs. He concentrated hard on the President's face next to his own on the monitor. He had missed perhaps the last thirty to forty seconds of the President's speech— and then Gavin suddenly realized that was exactly what the man was doing. He wasn't speaking to Gavin. He was speaking to all those votes out there. He was making a speech. Well, Gavin would put a stop to that soon enough. But for now he'd let the man ramble on for a few more minutes, because soon enough he'd have to do exactly what Gavin wanted.

"As I've stated," the President continued, "this administration will not bow to terrorism under any circumstances." His makeup was smooth and dry and concealed the flaps of skin around his jowls that had become greatly pronounced since he took office.

"But this administration—and this President in particular— has sworn before almighty God and the American people that nowhere in the world will we abandon a single American citizen held hostage by those who would destroy our way of life." Gavin was delighted with the graceful ease with which the President managed to move from a solomn vow not to bow to terrorists to a solemn vow not to abandon any American citizen held hostage. He had taken a position firmly on both sides of the fence. He was strong and realistic, yet he was compassionate and humane. Gavin begn to feel more in control. He let the President continue uninterrupted.

"Mr. Risen, you along with the American people have heard my position on terrorism. There is no conceivable way you can get away with this. There is no conceivable way this act will impress the American people in favor of your cause—whatever that cause may be. It has only enraged the American people and decent people on every conceivable side of every political issue everywhere on earth. There is just no way you can win. I strongly suggest that you take this opportunity to release your hostages at once. If you do so, I can promise that you will *not* be harmed. If you forsake violence, violence will not be used against you. Beyond that, I promise nothing. The American people and their President do not make promises to a terrorist. Not now. Not ever."

The President's voice faded under a swelling of music in Gavin's mind that mixed with the strange murmers of an unseen crowd, as Gavin looked at the face of the man on the left side of the screen and did not recognize it as himself. It was as if he had entered the middle of a late night movie and didn't know whether he was simply watching it or whether he had actually entered into the truth and timelessness of the film until he had passed from the role of spectator to performer. He moved his right hand softly across the stubble of his cheeks and watched as the man on the television monitor next to the President made precisely the same gesture, following Gavin's directions flawlessly. Gavin tried to remember what the movie was about, but his memory failed him momentarily, and then a phrase the President used generated a flash of recognition someplace in his brain. The movie was about a man who took over a television station in Miami and was holding a newscaster and crew hostage. The President was trying to talk the man into forsaking any ideas of violence. But who was that playing the President? Too heavy for Andy Griffith. Too fair for Martin Balsam. Could it be Carroll O'Connor? Maybe and then maybe not. And who was that playing the role of the man who had taken control of the television station? The man with the gun and the grenades and the black box—the man who scratched his cheeks when Gavin scratched his cheeks—the man who looked so much like Gavin—what was his name? Gavin would think of it in a minute.

"Do you understand, Mr. Risen, do you understand what I've been saying? We will cooperate only to the extent of protecting the lives of the innocent people involved. But we will not be dictated to by terrorists."

Gavin Risen decided that it was time to turn the political speech back into a major news event. He cued the performer who resembled him so greatly and then watched with a curious sense of artistic detachment as the performer on the left side of the screen spoke the words almost as fast as they ran through Gavin's mind.

"Mr. President, my fellow Americans, any possible viewers elsewhere in the world, and future generations, it is vital that one thing be cleared up right at the start." Gavin wiped an irritating drop of salty perspiration out of the corner of his left eye. Sure enough, the actor portraying him on the screen copied the gesture with uncanny speed and accuracy. "The President made the same mistake that the unfortunate Dr. Dukoff did. It's a mistake that a lot of people out there are probably making right now, too." Gavin turned up the volume of his voice. "I am not a terrorist. I have never been a terrorist. Unless of course, you consider it terrorism to entertain, to bring a truly creative new art form into being, to give birth to the future." Gavin watched proudly as the President listened to his words respectfully, eyes squinting as if trying to see directly into Gavin's mind on the other side of the screen.

"But you will all understand that in time. The important thing to remember is that I am not a terrorist. I am not going to try to make a deal for the release of any political prisoners. I am not going to ask that some unrecognized political state be recognized. I am not trying to call attention to horrible prison conditions. Or the evils of capitalism. Or any issues of so-called relevance."

Gavin paused, but he held his hand up quickly, indicating to the President that he was not quite finished, that he had more to say. The silence spiraled out over a stretch of fifteen seconds, growing increasingly deeper. Gavin inhaled and it was almost as if he could smell the odd perfume of a Big Mac. Special mayonnaise-based sauce blending with pickle and flour and beef and cheese. He could almost taste it. But there would be time for that later. He lowered his hand and spoke again. "I am not calling attention to conditions in Africa. I am not calling for an end to capital punishment, or the rehabilitation of wounded veterans of Vietnam. I am not calling attention to anything or anyone but myself. Do you understand that? I am simply calling attention to myself. I am my cause. The only deal I want to make is that you watch me for a while. Just watch me. Look at me. All of you. If you watch me for a while, none of these people will be hurt. I promise you that. But the minute the camera goes off me, they're dead. All of them." Gavin paused again, then spoke very slowly, his voice sounding not quite as hollow and mechanical as it had previously. "All my life, I have been watching everyone else. Now it's everyone's turn to watch me."

Gavin nodded toward the President to indicate he had concluded his comments for the moment. The President spoke softly, as if he were talking to a visiting dignitary he wanted to make certain not to offend. "How long, Mr. Risen? How long do you want us to watch you?"

"Not too long, I don't think," answered Gavin. "Certainly not years or even months, or weeks for that matter."

"Mr. Risen, you cannot tie up the nation's networks for days, if that is your intention."

Gavin shook his head slowly from side to side, as if he found the President's inability to comprehend amusing. "Don't you understand? Haven't you been listening, Mr. President?" He picked up the Colt Python in an angry gesture, and pressed it hard against Roger Tatum's head. The picture on the left side of the screen expanded so that both Gavin Risen and Roger Tatum were visible. The newscaster no longer looked frightened or nervous, merely resigned. "It's like I've been saying, the minute the cameras go off me, off goes Mr. Tatum's head. Why is that so difficult to understand?"

The President's eyes drooped for an instant in a flash of defeat, and then he spoke, again very softly. "All right, Mr. Risen. I understand. What is it you want us to do?"

"For openers," said Gavin methodically, as if the lines had been rehearsed a hundred times, "you can say good night to your viewers, Mr. President. And then you can just settle back like everyone else and watch me." Gavin smiled again in his mind but he knew that none of the millions of people watching his face knew he was smiling. And then he spoke again.

"This show," he said, "still has a long way to go."

17

The dryness in Gavin's throat had reached the point where he was having considerable difficulty speaking clearly. And he knew now that he must soon make arrangements for food and water and transportation. He realized that he would probably have no problem with food and water, unless of course, they tried to drug him into unconsciousness. Better not take any chances, he thought. Make sure anything you eat or drink is absolutely safe. Make sure Roger Tatum tries it first. Make sure—

He did not know exactly what it was that had moved in the room, but something was out of balance. It wasn't the movement of the cameras that bothered Gavin, he had allowed for that. No, it was something else. Something wasn't right, and he wondered whether perhaps when he had been concentrating on the monitor and his own miniature television set, someone had managed to slip into the studio and even now was crouching out there behind a chair or prop, waiting for the opportunity to rush Gavin, wrestle the Colt Python from his hand and complete the most heroic rescue of hostages ever carried live on national television.

Gavin's head remained stationary, facing the camera, but his eyes moved in their sockets like mobile cameras penetrating every corner and recess of the room. It had been over two hours now since Gavin had spoken to the President, and he was acutely aware that elaborate plans could have been formulated as to the best method of securing the safety of the hostages. Perhaps a handful of police, or even a single, carefully trained antiterrorist specialist was out there somewhere behind those white hot lights, scattered pieces of equipment, furniture, and props. Or perhaps they had already started to pipe in an odorless gas that was affecting Gavin's perception and would momentarily render him helpless. Or maybe he was simply worn out and the first heavy flow of fatigue was beginning to play games with his mind.

And then he knew what it was. She had moved. The assistant director, the woman with the headsets, had managed to edge closer to the exit door at the rear of the studio. Gavin had never seen her move a step. It seemed to him that she had been standing still on the very spot where she had been when Gavin had first taken over control of the room. But now it was obvious that she must have moved a good ten to twelve feet backwards during the intervening hours, until she was now at a point where she could turn and make a dash for the rear exit door and perhaps reach it before Gavin could react by picking up the Colt Python, aim it, and squeeze off bullets until one caught her at the base of the spine or in the back of the head, exactly halfway between the ears. She stood stiffly now, staring at Gavin as she had stared for so long. He was conscious of Roger Tatum asking him a question dealing with the worldwide reaction to terrorism, and then he felt the Colt Python, a cold, hard, heavy weight in his hand, and his fingers tightened around the stock as he sensed the break was about to come, and then the woman spun quickly and was headed for the rear door, her hard heels making castenetlike clicks as they moved across the surface of the studio floor. Gavin's arm extended full length and then jumped up and down slightly as the explosion came at the end of his fist, a microinstant of flame burning a roaring, violent, and by now familiar sound into the the ears of millions of viewers. Another sudden blast, and the woman, who could not be seen on camera, felt as if a piece of soft fruit or some vegetable like a tomato had been forced through her skin and then set on fire, strange flames spreading across her back, down into her buttocks and legs and at the same time reaching up to her shoulders and moving down through her arms and hands to her fingers, which were now reaching the last few inches for the handle on the rear-exit door. But they never made it. Instead, they tightened into tiny little fists that forced fingernails into the soft skin on either hand, and before she could unclench them she was dead, falling to the floor with such a sudden loss of grace that even Gavin Risen was taken a bit by surprise. For a second or two he had thought she might make it and had even found himself strangely hoping that she would, so that his adventure might turn in a new uncharted direction. He turned the Colt Python and again pointed it at Roger Tatum.

"Don't move," said Gavin. "Don't move, Mr. Tatum. Or I will have to do something I don't really want to do." Gavin waited a moment until he was certain that Roger Tatum would remain passive, chained to his arm like a silent dummy awaiting the next cue from his ventriloquist. Confident again that Roger Tatum would play his role obediently until the end, Gavin once again turned his attention to the camera with the bright-red light poking out of its head. Gavin spoke into the camera, directly to his audience.

"I think you people out there deserve an explanation of what just went on here. I'm only sorry our cameras didn't capture it all." Gavin paused and turned toward the other camera. "Pick up a shot of her. I want the control booth to split the screen so that our audience can see both her and me at the same time." Gavin now turned his gaze toward the monitor, waiting for his instructions to be obeyed. Within ten seconds they were.

The left-hand side of the screen filled with the prone figure of a woman, blood circling and spreading around her fallen body like a leak slipping out of an unseen faucet. Gavin Risen's face filled the right-hand side of the screen. "I just wanted you to see what happened here," said Gavin. "No one tried to enter the studio. No one tried to harm me. But this woman, who was here from the very start, tried to leave, and I just couldn't allow that. If I had let her go, next, one of the cameramen would want to leave, or Roger Tatum, and we'd have absolutely no show at all. Right?"

There seemed to be a slight movement in the woman's left leg, and Gavin wondered for a moment if the audience might be concerned that she was in pain or perhaps still had a chance for life. That would justify the authorities storming the studio, even if it did risk harm to other hostages. Gavin realized, too, that time might be starting to close in on him anyway. Sooner or later they would come after him. He knew that. But it had to be on his terms. Under his direction. "After all," he thought, "who is running this show?"

"Kill the camera on her," he said, "and use my face on both sides of the screen." Gavin stared again at the monitor and in a few seconds there were two of him there, electronic twins entertaining an entire nation. He watched as both of them spoke simultaneously. "I think it's only fair to make you aware of something now," he began, his voice cracking slightly from fatigue and dryness. "You've been an excellent audience, and I promise that if you'll be patient just a little bit longer, everything will come out all right. Roger Tatum won't be hurt. And neither will either of the cameramen. Nor will anyone else." Gavin felt pressure on his face muscles to form a smile. They strained frantically but could not quite bring it off. "When I have spoken to you from time to time—both on this telecast and through the characters on my tapes—I have implied that you will, in the end, understand everything. I think it is now time to make that understanding possible." He looked toward the camera on his left and said, "I want my face wiped off the left side of the screen. Bring in Roger Tatum there. And keep me on the right side." Gavin Risen turned to face Roger Tatum for an abbreviated moment and then glanced back at the monitor to make sure the newscaster was beside him there as well. Again he turned his gaze directly toward the camera in front of him.

"What you have witnessed—not only today, but over the past months—has been the greatest achievement in the history of television." Gavin Risen paused for effect. "What we have managed to do is conduct a massive experiment on the ability of television to present planned events of such convincing reality that virtually everyone in the audience of millions believed that what they were witnessing was actually the truth. Well, in truth it was a fabrication or series of fabrications aimed at revealing to all of us that what we see is not always what we should believe.''

Gavin nodded into the camera as if he were revealing a secret that would suddenly make everything clear to everyone watching. ''No,'' he went on, ''Tawny wasn't killed, because Tawny was simply an actress. Or should I say actor. Or female impersonator. No. The man in the mask wasn't murdered. Nor was the school-teacher, nor the police chief. They were all professional actors, carefully made up to disguise their real appearance. The techniques we used to make you believe that they had been shot or had their heads cut off were simply the most modern techniques known and available to every filmmaker. But once we had the authoritative news people assure you that they and the police had examined the tapes meticulously, and indeed, actual murders had been performed, you were ready to accept anything and everything you would see in the future, including this telecast. But really. How can you be sure that this telecast is live right now? Or whether it was taped days ago? Or even weeks? Or months? Don't you realize that Dr. Dukoff here is no more dead than you or I? That the woman you saw bleeding to death before your eyes a few moments ago is really quite healthy?'' Gavin moved his hand across the stubble of his beard, its sharp edges stabbing his fingers like hundreds of miniature knives.

''The President's part, of course, was a bit of a challenge. But all we did was piece together bits of speeches he made that were filmed but never shown before on television, and then show them next to my face and make it seem like he was speaking to me. Answering my questions. Reacting to my actions. Of course, there was some tricky dubbing involved, especially where he mentions me by name. But we have the technology for that, right, Roger?''

Gavin Risen glanced again at Roger Tatum but continued talking, his voice spewing out words with the same methodical precision it had begun the program with so many hours ago.

"So my friends, some of you are going to be furious to realize that this was an experiment, no matter how well intentioned. But some of you will realize the purpose for which it was done. In just a few moments, I am going to ask Tawny and the masked man and Ms. Sheridan and the police chief to come in here and appear as a group before you. I am going to ask Dr. Dukoff to get up from the floor and tell you his real name and occupation. And I am going to ask the dead woman lying on the floor at the rear of the studio to come back to life and step up here in front of our cameras and explain her role in our play."

Once again Gavin Risen paused, as if waiting for the scope of his comments to circulate around the nation. He could almost hear the screams of outrage reaching into the studio.

"But before I bring our cast back to life, I would like to personally thank Roger Tatum for playing his role to perfection. Roger, anything you'd like to say?"

Roger Tatum's eyes were those of a returning prisoner of war, clouded with questions that can never be answered or understood by anyone else. He turned those eyes toward Gavin Risen.

"You're crazy," he said softly. "Take the cameras off him. I don't care if he does kill me."

The gunshot came just as Roger Tatum finished his statement, punctuating the words with a fierce finality.

18

"We have entered the final phase of our telethon," said Gavin, his eyes tired, red, but still intense. Roger Tatum's face filled the left side of the screen next to Gavin, but the newscaster's blank expression indicated the man might no longer be aware of what was going on around him. An instant after Gavin Risen had squeezed the trigger of the Colt Python and sent a bullet burning past Roger Tatum's ear at a distance of less than an inch, the newscaster's features transformed themselves into a mask of total indifference, unconscious witnesses to events they refused to accept.

"I have a proposal to make," said Gavin. "Notice, I said a proposal, and not a deal, because I am not suggesting that I will harm any of the people here if my conditions are not met. But still I think it would make very good sense to meet my conditions since they are quite simple, they will cause no harm nor risk to anyone, and if they are met in good faith, then this program can be concluded successfully in a short period of time."

"What are your conditions?" The voice was as flat and mechanical as Gavin's, coming from Roger Tatum almost as if on cue, and without any genuine awareness of what it meant.

"First," began Gavin, "I will want a plane. A DC-10. Not to skyjack or anything like that, but simply a plane to fly myself and my companions here safely to New York." Gavin gestured with his hand, indicating that "companions" meant those present in the room with him. "Naturally," he continued, "a pilot must be furnished, along with ample supplies of food and drink for our flight to New York." He hesitated before speaking again and wondered if the plug would be too obvious, too blatant. "For myself," he went on, "I want two Big Macs with a large order of fries and two chocolate shakes. I want them on the plane, and the plane ready to leave from Miami International Airport within two hours. In addition to my food, similar or duplicate orders will be placed for my crew here, who of course, will accompany me on my trip. Appropriate television equipment should be aboard the plane so that we may continue our telecast in flight. I know this will be complicated. But it can be done. And it will be done."

Gavin's manner of speech now was crisp, authoritative. He did not know whether the authorities would cooperate with his requests or if they would try for a rescue before he and his crew could leave the studio. Nontheless, he felt in control. The show was going well, not exactly as he had imagined in his mind over the years, but well enough, he thought. He glanced at the miniature television set in his right hand and flicked the channel selector with his fingertips. There he was, still there, on every single channel. Again, he felt a sweet, tickling sensation where his pants pulled tight around his crotch and he could sense a stirring there, a surge of energy. His mind's eye tried to peek into a million homes and see how his image—how he, Gavin Risen—was affecting so many different people. They were all his audience now. The college professors. The fat lawyers. The illiterate kids. The ones doing twenty to life in prison. The empty shells lying in V.A. hospital beds with empty spaces in place of limbs and ears and noses. The hard-core regulars at Reinhart's Tavern, hypnotized by the image of the man who once emptied their ashtrays and flushed their toilets and mopped up their vomit. Would any of them recognize him? He doubted it because so few of them had ever seen him, and then only fleetingly. College kids were out there watching him, eyes hazy with marijuana and Quāaludes, looking at the lump-lump who had bumped their favorite shows off the air. Tennessee was watching him. And Texas. And California. And Maine. And New Mexico. Hundreds of places he had never been and never would be in that frail body of his were now tuned to Gavin Risen with an all-encompassing fervor that guaranteed him a place in their history as long as anyone living in any of those places was still alive. And even beyond that. Lovers in motels and people waiting at airports and shoppers in stores and toll collectors on lonely stretches of deserted highways were watching him. The CIA and FBI and the President were probably watching him even now and weighing their decision whether to let him have the plane he requested or storm the studio and get the whole thing over with once and for all and get this impossible asshole off America's airwaves before he drove the entire nation insane, if it wasn't already. They just didn't understand. They didn't understand what he was accomplishing. They were the real assholes. Especially if they tried to stop him now.

Gavin Risen cleared his throat, but when he tried to speak his voice collapsed into a harsh whisper that was barely audible to most of his audience. "Don't get the idea . . ." it began, and then stopped suddenly before Gavin held up his right hand in a gesture asking patience from those listening. Gavin lowered his hand and his eyes gazed out at the millions upon millions of faces he would never see and he wondered how many of the people belonging to those faces appreciated the sacrifice he was making on their behalf. He had virtually given up his life to provide them with a few hours, or at best, a few days, of enlightenment and original entertainment. Did any of them realize how exhausted he was right now? Did any of them realize the strain that was placed upon him now by being the center of attention of an entire nation and for all he knew, of many nations by now? Especially since virtually all of his life, except for the few brief hours when he had auditioned his cast and created his tapes, was spent as an observer, as a spectator, watching other men pull triggers and climb mountains and play tennis and sing folk songs and dance and answer questions and ride horses and kiss women and swim underwater and fight fires and fly planes and kill other people and sometimes even themselves. For over thirty years, he had watched them night and day, never fully realizing the amount of energy it took to actually do something, to actually be the message rather than simply the one who receives it. And he *was* the message, make no mistake about that. All of those hundreds of millions of eyes out there were receiving the same message at the same time and the message was, "This is Gavin Risen." But still, the strain, the responsibility, was more than one man should have to bear. Perhaps that was why he had selected Roger Tatum to be his co-host. But the truth was that Gavin had been disappointed in Roger Tatum's performance so far. Here he had given Roger Tatum what was probably the single biggest television news story ever, and the man had acted like an amateur rather than a coolly controlled, superbly informed news commentator who knew how to conduct an interview and channel guests' answers in the direction he wanted. "Oh well," thought Gavin, casting a glance at Roger Tatum. "Perhaps he'll get back to his regular form on the plane."

Gavin tried to speak again, and this time his voice was clearer and slightly stronger. "If my conditions are met, if a plane is provided to fly myself and my crew to New York, I promise the entire viewing audience that I shall allow the cameras to be turned off me and regular programming can be resumed shortly after we reach New York. If, on the other hand, the plane is not provided, I really can't say exactly what will happen." Gavin paused. A shadow of light seemed to shape his lips into a sinister smile. "But either way, be sure to stay tuned. Because this is going to be a really big show. A really big show."

Eternity was everywhere, clear and endless and constantly creating miniature puffs of pure-white cobwebs that walked across the horizon, then drifted off to become silver silhouettes etched against the vast blue screen that was the sky.

Gavin was a feather and a phantom floating through the illusion of space, knowing that time had disappeared and that his own private visions transcended the reality of the rocky hills and patches of gray water and stale yellow fields that glided below his eyes in eerie silence. He stretched his legs and arched his back in a painful bow, the action causing aching nerves to explode like hot bullets throughout his spine and legs.

The plane banked slowly to the left as he had instructed so that the camera could get a better shot of the wintry countryside below. He checked the small screen that now almost seemed a part of his hand, and he could see how superior the image of the land was on the split screen than it had been through the airplane window. It was clearer, more definite. And it was neatly bounded by the borders of the screen, giving the eyes a point of focus that could never be found in nature.

Gavin felt the ecstasy of pure knowledge surrounding him now like a vapor of light filtering in through his eyes and ears and skin and stirring a sense of oneness with his destiny that made him understand with an awesome clarity the meaning of every moment he had ever lived.

He turned his gaze toward Roger Tatum, crouched in a seat across the aisle, slowly sipping the final drops of a milkshake. From the moment Gavin had hammered open the handcuffs that had bound Roger Tatum to his side for endless hours in the studio and let the newscaster move a few feet away from him, Gavin had noticed that the man seemed to become more relaxed, more aware of what was going on around him.

"This is the captain speaking." Gavin's eyes immediately moved from Roger Tatum's face to the front of the plane. "I am sorry to interrupt, Mr. Risen. But it looks like we will be experiencing some weather in a few moments. Nothing major. But it could get a bit bumpy back there so I thought I'd let you and the other passengers know it would be a pretty good idea to keep your seat belts fastened until I tell you otherwise."

"Take that seat," Gavin commanded the man holding the minicamera on his shoulder, in the aisle just slightly forward of Gavin's own seat. "Sit down right here," Gavin said, indicating the middle row of seats across from him on the almost empty ghost ship of a DC-10 that even now was beginning to tremble slightly at the gathering storm the captain had spoken about just seconds before. "Sit down here," Gavin said. "But keep that camera on me every second no matter how we bounce around the sky. I want our viewers to experience this with me."

For a fragment of an instant Gavin believed the grenades had exploded, so violent was the sudden drop in the plane's altitude. The cameraman lurched forward and then fell back, toppling across seats and dropping the camera to the floor. Gavin felt his stomach erupt as fear burned like streams of lava shooting wildly throughout his body. The small television set fell onto the empty seat next to him and his hands gripped the armrests, squeezing them with frantic power. Now the plane plummeted again, seemingly forever, and Gavin closed his eyes and concentrated on the screen in his mind, where Pappy Boyington and his Black Sheep were bouncing across the sky with a hundred zeros in hot pursuit as Japanese battleships floated below, peaceful props like sleeping children resting on top of the Pacific. And then suddenly a Jap pilot crashed through his cockpit and clutched Pappy tightly by the throat with both hands, and when Gavin opened his eyes he could see that the Japanese pilot was Roger Tatum. He felt as if his neck was on fire where the newscaster's hands tightened harder and meaner and madder, as if they were trying to reach each other through Gavin's skin. The plane bounced toward the sky and Gavin could smell a sour mixture of pickles and mustard and milk as the newscaster screamed something in his face, but Gavin could not hear the words because the sound of his own gagging roared in his ears and his eyes misted over with tears as blackness started to grow out of the ceiling and fill the space above the newscaster's head, and Gavin knew that he was about to die forty thousand feet in the sky, unseen by all those hundreds of millions of eyes that had been watching him since yesterday. And then this blackness moved away as the plane steadied, and Gavin could see the other cameraman over the newscaster's shoulder, only the cameraman was not going to leap on Gavin and help the newscaster kill him. The man was doing what he was supposed to do. He had the camera pointed toward Gavin and the newscaster and he was filming Gavin's death. The intense pain in Gavin's throat did not block out the thrill that moved through his body as he realized that he would not die in vain. With a violent effort he twisted his head to the right, and his own hands clawed at Roger Tatum's fingers. And then he could see it. The miniature television set, lying on the seat next to him. He could see Roger Tatum's back on the screen and part of his own face, bulging eyes included, and he could tell by looking at his own eyes that he did not have more than a few seconds of consciousness left, but that didn't really matter very much anymore because now millions could see his death and the drama of his life would have meaning for all of them. He moved his hands away from Roger Tatum's fingers and then along his own chest and down his side, seeking the pouch so he could pull the pin from a grenade and end this live telecast with bits of his and Roger Tatum's body being blasted into the camera.

And then he saw something on the tiny screen that caused his aching eyes to focus harder. A small black dot two seats away from him on the very edge of the screen. His eyes narrowed for a closeup, but he knew even before he could see it clearly that the black dot was the Colt Python. He moved his hand away from the pouch and stretched his arm as far as it could reach, using the meager energy he had left to force both himself and Roger Tatum as far as he could to the right, and then his fingers were scratching feebly across taut fabric until finally he felt the cool, hard plastic butt of the Colt Python and even before he realized he had pulled the trigger, he could feel warm chunks of Roger Tatum's brain and face and moustache on his own skin, hot blood stinging his eyes and tasting sweet and sick on his lips as the dead man's hands relaxed on his throat, and Gavin looked up past what was left of Roger Tatum's face to make certain the cameraman was still doing his job, that he had gotten it all.

After he had pushed Roger Tatum's body away from him, Gavin moved to another seat three aisles further back from where he and Roger Tatum had struggled so violently. He simply motioned for the cameraman to keep his camera focused on him, and then sat back and eased his fingers along the throbbing skin on his neck where he could trace impressions left there by Roger Tatum's fingernails. The remainder of the flight to New York was telecast in silence, except for an interruption by the captain, who announced that they would be landing in about twenty-five minutes.

Gavin stared directly into the camera without making any attempt to speak. He was trying to sort things out in his mind and come to some sort of modified plan to put in operation once he reached New York. He could sense that Roger Tatum's death would probably rule out any further cooperation or restraint by the authorities. He imagined that even now snipers might be moving into place at the airport, honing their sights on the spot where they would fire hundreds of bullets into Gavin's body as soon as he was a safe distance away from the plane, sacrificing only the life of the cameramen, and perhaps the pilot, along with Gavin's when the grenades exploded. Or when the black box with the buttons on it erupted with enormous devastating power when someone tried to defuse it after Gavin's death.

"But what would they do," thought Gavin, "if I simply surrender? Suppose before we land I simply make a statement that I have accomplished my objectives and that I am freeing the cameramen and pilot and wish to surrender quietly, without any violence. They couldn't very well kill me then," thought Gavin. "At least not for a while. At least not until after my trial."

Gavin continued to stare silently into the camera, but his mind was becoming highly stimulated at the prospect of being the defendant in a major trial that might very well be televised. The only problem with that though, was that they would never let him have a television set or monitor in the courtroom so he could see himself testifying. In fact, he probably wouldn't even be permitted to watch videotapes of the trial or evening news reports or anything associated with the trial. So really, what good would it do him to have his trial televised if he couldn't see it? Anyway, the idea of surrender really wasn't all that appealing to him. After all the attention he had attracted nationally, and by now he was certain, internationally, the act of surrender would be so anti-climactic, and surely disappointing to his viewers. No, he would not surrender. He would go ahead with his original plan, the way it had been written on the script in his head long before he had even met Tawny or the police chief or any of the others. He would just have to take his chances that the snipers' bullets wouldn't hit him or some rescue crew overpower him. But even if they did, at least the ending would be far more entertaining and dramatic than a passive surrender.

And then he thought about making the ending as spectacular as he could, perhaps killing the pilot while they were flying over New York and then trying to guide the plane directly into the twin towers of the World Trade Center. That would make a good ending. After all, he thought, look at all the attention the man got who merely climbed one of the towers. Television interviews, offers for books, films. He became a national celebrity overnight, a folk hero. But just think how much more colorful and spectacular it would be to knock the towers down in flaming wreckage, rather than merely climb one to get to the top. It could very well be the most spectacular airplane crash in history, and Gavin began to visualize himself at the controls of the plane with the minicamera in front of him so he could show everyone exactly what the impending crash would look like from the pilot's point of view. The towers, appearing at first like double black boxes baking in the sun above New York, glistening with stone-hard beauty that seemed to draw Gavin and the plane directly toward them, and then they were looming larger each second in front of Gavin's eyes until he could actually make out individual windows and then he was even close enough to see people in the huge rooftop restaurant, moving about frantically as they realized the plane was heading straight for the buildings, and just before the nose of the plane made brutal contact with the monumentlike skyscrapers, Gavin used his special abilities for close-up viewing and focused on the face of a fat, fiftyish man in glasses who stood frozen at the window, his mouth wide open in shock or perhaps in the act of making a silent scream. And then Gavin tried to guide the plane straight into the man's mouth. And then everything disappeared.

Gavin blinked for a long second and when he reopened his eyes he was still there in front of the camera. He calculated that they were only about eight or ten minutes out of New York now, and if he wanted to end the flight with a spectacular crash into the towers of the World Trade Center, he should probably start moving about now. But then he began to think that even though he no longer had Roger Tatum as a bargaining point, he still had the cameramen and the sound technician and the pilot, and they certainly were worth something. The question in his mind was, were they worth two or three more hours? Could their lives buy him enough time to complete his telecast the way he wanted. A fast rush of steamy clouds raced by Gavin's cheek and he realized that the plane was beginning its descent. Within a few moments he would be on the ground in New York, and he would either be dead very quickly or still have a chance to do what he now felt more strongly than ever must be done.

The sun was a dirty yellow lemon in a sky turned sick and sour by smog. Below, the skyline of New York began to pop into view between scurrying clusters of clouds, like silent steel knives stabbing at the low-flying plane. Gavin had seen the view many times on telecasts, and found those views more dramatic and memorable than the one he could get simply by looking out the window. He looked again at the small television set by his side and for no particular reason traced his finger over the image of his own face, and he wondered how many millions of people in New York were watching him at this instant. For the first time in perhaps fifteen years, his mind returned to Doctor's Bar, and he could see the drink-reddened faces and ugly little eyes glaring up at the magic little black box on the shelf in the corner above the bar. How many of those people might be in Doctor's Bar right now, eyes older now, features lost behind inches of bloated flesh and broken blood vessels, staring at a supersize screen that lined the wall where that very first television set used to sit behind the bizarre-looking magnifying glass? Did they remember him? Did they realize he was the same little boy who used to lie upstairs immobile in a hospital bed and meet the most wonderful people in the world within the world of his very own television set? Was Big Teddy still there? And what about Hattie? And Will, the Indian? And if any of them were, did they remember or even care about what happened to Veronica? And had it dawned on their drink-fogged brains that Gavin Risen, the high-flying star of the greatest show in television history, was really not crying over Veronica the night the television set fell into her bath and stopped her heart and a very bad dog-food commercial in the same instant.

"Five more minutes and we'll be on the ground, Mr. Risen. Fasten your seat belt." The captain's voice was calm, matter-of-fact, as if he were making a routine announcement for a routine landing.

They were out over Queens now. That must be Shea Stadium over there, and the Triborough Bridge. The plane continued to descend, and Gavin could see the morose monotony of boxlike houses dotted by occasional frozen swimming pools and streets lined with mounds of dirty snow bulldozed back from the last storm. Legions of nervous little ticks scurried back and forth across the surface of the city as the streets loomed suddenly larger and Gavin could see the ground coming up to meet the plane and then they were coming down over the water, but they were much too close to it and Gavin began to wonder if the pilot might not be under instructions to ditch the plane in the water just short of the La Guardia runway. The water came closer and closer now and Gavin could feel his teeth bring blood from inside his mouth, but his expression never changed as his hand squeezed the butt of the Colt Python and he prepared to fire a bullet into the pouch and then they were over the runway and the gray ground greeted the wheels with a whining scream and Gavin's neck snapped suddenly back, but he managed to keep his eyes locked to the camera, and by the time the plane rolled to a stop he was ready to speak again to his audience all over the world.

19

The wind was an icy razor that cut across Gavin's face with a quick cold pain he hadn't felt in all the years since he'd left New York. He stepped through the DC-10's doorway directly onto the portable steel staircase, poking the barrel of the Colt Python gently into the back of the pilot who preceded him by a single step. The cameramen had already descended the stairs and were now aiming their cameras at Gavin, who was virtually obscured behind the large frame of the uniformed pilot, a tall, beefy, fiftyish man with a deep Florida tan and teeth so white and straight they looked like a boxer's mouthpiece.

Gavin moved his head slightly to the side so he could see around the captain's body and across the open runway. There was not another plane at the airport. Obviously the entire place had been closed to traffic. But Gavin knew that the airport wasn't totally empty. Somewhere in the buildings or behind a parked runway vehicle or at boarding areas he couldn't see, there were people who were waiting quietly, patiently, for the perfect moment to pull triggers, with all their sights aimed at a spot the size of a dime in the exact center of Gavin's forehead. And if one of those bullets missed and hit the pouch of grenades killing Gavin, the pilot and the cameraman, as well as crippling the DC-10, well, that would just be tough luck. But maybe all the bullets would fit, one after another, into that imaginary circle on Gavin's forehead.

"Don't move," said Gavin suddenly to the pilot. "Don't go down the stairs. Don't move another inch." Gavin pulled the barrel of the Colt Python from the captain's back and moved slowly backwards out of the winter wind and into the plane. He was still close enough to the pilot that he could put a bullet through the man's body before the pilot could complete a step.

"Do you see anyone out there?" asked Gavin in a voice loud enough to be heard even by the cameramen at the base of the stairs. There was silence for about fifteen seconds while the captain's head turned slowly as his eyes scanned the seemingly deserted airport. "Don't try to fool me," said Gavin, "because if I go, you'll go with me."

The captain continued looking for another ten seconds and then said, "I don't see anything at all."

Gavin realized that he was now off camera, that millions upon millions of people were now watching the captain. But that wasn't important. "Can you fly a helicopter?" Gavin asked the captain.

The captain answered, "Yes. I flew them in Korea and a few times since then. But I haven't flown one for about six or seven years now." The captain started to turn to speak directly to Gavin but he froze quickly at the sudden loud crack of the Colt Python.

"I told you," said Gavin, "not to move. There are millions of people out there watching you. And you wouldn't want them to see you with your head blown off, would you?" The captain did not answer because he knew there was no need to; his silence communicated clearly how well he understood Gavin.

"All right," said Gavin, "everyone back into the plane. I've got some final words for our viewing audience before our story ends. When I count to three, everyone start moving slowly back into the plane. One. Two. Three."

"I want a helicopter," said Gavin, his image clear and sharp on the small television set in his hand. "The helicopter should be flown out to our plane and left within ten feet of the landing stairs." Gavin's voice revealed a nervous tremor, and his tone was slightly higher-pitched than it had been. He glanced in the direction of the door as if he expected a rescue crew to burst through it at any second. "It need not be a large helicopter," he continued. "Just as long as there is a seat for my pilot and myself. I shall not harm the rest of my crew. They shall be left behind here at the plane and my telecast will be over. And when I have reached my destination my pilot will be released unharmed!" Gavin's tongue slid over his lips and then hid again in his mouth. "On the other hand, if the helicopter is not left abandoned ten feet from the landing stairs to this plane within thirty minutes, I shall blow up this plane, myself and my crew." He nodded toward the camera as if it were a person. "It is your decision whether the final part of our story shall be peaceful or violent." Gavin stopped talking and paused for a moment, seemingly to search his mind to see if he had forgotten anything. Then he spoke again. "The helicopter should have a full load of fuel, and a portable television set, the screen about ten or twelve inches. I would also like two more Big Macs, two large orders of fries, and two chocolate milkshakes for my pilot and myself." He couldn't resist his next line, although he wondered if everyone in the audience would understand it. He pointed his finger at the camera and said "You, you're the one I'm doing this for. You sitting out there in your living room. You are the reason why I planned this show for Sunday. I wanted to make sure as many of you as possible would not be at work, so you could stay home and watch my show. And that's what this really is ladies and gentlemen, a show. 'The Gavin Risen Show,' starring yours truly."

Gavin glanced again at the door and then spoke directly to his crew. "I want one of the cameras over in the doorway, so you can shoot across the runway so that I can see that no one or nothing except that helicopter comes near this plane." The stinging chill of the New York morning had moved into the plane, invading the bodies of the television crew, pilot, and Gavin Risen, who had to concentrate to keep from shivering. Time passed with little said, as Gavin continued to gaze directly into the camera until he heard a muted but steady sound coming from outside the plane, growing gradually louder and closer until he was certain that it must be the copter. Gavin rose from his seat and moved toward the door. The engine noise was quite loud now, and the copter hovered about fifteen feet above the door of the plane, a strange mechanical animal suspended in space. "Pick it up," directed Gavin. "I want the screen split again so I can see both the copter and myself." Gavin returned to his seat and again picked up the small television set. He held the set in his left hand for a moment before the screen was divided in two and then quite suddenly it appeared on the screen that the furiously rotating blades of the copter might slice off Gavin's nose. The humor of the scene was not lost on Gavin, as he yanked his head back quickly as if to avoid the whirling blades on the other side of the screen.

Overhead the sky had become a dark gray wall, sealing off the sun and now beginning to shed soft white circles of snow that floated down gently toward the earth until the chopper's blades blew them into frenzied little white cyclones. "What are they waiting for?" whispered Gavin to himself as well as his audience. Gavin had barely spoken the words when the copter began to descend again, a gloomy praying mantis about to drop down on its victim. The copter came lower and lower, its engine noise blocking out any words Gavin might try to say, and then it was visible in the doorway parallel with the plane. Gavin tensed visibly as the copter continued to drop and then he could no longer see it and the air was suddenly still except for the final few whirrs of the blades after the engine was cut off. Gavin looked at the small television set and focused his total attention on the copter that only seconds ago had been nearly close enough to touch. The door on the pilot's side of the copter swung open and a medium-size man dressed in leather jacket, blue jeans, and New York Yankees baseball cap jumped out. He slipped to the ground and then quickly rose and took two steps toward the plane and then stopped. He cupped his hands around his mouth and yelled, "Your copter's here. It's filled with gas. Your food is right under the copilot's seat. The copter is empty. There's no one in the copter. It's all yours." He shouted the words rapidly, underscoring the fact that he wanted to get his role in this bizarre scenario over as quickly as possible. Even before the word "yours" was fully formed and out of his mouth, he turned and sprinted across the open runway toward the landing ramps.

"Gentlemen," said Gavin Risen, his voice a mechanical monotone, "get ready to turn off your cameras."

20

They were gliding above the city in slow motion, passing close enough to office buildings and hotels to see figures moving in the windows. As they flew closer to the heart of Manhattan, they could see windows opening and people pointing toward the copter. Gavin looked down and he could see two men in white shirts standing on a rooftop. They had rifles in their hands, and as the copter passed almost directly over the men's heads at a distance of about one hundred feet, Gavin could see the rifles raise in unison, hear the almost simultaneous reports of the rifle fire and then a sudden "ching" sound as one of the bullets ricocheted off the steel surface of the copter. "Up. Go up higher," said Gavin, and the copter immediately soared upward, reducing the two men in white shirts from the size of an inch each to almost invisible white dots in the space of a few seconds.

There was activity on many rooftops now, tiny specks of life scurrying about excitedly at the opportunity to see and perhaps participate in an event that was holding the entire world a captive audience. Gavin looked up from the frenzy below and his eyes focused quickly on the familiar face on the television screen. He turned up the volume, which he had lowered only moments before. The man on the screen was speaking, but even with the volume on maximum, Gavin had to strain to hear Danton Morris's words. "The helicopter has been seen heading toward down-

town Manhattan, perhaps in the direction of Times Square. Police, Coast Guard, and other military helicopters, along with
newscasters equipped with television cameras, are being sent into
the area, as are numerous police, fire, and emergency ground
units. As of this moment the borough of Manhattan has been
placed under martial law. All residents and people in the area are
advised to stay indoors. Stay off the streets. The police also
request that you stay away from windows and not go out on fire
escapes or onto rooftops. There is no way of knowing at this time
if Risen plans any attempt at mass violence, but we have been
advised that if the authorities can locate the copter in a spot that is
not densely populated, such as the Wall Street area, where all
offices are closed today, as it's Sunday, they will attempt to
destroy it by whatever means necessary.''

Danton Morris was his usual distinguished self, totally un-
flappable and precise, no matter how perilous the situation. Gavin
had admired the man for years, perhaps trusted him more than any
other newscaster or television personality he could think of.
That's why he was especially pleased that Danton Morris was
covering this phase of the program. He knew he could count on
Mr. Morris to give him factual, objective information. He turned
the channel selector quickly and there was Harris Winslow at La
Guardia Airport, standing in front of the DC-10, talking to the
members of Gavin's crew. Gavin had never been pleased with
Harris Winslow's method of interviewing people. It was too
pushy, too prying, it was as if he were always putting his own
words in their mouths. ''Did you see any sign, anything at all that
might have indicated that this suspect, or madman, or call him
what you will, may have been connected with any terrorist or-
ganization?''

Click-Click. So much for Harris Winslow. Gavin kept turning
the channel selector rapidly, pausing as each channel clicked on
to determine what program was showing. Every channel, even
the independents, were covering the Gavin Risen story. Gavin
felt a triumphant surge of emotion. He no longer held the television cameras hostage. He was no longer forcing television to

focus on him. They were doing it now out of their own free will. Every channel in New York. And perhaps in the entire country. All of Europe was probably watching him, too. And Asia. And maybe even Africa. Him. Gavin Risen. One man. He was teaching the entire world a lesson it would never forget. Gavin flicked the channel selector back to Danton Morris's report, but when he did he did not see Danton Morris's familiar face on the screen. Instead, there was a tiny black dot moving across a dull gray background. The camera moved in closer, and then Gavin could see that the tiny black dot was a helicopter. He could see that the snow was starting to fall harder now, coming in great white sheets that surrounded the small black dot. And then he heard the deep clear voice of Danton Morris. "That's it," said Morris. "That's the helicopter that only moments ago left La Guardia Airport, carrying with it one Gavin Risen—a name that by now has become infamous around the world—and one John Duechen, a senior airlines captain now held hostage by Risen and presently piloting the helicopter you see on your screen."

The windshield wipers on the copter were racing back and forth frantically as large white discs of snow appeared for an instant on the windows and then vanished quickly. Visibilty was beginning to grow more difficult, and the captain looked at Gavin as if to communicate his apprehension through his eyes rather than his voice. But Gavin's own eyes remained locked to the television set, obviously convinced that the scene shown on the screen was more real than the snowstorm that was swirling more desperately around their tiny craft.

"Their position is estimated at somewhere between Seventy-first and Sixty-fifth, between Madison and Lexington. Other military craft in the air have been advised of the Risen helicopter's location, and they may now be on their way to try to force it out over water or at least out over less populated areas."

Gavin smiled in his mind. "Good old Danton Morris," he thought. "You can always count on him to give you the latest news first. And give it to you straight." The captain again took a fast nervous glance at Gavin, who now turned to him and said almost softly, "You have been doing an excellent job, captain. I'm going to do everything I can to see that you get out of this alive. Now, take me to the corner of Forty-ninth and Seventh.''

Below, skyscrapers stood at silent attention, and then Gavin could see something rising up from between two of the tall buildings, floating higher and higher until it was above the buildings and closing the gap that separated it from Gavin's copter. It was perhaps a mile away and was heading straight toward them, but somehow the captain didn't seem to notice it, so intense was his concentration on guiding the helicopter through the snow-shrouded visibility immediately around their copter. The captain spoke. "I don't know how you expect me to find any place in this city. Especially in this kind of weather. I'm not a helicopter pilot, damn it. I'm doing everything I can to keep the goddamn thing up here as it is."

The dot that was the approaching helicopter loomed closer now, perhaps three-quarters to half a mile was all that separated them.

"The latest report is that four military copters seem to have the Risen copter fixed in a target area between them all and are now closing rapidly." Danton Morris's voice was matter-of-fact, as if he were simply reporting a routine police chase after a stolen car. Gavin looked at the television set and he could tell from the size of his copter on the screen-shot from behind that the copter trailing him was managing to close ground.

A great gust of wind whipping up from below seemed to grab the copter and hurtle it skyward, causing Gavin to lurch forward and the captain to fight the controls as the snow pounded down harder now, ice-white bullets strafing the thin armor of the copter that surrounded the two men some fifteen hundred feet above the frozen sidewalks of New York.

"Police are putting up roadblocks to keep all traffic from entering a mile-square radius in downtown Manhattan. Traffic is already pouring out of the area, and thank God it's Sunday or otherwise there would be horrendous traffic jams." Gavin pushed his body away from the control panel, and steadied himself back into his seat. The approaching copter had disappeared behind the screen of heavy snow and then he saw it rising over the shoulders of a cluster of slablike buildings below and to his left.

"Do you see it?" asked Gavin, his voice quietly communicating tension.

"I do," said the captain. "I think the best thing you could do is let me set this thing down before they blow us out of the sky."

"As our cameras show you," the voice of Danton Morris interrupted the captain, "the Risen copter is much closer now than it was even three minutes ago. Notice that dot in the top right hand corner of the screen. That's a military copter closing in fast on Risen from another direction."

"Take us down," said Gavin. "We're going down. But follow my directions every inch of the way."

The captain made the appropriate adjustments and Gavin's eyes began to search the helter-skelter topography of rooftops, looking for a guidepost, and then he saw it.

"Over this way, to your left." Gavin was unfamiliar with the skyline of New York, but he had familiarized himself with some of the most important landmarks and addresses. The snow continued to cloud his vision but he was able to pick up Rockefeller Center and then, a few blocks south, the *New York Times* Building. "The Risen copter seems to be trying some evasive tactics now. Either that, or it's starting its descent, possibly to land on a city street or a rooftop. Or who knows what. He may have located the target he's been looking for and is now trying to reach it before the copters close in." Gavin could not help but admire the detached professionalism of Danton Morris. He wondered for a moment if all of this was real, if any of this was real. Or if he and Danton Morris and the captain and all the people in the other copters weren't merely performers in some great and grand "made-for-TV" movie. The people he had seen in the buildings and the rooftops were simply extras and the skyscrapers mere cardboard props. How had he gotten into this movie? He tried to recall how it all happened but his attention was diverted by the sudden appearance of the building he had been searching for. He was sure that was it. Looking like a giant shaft of cold black marble, solemn and impersonal and waiting for him to come and end his drama here.

"Down. Take me down right here. Right to that building there. Get me close to the rooftop. Within ten feet. You won't even have to land. And then you'll be free to go." Gavin pointed his finger at the bleak tower and the captain nodded that he understood. The helicopter began to drop faster than Gavin imagined it would and for a split second he thought they had lost power and would crash right onto the roof. But the captain seemed to have the copter under control and the rooftop was only fifty feet below them now and slightly to the right. The descent continued more slowly now and Gavin could see where the hard white snow was sticking to the rooftop. It came closer. Still closer. He could see an archway and a door. Now only thirty feet to go. Gavin looked up to see how close the other copters had come and he was relieved that he could see no trace of them anywhere. Perhaps they had gotten lost in the chase amid the maze of buildings and the snow, which was coming harder now. Twenty feet, maybe less. Gavin looked behind his seat and found what he had hoped would be there. A strong length of chain bolted to the floor. Attached to the chain was a wide leather belt that served as a seat. Gavin had been prepared to jump the final ten feet to the roof of the building, but he knew that such a jump could break an ankle, or even set off the grenades, in which case he need not worry about his ankle being broken or about anything else ever again. And, of course, if the grenades went off now there would be no television cameras to show his death to the world.

"We're at about ten feet now," said the captain. The helicopter stopped in midair and hovered above the roof like a giant eagle inspecting its nest. "All right," said Gavin, "this is close enough." He slipped the small television set into the large outside pocket of his jacket. He then bent, placed a loop of chain and the wide leather belt at his feet, then lifted them over his feet and up his legs, over his hips, until they had tightened around his waist and buttocks. He pointed the Colt Python directly into the face of the captain. "You are to keep this copter right where it is until I lower myself safely onto the rooftop. If you try to shake me by starting to move forward or up too fast, chances are excellent I will have time to put a bullet into these grenades and blow you out of the sky. If you do as I have instructed, you will be all right. Do you understand?" The captain nodded, but before he could ask the question he had formed in his mind, Gavin was out the door and lowering himself quickly toward the roof below. The wind came rushing at Gavin in ferocious blasts, churning corkscrews of frigid air that almost lifted him back up into the helicopter, but instead swung him out over the edge of the roof in a frightening arc. The chain felt like links of ice in his hands as he lowered himself the final few feet, pain freezing into his fingers, and then one foot felt something solid beneath it. His other foot touched down. He slid from the leather seat, let it drop around his feet, then stepped clear of the seat and the chain. The helicopter lurched forward, then quickly upward. Within seconds it was sliding through a maze of snow and skyscrapers. It appeared to be heading toward Park Avenue. Again the wind came at Gavin with a frantic fury, as if it were an enemy consciously trying to destroy him. His already tense body stiffened still more as he braced himself to keep from being blown off the roof to be dropped forty-two stories to his death. He could see the helicopter descending over near Park Avenue, and he realized that the captain wanted to get down on the ground as fast as possible before some skilled marksman perched on the roof of any of dozens of buildings nearby hit either the captain or the copter in a critical spot. He was amazed that he could still hear the engine at this distance, and then he realized it was the engine of another copter, coming almost straight at him now, about one hundred feet above his head. He wondered if the pilot of the approaching copter had seen him set down on this rooftop. Or if anyone in any of the other copters had. If that was the case, they'd all be swarming down on him within seconds. But maybe they hadn't seen him. Maybe the captain was the only other person who knew exactly where Gavin Risen was at this precise moment, his face being lashed by cold tunnels of air and hard, driving snow. But the captain was probably on the ground by now, and certainly he was telling everyone what Gavin had done and where he was at this very moment. But did the captain really know which building Gavin was on? After all, he had only flown over it for a few seconds during a snowstorm with his own life very much in danger. He probably hadn't been concentrating on the building itself, and possibly he could not pick it out again.

The approaching helicopter veered to the left and then plummeted sharply downward and disappeared behind a glass and stone tower that seemed to Gavin to be taller than the building he was standing on. And he certainly hoped he was standing on the right building. From all that he had read about the building itself, about the address and the surrounding area, he was quite confident that this was it. He reached into the large pocket of his coat and his hand felt the plastic case of the small portable television set. It, too, felt cold. He pulled the television set from his pocket and he was suddenly no longer alone. Now someone was up here with him to share his glory. Danton Morris was speaking. Gavin turned up the volume because he knew Danton was talking about him, and he didn't want to miss a single word.

"Apparently they've lost sight of the Risen copter," said Danton Morris, wool ski cap pulled down on his head, scarf tight around his neck, gray overcoat adding thirty pounds to his appearance. "We've set up our news report headquarters here at Rockefeller Plaza and are in constant communication with our own network news copters in the area, as well as with police and military forces in Manhattan, which, by the way, now seem to be everywhere. In the air. On the ground. Getting ready for whatever might happen, for whatever madness Gavin Risen may have in store for the city of New York."

They didn't know where he was yet. No matter. They would know soon enough. Gavin walked slowly to the edge of the roof, stepping into the wind now so that each step became an effort. But at least it was better to have the wind blowing into his face than pushing at his back. This way, he would not be blown off the roof.

"The last positive fix on the Risen copter was in the area of Forty-ninth street and Seventh Avenue. There's also been an unconfirmed report that the copter actually set down on a rooftop in that area and an air search by the copters is being conducted at this moment." Danton Morris brought the back of a gloved hand to his lips, to warm them, if only for an instant. "The weather conditions have become atrocious," he continued. "It's amazing to me that none of the copters has crashed into a building or even another copter. I am certain they would have been ordered down by now, if it were not for the seriousness and incredible drama of this event, which has captured the attention of the world. Even now, what you are seeing in your homes in New York and Texas and California, and all the states, is being carried live, by satellite, to Europe, Latin America, and, I believe, Africa and the Far East as well."

The icy winds and hard pellets of snow no longer bothered Gavin Risen. The light from the television screen was warming him, as were the words of Danton Morris. He stepped up onto the ledge of the rooftop. He could move no further. One more step would send him to the frozen sidewalks below. But he knew that he was far more visible now. It was only a matter of time before one of the copters would spot him, a tiny speck on the snowswept roof of one building, on one street, in one city, in one country. A tiny speck whose image would soon fill the eyes of the world.

"This report is official," Danton Morris's tone was urgent, even excited. "The Risen helicopter set down on Park Avenue just moments ago. But Gavin Risen was not in it. Risen had forced the pilot to let him drop a chain ladder onto a rooftop in the vicinity of Fiftieth Street between Fifth Avenue and the Avenue of the Americas. The military and police copters in the area are closing in on that area. So are police and military ground squads. We are sending camera teams and field reporters into that area to try to bring you the fullest live coverage possible, if we are in fact, to witness the end of Gavin Risen's reign of terror."

Gavin stood on the ledge, wavering slightly in the wind, eyes glancing upward from the small television screen and the face of

Danton Morris toward the gray infinity of the New York winter sky. The helicopters would be here any second. Gavin felt a wonderful sense of anticipation. His eyes were stinging with cold pain as the snow came at him thicker and crueler now. But it did not matter. He was passing beyond the physical laws of reality, beyond concepts of pleasure and pain, beyond ordinary mortal concerns for survival. He was here and soon he would be everywhere. And then he heard it. A soft steady hum coming from the clouds. And he began to recall those moments when he had first seen the great old movie version of King Kong on television, with Kong standing defiantly atop the Empire State Building, swatting feeble fighter planes away like pesky flies.

He saw three of them simultaneously, even though they were approaching him from different angles. He wondered if they had seen him yet, and he was tempted to wave but instead waited patiently, the snow now covering him like a white ghost.

"We think we've picked him up. One of our aerial camera crews thinks they've spotted Gavin Risen. There. See it? That may be him. Standing on the ledge of that building. It certainly looks like a human figure from this distance, doesn't it?"

Gavin glanced down at the small television set he held in his hands, and he could see now what he looked like from the sky. Once again, his image was reaching all over the world, uniting all nations and all men in a single experience, a shared moment, a sacred memory for future generations.

"That looks like it's him, all right. Our aerial crew has identified his location as atop the CBS Building. He just seems to be standing there like a statue. He must know he's been spotted by now, but he's making no attempt to escape or hide."

Gavin wondered if the military and police copters would simply come in close enough to use rifles or machine guns to blast him off the rooftop, risking the explosion of the grenades and whatever damage they might do to the building or the streets below. The wind sang in his ears, a simple melody with words, and he could hear the chanting coming back to him, the chanting he had first heard years ago on television. The voices swirled about his head, shouting in the wind, "The whole world is watching. The whole world is watching. The whole world is watching."

The helicopters were close now, so close that an average marksman in one of them would have been able to hit Gavin in the head with a single shot. But nothing happened. The copters simply hovered in the air about one hundred feet away from Gavin, as if awaiting instructions about what to do next.

"He's just standing there, seemingly in a trance," said Danton Morris. "He has not moved nor acknowledged the presence of the helicopters in any way."

Without lowering his head, Gavin dropped his gaze to the small television screen. He saw his own face. It was a close-up.

"The power and versatility of our new minicameras is really revolutionary," Danton Morris commented. "The copters are about one hundred and twenty feet away from the suspect, but the picture you see gives you a clear impression of his face as if you were in the same room with him."

Gavin stood motionless on the ledge, waiting for the words he longed to hear from Danton Morris, and wondering when the bullet would be coming, and from which angle.

"The police and military are sending antiterrorist teams into the CBS Building at this moment," said Morris in clipped, precise tones that indicated the story might rapidly be building to a climax. "They're also sending marksmen into other buildings in the area. It's becoming obvious now that they want to try to take Gavin Risen into custody alive, but that they are prepared to kill him quickly if any possibility of escape presents itself to him. They'd obviously like to question him about possible terrorist connections, but they don't want to take any chances on his terrorizing this city, and the country for that matter, any more than he already has."

"Why doesn't he say the words," thought Gavin, "the words that I'm waiting for?"

Five minutes passed. An eternity passed. And nothing happened. Gavin didn't move. The helicopters didn't move. And then Gavin saw a window in the office building across the street suddenly open. Then another window. Then another. Then a dozen. Then what must have been a hundred. Thin black snakes that were the barrels of rifles poked their heads out of the windows. Suddenly the helicopters raced their engines and began converging slowly on Gavin. Behind him he heard the door to the roof blast open. He turned his head and saw a column of twenty or more soldiers moving across the rooftop toward him, machine guns and rifles pointed directly at him. He turned his head back toward the approaching copters and then down at the image of his own face on the screen. Above the roar of the engines and the crunch of footsteps behind him, coming closer each second, Gavin could hear the lonely music of the wind and the steady voice of Danton Morris.

"This looks like the end. They are closing in." There was a pause and then Gavin could hear nothing else but the pure electronic sound of Danton Morris's voice. It was as if the helicopters and the wind and the approaching footsteps had been wiped off some soundtrack so that he could concentrate fully on the newscaster's words. "I have just been informed that what you are watching now is the single best-witnessed event in the history of the world. People from every nation are now watching the same image you see on your screen: the face of Gavin Risen. People who don't speak the same language or share the same religious or political beliefs or share the same values are now sharing a moment in time that will stay with us all, for all of our lives."

Gavin raised his arms until the small television screen was almost parallel to his face, so that he could look directly at his own image without blocking his face from the television cameras that were televising that image to the world. The copters were almost on top of him now. He could sense that the soldiers behind him were about to reach out and grab him and then he took that one simple step into eternity, his left foot moving out over the edge of the ledge and then he was flying downward through a cavern of wind, holding the small television set in front of him as he fell, watching his body hurtling down, knowing that these images would be his final gift to his audience all over the world, knowing that these last exploding images of Gavin Risen would be shown over and over again, even to generations yet unborn, and that he would be with them all, now and forever, until the end of time. He was the first person to bring it all together, to make his life and death an adventure for all mankind, to become writer, director, performer, spectator, victim, and executioner simultaneously in front of the eyes of the entire world. He was the first. But surely others would follow. The snow and the wind whipped past his eyes, but his eyes focused only on the black dot that was himself and that was now a part of everyone and eternity. And he kept watching it grow smaller and smaller and smaller until . . .

the end.